WORKBOOK PRESS LLC
187 E Warm Springs Rd,
Suite B285, Las Vegas, NV 89119, USA

Website: https://workbookpress.com/
Hotline: 1-888-818-4856
Email: admin@workbookpress.com

Ordering Information:
Quantity sales. Special discounts are available on quantity purchases by corporations, associations, and others. For details, contact the publisher at the address above.

ISBN-13:   978-1-957618-16-6 (Paperback Version)
                978-1-957618-17-3 (Digital Version)

REV. DATE: 1.26.2022

CRACKED PORCELAIN

ACTS OF ABUSE PART ONE

A complete fictitious story about Ruth Ashley and her life as a nurse and model following her harrowing life and looking in to her past experiences of abuse. This story shows highlights the many emotions and nightmares as well as other effects following experiences of abuse. It also deals with lesbian relationships and societies reactions to same sex relationships, as Ruth discovers her own sexuality amidst the chaos and animosity around her. Some people may find this book disturbing particularly if you have experienced abuse of any kind, whether it be physical, mental, psychological or financial. You are advised to seek help if this is the case you can find useful websites at the end of the book.

DEDICATIONS

This book is dedicated to people who have made a difference to our society, the voices of the people who are not afraid to speak out and be noticed. I speak of many people who have even given their live for a cause because their voice matters. I speak of people who speak out about the oppression and the abuse, as well as those who fight for the weak and encourage the strong to be with them. People like Martin Luther King, Nelson Mandela, John and Yoko who have made their feelings known about peace and to Emma Watson for her remarkable speech on sexual equality. For the gay pride that makes a difference to the gay population and their freedom, Manchester pride has an impact on the city (Don't forget the festival every August). I could name many more like the many crises teams, some of which are featured on the back of the book. I also refer to the mental health teams all over the world who have a difficult task in helping those less fortunate than ourselves, may they be rewarded for their efforts.

Thank you as usual to all my family and friends

for your support in my endeavour to get my message across, I speak of hope, freedom gender equality and fighting against all kinds of abuse. Thank you Gemma, Jeni, Mike and Dan may you all reach your ultimate goals in life and whatever you do I am proud of you all. A special thanks to Rachel Day for her editing work and interest in my projects and thank you to my friends and colleagues for their support unfortunately I am not able to mention them all.

CRACKED PORCELAIN

IN THE BEGINNING

In a dark room a dim light was shining on to an attractive large porcelain vase which stood on a polished wooden table. It was decorated in flowers, which were finely painted on both sides; the rim had a painted gold bow with two ribbons hanging down. They both the flowers and the ribbon seemed so real. The room was in silence and everything in sight was neatly in its place, porcelain figurines placed strategically on a shelf and porcelain masks displayed neatly on a wall as if they had some symbolic meaning. The masks had been painted by hand; some of them were western and the others oriental. Whoever had put them up must have measured the distance of each one because they were placed apart perfectly.

Suddenly the silence was broken by a loud bang, as the vase seemed to explode and shatter into a thousand pieces. Fragments of porcelain went flying into air in all directions landing all over the floor. This was followed by further sounds as the shelves fell and the figurines fell onto the carpet, the masked were also damaged as a baseball bat smashed against a wall. The vandals were two heavyset men wearing masks with menacing faces to terrify their victims. Following the ordeal the room was a mess, everything was quiet again but the body of a forty-year-old woman lying half naked on the floor battered and covered in blood. Another person was in the room, she was a teenage girl also half naked sitting staring at the body with her bright blue eyes. She had long blonde hair and a glowing complexion, she was trembling and tears were flowing onto her cheeks. The girl was obviously traumatized by the event what she saw must have been horrific and she was experiencing flash backs of the incident. She also had blood splashed across her face and bloodstains on her hands and clothes.

The police and ambulance crew arrived talking to a woman with short mousy coloured hair and a slim body, she was holding a photograph of the two victims. The woman kept crying then looked across at the young girl who remained silent with her eyes transfixed on the body.

"So you are Laura Brown the victim's cousin?" One of the officers asked.

"Yes I am Sarah's cousin, can I go to Pamela now?" Laura asked pointing to the teenager.

Laura was a thirty-five year old woman with fair hair, who was very close to Sarah she had looked after Sarah since she was diagnosed with multiple sclerosis, helping her with her cleaning, cooking and anything else she needed. Laura's boyfriend used to assist too. They entered the place and discovered that there was a problem when the kitchen was a mess, then when they entered the living room they discovered the meaning for the mess. Sarah had Obsessive-compulsive disorder (O.C.D) so they knew something was not quite right, but to find such a horrific scene was too much to deal with. Laura screamed hysterically and had to be calmed down by her boyfriend Colin who was trying to control his own emotions. But they had to think about Pamela and what was best for her witnessing and being a victim of rape and murder.

Pamela remained still sitting rigged by now and staring coldly to the place where her mother's body was, she continued to see images of the men who terrorized her. Laura tried to get a response but Pamela never moved even when Laura hugged her and kissed her on the forehead but still no reaction.

When Laura eventually got through to her, she took her to her house and looked after her with her own children Janet, Alison and Rebecca. She tried to make Pamela feel at home having her own room due to sleep disturbances; she would have nightmares and wake up screaming. She knew all about her childhood as a model and other trauma's from her past, Laura encouraged her to do modeling but she was never the same confident girl that used to advertise soap and other products. In fact Pamela had developed multiple personality syndrome as her coping mechanism, she had the personality as a child called Anne then a person called James who protected her. She even created voices for each personality raging from high pitched to deep voices some were quite frightening. She also found it hard to form relationships with boys and often beat them up as she put it.

Laura thought back to Sarah's childhood and the life she had. Sarah grew up with a friend called Kevin and really that was the start of her problems as she was so obsessed with him. They used to play with plastic dolls and action men, Sarah's OCD began then when she used to back the dolls clothes away in small boxes each colour coordinated and according to size, shape, even the army uniforms had to be organized. Kevin used to get annoyed by her OCD and told her so in plain terms. Laura remembered when Sarah's parents were packing to move house how Sarah would unpack and pack again until everything was perfect.

Plastic dolls and action men

It was a warm day as the sun was shining through a conservatory window onto a box of toys. All around these were other boxes already packed and sealed ready to be moved. The open box containing the toys consisted of plastic Barbie/cindy dolls and action men with sets of clothing neatly packed at the right hand corner. To the left was one single action man wearing an army uniform each doll was in good condition, obviously well looked after by Sarah. She particularly paid attention to the action man, but tended to put the uniforms on the female dolls.

Suddenly there was movement, as a small Sarah

aged four appeared she began running around with a Barbie doll in her hand. A boy called Kevin about the same age was chasing her with an action man in his hand; they were running around the box of toys. The girl had dark hair, which was tied with ribbon into pigtails; she had a pretty face but a pale complexion. The boy had fair hair and was also quite pale. Strangely enough they vanished as quickly as they appeared looking transparent before they vanished like ghosts or memories of their former selves.

But who were these two children who had once ran around this house playing it seemed that the girl Sarah once lived here while Kevin was invited to play at her house. Sarah left there with her parents and the packed boxes were present because they were moving. Sarah was older and reflecting back to her life at the home in her childhood, her parents had to move due to being in debt. They had fallen on hard times Sarah was their only child and they used to dress her so perfectly like a toy doll. She was brought up to be elegant and a lady despite their depts, her mother was obsessed with Sarah being clean and tidy to the degree that she made Sarah wash her hands three times before meals and made her shower twice a day. This is known today as obsessive-compulsive disorder (OCD) and Sarah's mother displayed more than the average person with such a disorder. The condition was so bad that Sarah questioned her own cleanliness and often looked in the mirror checking her skin, making sure there were no spots or blemishes. Sarah like her mother-loved porcelain ornaments especially porcelain masks. But her mother never liked the masks or the fact that Sarah always wanted to paint them.

Sarah played happily with Kevin as a child; at her parents' home they never seemed apart playing mainly with the plastic dolls, they imagined that they were grown up and either at war together or getting married. Kevin's mother seemed to get on well with Sarah's mother but never really socialised together. Sarah and Kevin even spent time in school together they were inseparable other children considered Kevin odd because he preferred to mix with the girls. He was called sissy and other random names because he preferred female company. His idea was that girls were more loving and understanding while boys just wanted to fight.

As they became a little older they played tennis

together Sarah liked competitive sports and was in the tennis and netball team. She wanted to get involved in most competitive sports and was fearless as she challenged most people.

Kevin liked history and would never fail to attend his classes; Sarah was more interested in pottery and produced many shaped pots. But she had a fascination for masks mainly the ones made out of porcelain like the oriental designs. She loved to paint masks to her own style and kept many masks in her family home. Her parents considered this a morbid fascination and tried to deter her from this hobby, but Sarah was obsessed and continued collecting these masks.

Kevin was attending history class one day when the teacher was discussing historical battles with all the gruesome details. He showed pictures of soldiers in battle in gory detail; Sarah was not amused and sat sulking in a corner. Kevin was a typical lad who wanted to see more fixated by the uniforms and weaponry used in battle. The teacher Mr Grimshaw was an older man in his fifties with hardly any hair and a thin moustache, who wore corduroy trousers and a tweed jacket. His nose looked an odd shape almost like a beak and his eyes were like tiny marbles that gazed at people as if they had crawled up from the ground. Most children hated him and felt uncomfortable in his presence especially Sarah who felt that such teachers should be anywhere but at school teaching her. He was a firm believer in corporal punishment as a main form of discipline and often used a cane to demonstrate his authority. A swift few strikes to the behind or hand would teach any child not to misbehave again in his presence.

Sarah preferred Mrs Strand a prim and proper teacher who was thin with a long pointed nose and a parting down the centre of her grey hair. She taught English and was very strict with her pupils, making sure they listened to all that was being said.

Sarah was developing into a beautiful girl, her complexion was slightly tanned and her large brown eyes were sparkling like diamonds in the sky. She also had a nice figure and could have made a great model, appearing in local catalogues or on posters.

The teachers often asked her what she wanted to do for a living; she would reply I want to be a tennis player. Although she didn't like history she did admire Florence Nightingale, the lady of the lamp. She liked the woman's courage and determination. But then she also liked other female historical leaders such as Joan of Arc, Cleopatra and Bodesia. She liked strong women who could face up to men, fearless and challenging like her own personality.

Sarah was known as a perfectionist but one who also developed OCD obsessive-compulsive disorder. She displayed this by the way she organised her room with clothes neatly stacked in order of colour. Her life was orderly and this could easily irritate people especially the hand washing and opening and shutting the wardrobe.

Sarah also liked uniforms and would cut magazines up and stick photographs of people in uniforms into her scrapbook. Just like the porcelain masks that she hung neatly on her wall, each one had to be in line not one out of place.

Sometimes Kevin would be irritated by her OCD and deliberately move a mask or untidy her clothes, but Sarah soon got them back in order. Kevin realised that Sarah was growing up and he had lost the girl that he once visited who played with plastic Barbie dolls while he played with his action men. They had known each other for ten years from infants to early teenagers and hardly ever argued about anything.

"Sarah you really are OCD I have never met anyone quite as bad as you" Kevin said laughing

"Honestly you know nothing my mother is much worse" Sarah replied unlocking and locking the front door four times.

"And will you stop it with that lock" Kevin said taking the keys off her.

Then suddenly Kevin was told about his mothers diminishing mental health condition, She was suffering from depression and this was putting a strain on his father who eventually had her committed into a mental health hospital. He then arranged for Kevin to move away and live with his aunty Gladys in the south of England. It was a painful departure for Sarah and Kevin, the idea of Kevin leaving his family home his school and most important to him his dear friend Sarah.

The snow lay thick on the ground that day when Kevin had rushed around to her house to inform her of his bad news. Sarah already knew about her parents and about him leaving. She wanted to soften the blow by letting him know that she already knew she was told by her mother and so had time to prepare herself for the news from Kevin.

"Sarah I have to leave" Kevin said bowing his head

"I know you have to live with your aunt Gladys's" Sarah said sadly.

"I will miss you" Kevin said sincerely

"But of course you will" Sarah replied

"Did your mother tell you? Kevin asked

"Yes she found out last night you know how people talk" Sarah explained.

Sarah refused to reveal her true feelings trying to disguise her tears with her scarf, but behind her brave face lay a woman who was sad and felt as if her heart had been torn out. Sarah spent nights alone painting her masks; each mask was painted with tears running from their eyes. She began having nightmares about the war that was broadcasted on television and in the tabloids.

One war after another occurred over the years Sarah held the action man that Kevin once had, he wore a uniform that reminded Sarah of the soldiers on television. She dreaded the thought of Kevin in battle somewhere and possibly hearing of his death.

The years passed and Kevin had reached nineteen, he made a journey back to his hometown in order to contact old friends, but although he searched for Sarah she had moved away from home. Kevin was unable to find any trace of Sarah and had given up and returned to his aunty Gladys. He was certain that he would never see her again then one day he was sitting in a café and who should walk in the door but Sarah.

Sarah looked around the café and suddenly noticed a young man looking sad glancing at an old photograph of two young children smiling with toys all around them.

"Kevin" she said softly taking removing an action man from her bag .

"Sarah is that you?" He said with a smile

"This is yours" She said smiling back

They kissed and embraced at that moment Sarah dropped the doll on the floor the head became detached and rolled under another table.

"I am sorry" Sarah said racing under the table after the doll

"Sarah its not important leave it" Kevin shouted.

"Well it is to me" Sarah said picking it up.

Kevin realised how much it meant to her as sentimental value.

"I will fix the head back on but I would like you to keep it" Kevin said.

"Ok that sounds good to me" Sarah agreed

"So what have you been up to over the years, apart from looking beautiful?" Kevin asked

"I am working as a nurse, I trained as a cadet" Sarah said fidgeting with her bag

"A nurse that's nice" Kevin said watching her fidgeting

"So what do you do? Sarah asked

"I am in the army" Kevin said trying to reconnect the dolls head.

"Oh" Sarah stopped fidgeting "the army?" she seemed shocked as if she had been told that somebody had died "Why the army?"

"I have always wanted to join the army you know that" Kevin said confidently.

"I know but people get killed" Sarah said concerned

"People get killed in road accidents or by other means you can't say its just through war" Kevin tried to reason with Sarah.

"But those people don't go out to get killed" Sarah said sharply

There was a pause while both looked at each other both reflecting back at their childhood, the years of playing with plastic dolls and action men or playing tennis.

"Sarah we go back a long way, we have never fallen out" Kevin tried to reason with her.

"I know I just worry about you we are old friends" Sarah said knowing she felt more for him that she wanted him to know

Kevin was fond of Sarah but not in love with her, he considered their friendship as special but nothing else.

Kevin never mentioned his girl friend Jackie but after their meeting he walked Sarah to her hotel then headed to a bus stop and stood waiting for a bus, Jackie was already at the bus stop waiting for him. Sarah noticed them together kissing and her heart sank. Her hopes had been dashed by the presence of Jackie whatever plans Sarah had for them was over.

Sarah was in the nursing profession, in a sense she had followed her dream as a latter day Florence Nightingale. But not content with this she joined the military hospital dealing with wounded soldiers perhaps it had something to do with Kevin being in the army. Perhaps she thought she could watch over him as a nurse and maybe eventually win his love through helping him. She had thought about what Kevin had said in the café a few months ago. Sarah plunged herself into her career and proved to be a hard working nurse, she also soon gained promotion becoming a ward sister. She was strict but fair and continued with her OCD maintaining ward cleanliness and insisting that everything is put back in its place.

Meanwhile Kevin had joined the army and was being stationed abroad he was being sent to Malaya near rubber plantations. Kevin entered the army doing basic training, he longed to get through and get stationed somewhere abroad, Malaya was having trouble with gorilla warfare people were being ambushed and killed. When he arrived at the barracks he was orientated to the army camp by some of the regular soldiers and made to feel at home or this is what he led Sarah to believe. In reality he was probably having a rough time being disciplined as Kevin hated routine and found Sarah's OCD difficult to except so he considered being regimented worse. He did well on the assault course only because he imagined Sarah at his side as he combated most of the obstacles. Although he loved Jackie he found that he was thinking of Sarah whenever he was alone, remembering his childhood.

At the barracks other new recruits were discussing relationships some were single, some had girl friends and others were married. One soldier noticed a photograph of Sarah on the top of his locker and made comment.

"Is this your girl friend? She's beautiful" He said admiring the picture

"No she's a special friend" Kevin replied

"Oh come on she has to be your girl friend" He continued "She would not be displayed on your locker if she was just a friend. "Or are you gay?".

Kevin was shocked by his remark and very offended as he respected Sarah and hated anyone saying anything against her. Also although Kevin was heterosexual he respected other people's sexuality, he felt everybody had the right to do as they pleased as long as it didn't harm other people. His philosophy of life was to live and let live, therefore respecting other peoples religion, culture and sexuality. Sarah agreed with this principle and that's the main reason they remained good friends.

"I have explained things to you George so just except that Sarah is my friend and for your information I am not gay" Kevin said bluntly "I love Jackie"

"Well your sensitive" George replied

"Fuck you George I told you how it is" Kevin said angrily.

"Hey don't give me grief, I bet your woman wouldn't like you swearing" George said teasing Kevin

"I am marrying Jackie" Kevin insisted, "I love her"

"Are you sure about that?" George replied

"What do you mean by that?" Kevin asked angrily

"Its obvious you really love Sarah" George said

"I don't want to discuss it" Kevin said dismissively

"If you love Sarah you can't marry Jackie" George insisted

"Look its complicated and I can't think straight ok" Kevin said clutching the photograph of Sarah

"Ok mate but think about it" George walked away leaving Kevin bewildered.

Kevin was sent to Vietnam with his regiment facing a war that proved to be more that he expected it was not only jungle warfare but also a drug-educed nightmare. People were taking drugs to cope with the perils of war and Kevin had joined them, the whole horror of jungle fighting with an enemy who had experience in jungle life. After months in the jungle fighting and surviving the battle became more intense and the casualties became many.

Kevin was wounded by a blast from mortar fire; he was thrown into the air and landed on the ground unconscious. He woke up in hospital but had no idea where he was and what had happened. A flash from the blast blinded Kevin and shrapnel had entered his body. Sarah was in the hospital caring for the wounded when she saw Kevin; he was lying down with his eyes bandaged.

"Kevin its Sarah" She whispered in his ear.

"Sarah is that really you?" Kevin replied turning in the direction of the voice.

"Yes of course its me" Sarah said jovially.

"But I don't understand how did you get here"

Kevin said confused.

"I am a nurse remember and I too joined the army" Sarah said examining his bandages.

"I thought when that blast hit me that I would never see you again" Kevin said sadly.

"Now Kevin you don't think I would let you off that easy" Sarah said confidently.

"I guess not" Kevin replied.

"Besides we need to get you well" Sarah said mopping his brow.

Sarah nursed Kevin for months afterwards eventually he was well enough to go home he failed to regain his sight and it took a further two years to fully recover and once he could see again he planned to see Sarah and thank her for helping him.

Kevin was fighting his feelings for Sarah as he felt their relationship was as friends not lovers, but Sarah felt stronger than him that things could work. Kevin eventually went back to Jackie and they got married in church Jackie wore a white dress with a beautiful veil. But even then Kevin saw Sarah's face and not Jackie he even dreamed of lifting her veil and seeing Sarah.

He tried writing to Sarah but never received a

reply due to the fact that Sarah was still abroad and helping wounded soldiers. She also knew that Kevin was getting married and wanted to take her mind off the event. To bury herself in her work was the only way that she could deal with losing Kevin to Jackie. But Sarah had been involved with another soldier and admitted to her cousin Laura that she was using him as she loved Kevin and no one could ever replace him.

Eventually Kevin managed to travel to Sarah's hometown and she had just arrived on leave. Kevin had booked into a hotel near her home and awaited her arrival home. He noticed her heading for home and called to her.

"Sarah!" He shouted.

Sarah turned searching for the familiar voice but couldn't see him, Kevin was deliberately hiding.

"Sarah I was the one who was blind not you" He said laughing

"Kevin where are you?" Sarah shouted.

At that moment Kevin appeared and ran up to Sarah as she reached him he picked her up and spun round with her in the air. He then kissed her and put her down still holding her he smiled and spoke in a calm voice.

"I had to see you" He said.

"I am pleased you're here" Sarah said her heart was beating almost through her chest.

"Are you?" Kevin said a little bewildered.

"Where are you staying?" Sarah asked still excited and trembling.

"At that hotel" He pointed at the hotel nearby.

"Come and have a drink with me" He invited.

"But I am shabby from my journey" Sarah said pointing to her uniform.

"Its fine get you can clean up and change in my room" Kevin offered.

"Really" Sarah said suspiciously.

"Come on Sarah you can trust me we have been friends for years" Kevin was reminding Sarah of the years they spent together as friends.

"I know lead the way" Sarah insisted.

They entered the hotel and headed upstairs to his room, Sarah took her belonging to the bathroom and got ready for her shower. While she was in the shower she began to feel odd her legs were weak, never the less she continued washing and stepped out of the shower refreshed.

She changed her clothes producing a dress from her case and placing her make up bag on the side. She went dizzy again and sat on the toilet for a moment, her legs were tingling and she was frightened.

She eventually came out of the bathroom and looked oddly at Kevin then placed her bag on the bed. She looked back at the bathroom then at Kevin who stood bewildered at her.

"Are you alright you spent a long time in there?" Kevin eventually said.

"Yes of course I am women take a while to get ready you know" Sarah said sharply.

They headed downstairs to the bar Sarah sat at a table while Kevin headed to the bar. When he arrived back to Sarah he was holding two drinks and a menu under his right arm.

"I thought you might be hungry" He said offering Sarah the menu.

"Yes I am starving" Sarah said smiling "And I am sorry about earlier I suppose I am nervous"

"But why its only me" Kevin said jokingly

"I know perhaps I am tired from travelling" Sarah admitted

"I really can't believe that we have so many

years behind us" Kevin said.

"Yes the times we played together with my plastic dolls and your action men" Sarah began to relax and felt comfortable again in his company.

The evening passed and it was soon ten o'clock in the evening they returned to the hotel room, Sarah picked up her bag, then turned around to face Kevin. He was gazing into her eyes and began to speak to her in a gentle voice.

"I have missed you" Kevin admitted "I think of you often"

"Don't do this" Sarah said upset.

"Sarah I love you" Kevin confessed.

"No this is wrong, what you are saying is wrong" Sarah said

"No you know it isn't, we were meant together" Kevin said gripping her shoulders with his hands.

Sarah's bag dropped off her shoulder and landed on the floor, Kevin then kissed her tenderly on the lips. Sarah became hot and confused she returned a kiss and he began to kiss her neck. She pulled back and screamed at him.

"No that's enough Kevin" Sarah shouted "Your not being fair"

"Please forgive me Sarah" Kevin said upset.

Sarah bent down to pick up her bag then turned around to Kevin who was now sitting on the bed. She walked over to him removing her dress and kneeling down to him. She kissed him and began to remove his shirt she had become the seducer and was doing what she always wanted to do. Kevin responded by removing the rest of her clothes, she then kissed his naked chest and he coursed her breasts. She continued to kiss him and brushed her hands down his body, while he caressed her buttocks before long they were making love through the night.

By morning they were both naked on the bed, Sarah was the first to wake up and watched Kevin sleeping, she knew that this was a moment of weakness for both of them and that guilt would set in. Kevin had to go back to his wife and she needed to clear her head. Is this what its like to be a mistress how very uncomfortable having to share a man in this way. Sarah had to think about what she was doing, she was so confused Kevin was her friend from childhood they were friends that crossed the boundaries in a moment of weakness. Its no good Sarah thought I can't justify what I have done by bringing up our friendship and using that as an excuse to make love to a married man. The thoughts continued as Kevin began to wake up Sarah stayed in bed in his arms and smiled as he woke and looked at her.

"Good morning" Kevin said kissing her forehead.

"Good morning" Sarah said kissing him back.

"No regrets?" Kevin asked her.

"No not at all" Sarah replied although inside she was feeling differently, but unable to discuss her true feelings of guilt in case she spoilt the moment.

Later Sarah left the room for home and Kevin left for the station to return to his wife, they met regularly after this for a few months then they were both stationed abroad. Sarah went to Germany and Kevin returned to Vietnam. Then Sarah discovered that she was pregnant and had to make a decision whether to tell Kevin or not. She had even contemplated abortion, after all her career was now compromised but this was a love child that she could cherish forever as a part of Kevin if she couldn't have him she could have his child.

Kevin regretted betraying his wife and cheating on her and returned to the family home. Sarah was pregnant but kept the baby a secret; she gave birth to a daughter who she named Pamela.

Pamela was blonde and beautiful; she was regarded as Sarah's pure treasure just like her porcelain ornaments like her mask. She attended school and was very clever, she attracted all the boy's attention and knew it she teased them and then sent them away not wanting to know them. Pamela was brought up in the modelling world Sarah wanted the best for her and her perfect daughter had to be treated well as her own angel. After Pamela's birth Sarah was having further problems with her health the tingling in her legs lasted longer at times her legs were numb.

Kevin went back to the battlefront and was killed in action; he was literally blown to pieces his head separated from his body just like his action man as if it was destined to happen that way. His body was flown home and a military funeral arranged. Kevin never knew about Sarah's secret and what was worse not long afterwards she developed Multiple sclerosis and she deemed that it was a punishment for having an affair with Kevin and having his baby. Kevin died with the photo of Sarah in his hand a sudden explosion near their camp killed him and a few of his colleagues. George went to visit Sarah in order to explain what had happened her address was in his notebook, which he kept on him at all, times. When George turned up at the doorstep Sarah knew what had happened and collapsed in shock, fortunately she was with family and friends who helped her to a seat.

"He really loved you Sarah, but his heart was torn in two" George explained.

"I know how he felt about me" Sarah said.

"He mentioned your name when we were in the jungle" George said.

"Saying what?" Sarah asked.

"That if he had his time over he would have married you" George wanted to say more but at this point a child entered the room, it was Pamela aged three.

"This is Pamela, she is Kevin's daughter" Sarah announced.

"He didn't mention her" George said with tears in his eyes.

"He didn't know" Sarah admitted "But Pamela is the best thing that came from us and the biggest reminder of him"

"I can see Kevin in her" George said looking at

Pamela.

Sarah got up and went into the bedroom she looked in the wardrobe and found a box, she returned with an action man in her hand.

"I repaired the head on his action man" Sarah said handing it to George.

"He broke it when we were playing as children"

George looked at the porcelain masks that were displayed on the wall; one of them was cracked down the centre. He knew what Sarah was like about perfection so he never mentioned it, but Sarah noticed him looking at them and seeing the crack removed it from the wall in disgust.

"My work but this one is cracked so it needs to go" Sarah said throwing it in the bin.

"Your very good" George said touching one of them.

"I try my best to make them perfect" Sarah said trying to draw him away from the wall in case he disturbed any of them.

Sarah's cousin Laura called to him realising that Sarah wanted George to get away from the wall.

"Would you like a drink George?" she asked.

"No thank you I must go" He passed a porcelain

vase, which was stood, on a table near the door it was the most attractive ornament in the home decorated with flowers and a swirling pattern.

Sarah began to cry watching George leave seeing a uniform going out of the door like Kevin's

Pamela rushed over to her mother seeing her upset "Its ok mom everything is ok" she said trying to console her. Laura felt helpless as she looked on also crying.

Pamela was a beautiful child with her blonde hair and blue eyes soft unblemished skin and perfect white teeth, she was quiet but very confident walking so gracefully across the room. She was taught how to perform in front of the camera and could model children's clothes better than any other child; she was like a miniature adult modelling clothes and in soap adverts. Pamela was known for some of her television appearances as she appeared in adverts she was also on posters advertising various products. Pamela became the angel of child modelling whom many mothers admired across the country. She had the walk and the talk and she was making a lot of money for her disabled mother. They lived in a bungalow adapted for her and her needs. Pamela was growing up and by now she had reached her teens, she had informed her mother about Peter explaining in detail what he said and done, he was her uncle who had abused her and threatened her to remain silent or he would tell her mother that she was no angel and not the perfect porcelain child her mother loved. "I am no longer your perfect porcelain child" she said disappointed, "I am cracked porcelain to you mother".

Sarah looked into her eyes and spoke gently "You will always be my angel" she said hugging her.

Pamela was growing up with her own nightmares as she was being molested by her uncle Peter and was threatened to keep quiet about it or her mother would be angry with her perfect daughter. He was finally exposed when he was caught molesting another child, he was a short fat man wearing thick glasses and spoke with a Scottish accent. A group of angry parents took the law into their own hands and killed him. He was caught at his allotment with the child she was taken away, he was beaten until he was unable to move, his shed was covered in petrol and his shed was burnt down with him inside. But this was nothing compared to the horror her mother and her were going to encounter in their home, a living nightmare was about to take place. One summer's night two men in masks armed with baseball bats broke into their home and smashed the place up including the porcelain ornaments. They then beat and raped both of them and killed Sarah leaving Pamela as cracked porcelain, a once perfect child part of her mothers porcelain cracked and no longer perfect. Pamela was having flashbacks about the attack these consisted of the rape and the terrible battering that her mother had and the blood splashed across Pamela's face. Pamela stood silent trembling staring at her mother's lifeless body, although she had tears streaming from her face she was unable to speak or react in any other way. Pamela often had nightmares and woke up screaming, she would only speak of a baseball bat being wielded in the air and smashing porcelain masks and other ornaments. Nothing about her rape or her mother's horrific death or the blood on Pamela's hands and face as she witnessed her mother being battered to death.

Pamela was then brought up by her relatives and suffered mentally by the trauma, she was said to have multiple personality or disassociate identity disorder. Her mind split into at least sixteen personalities and she created a hatred for men, she was often admitted to the psychiatric hospital. Often she would come in like a wild beast and left victims behind, her modelling career was surprisingly successful despite her condition. Pamela knew how to perform and left alone she would perform like an angel leading models onto the stage or catwalk. Her aunty Laura brought her up but found it difficult to manage her, when she would take on one of her personalities acting like a younger child refusing to acknowledge her real name. Laura was the closest person to her and knew more about Sarah than anyone else, she harboured many secrets never revealed at this time.

Beautiful

It was a hot summer's night the rain was pouring down and people were running down the street trying to shelter from the storm. Thunder was heard in the distance and the odd flash of lightening indicated that the worst of the storm was yet to come.

But despite the weather outside things were quiet at a local psychiatric hospital as the patients sat around the lounge areas or wandered the corridors unaffected by the weather condition outside. One lounge was filled with cigarette smoke as patients sat smoking and occasionally coughing or mumbling to themselves. Some would strike up conversations or fidget uncontrollably others just stared into space.

Two of the staff sat discussing previous events of the day, they then diverted to outside pursuits such as their social life. Kathy Duke was a well a plump and big breasted lady with short blonde hair about thirty-nine, while her colleague Ruth Ashley was a slim beautiful lady with peachy soft tanned complexion, she had long dark hair and a radiant smile. She was a little younger than Kathy about thirty, but quite mature for her age as if she had a lot of life experiences.

Suddenly Kathy let out a roar of laughter than startled a few patients while Ruth laughed a little lower.

"Honestly Kathy you make me laugh" Ruth said holding up her mug of coffee.

"Well you have to laugh honestly I have never had such a good time since we went to that bar" Kathy held up her mug "Cheers!"

Ruth adjusted her hair tying it back into a pony tail and securing it with a bobble her large brown eyes glancing up at the clock, the hands seemed to have stood still time seemed to pass slowly. Nothing was happening and they were in for a long shift, In fact the whole day was uneventful minus a few isolated incidents.

Suddenly the ringing of the office phone broke the silence, Ruth dropped her mug on the floor and it broke into pieces. Another member of staff ran to her rescue and helped her collect the fragments of the mug. She was an older member of staff who showed concern, as Ruth seemed quite nervous.

"It's ok only a mug not life or death" Ann said mopping up the coffee then noticing a slight cut on Ruth's hand.

"Are you ok" she asked concerned.

"Yes of course" wiping away the blood with a tissue. "It's only a scratch."

"I have seen you in a worst state after that boyfriend of yours got hold of you, what was his name Malcolm wasn't it"

"Yes Malcolm, well he's history believe me" Ruth said standing to her feet.

"Good you can do better than him" Ann said smiling "I've had a few sad bastards myself" she continued "None of them worth anything" Ann said with a sour expression on her face as if she had just sucked a lemon.

Ruth pondered for a moment and replied.

"He was a real psycho he must have been like it with others fits of anger and inner rage surging through him striking out at everyone and everything".

"Sounds like an animal he should be locked up" Ann said frowning.

"Oh he is, ask Kathy she was with me when he was arrested."

Ruth suddenly dropped the pen that she was playing with in her hand.

"Christ Ruth your nervous tonight" Kathy said with concern

"Sorry I suppose things are still on my mind" Ruth replied picking up the pen.

"Have we got an admission Kathy? Ann asked.

Kathy was looking shocked and found it difficult to speak at first "You could say that" said hesitantly "we do have an admission"

"So what's wrong it's not that late and it was getting boring" Ann said in anticipation of the pending news.

"No it's not late Ann but you won't like this" Kathy said waving a piece of paper in her hand.

"Not Jimmy the by polar or Caroline the schizophrenic" Ann guessed.

"It's bad isn't it Kathy" Ruth said worried.

"You really won't like this one" Kathy said she seemed very uneasy.

"for Christ sake tell us Kathy"

"Do you remember Pamela Brown?" Kathy said looking at Ann

"Oh for god sake no" Ann replied "Yes I remember Pamela from ward 35".Ann was an older woman large in size and loud she was also very opinionated.

Ruth noticed the look of dread on Ann's face and turned to Kathy "So who is she?"

Kathy hesitated for a moment and looked at Ann for support

Ann's expression changed from a look of surprise to a look of horror "One weird bitch, who brings this ward into an uproar" She paused then continued "A truly evil madam who is cursed by the devil himself"

"Kathy interrupted honestly Ann she's not that bad"

"How bad?" Ruth asked concerned for her own safety

Kathy sat Ruth down and placed her hand on hers "She has a few problems and has complex needs, she has quite a history of abuse and traumatic episodes that would turn your head honestly.

"Yes like the exorcist a mad fucker believe me" Ann said sarcastically.

Kathy looked at Ann in disgust "Why don't you prepare for our admission"

"Ok but don't say I haven't warned you Ruth" Ann said walking away.

Kathy took a breath and then continued to explain about Pamela to Ruth.

"Pamela Brown is a twenty seven year old woman who is suffering from multiple personality syndrome or disassociate identity disorder as it's called today". She stopped looked at the time then continued.

"Her mind is divided into a number of identities which manifest themselves in many ways mainly in various voices noticeable when she is interviewed or when she is annoyed with someone most of them she believes protect her. Pamela as the host is often hidden away by these other identities and she can become very dangerous to herself and others". Kathy looked at the clock again.

."You need to read her notes to know more we need to prepare for her arrival. The police have just arrested her and put her on a section 136 you know the police holding power, Dr Gilbert is on the way to the ward to meet her so expect fireworks" Kathy rose to her feet and beckoned Ruth to the office.

"I am aware of the mental health act of 1983 section 136 is when the police can take a person from a public place to a place of safety" Ruth said confidently.

Ruth followed close behind her still asking questions "Kathy what has she done this time?"

"Stabbed a man in the shoulder with a bread knife" Kathy replied "Oh and attacked a policeman, the police knew her and seeing her rocking and speaking in various voices assumed she had relapsed.

At that moment Dr Geoff Gilbert entered the ward dressed in a brown suit, a pale yellow shirt and a dark red dickey bow. He had a goatee brown beard and wore silver rimmed spectacles, which were stained in the corner of the left lens. He looked around for Kathy and seeing her began to speak in a superior manner acting as if he wanted to be anywhere rather on the ward.

"So are we expecting the bitch to arrive?" Geoff

said to Kathy and Ruth.

Kathy gave a look of despair and nodded "Yes we are expecting Pamela"

Geoff grunted, "I hope you are this time" Geoff was preparing an injection and then smiled "I will be prepared"

"Is this because of that war wound?" Kathy said pointing to a scar about 3cm long down the side of his cheek.

"Well the bitch won't attack me again" He said smugly

"Geoff you don't mean that, not you" Kathy said looking at him in disbelief.

"I don't believe you Geoff honestly this woman has experienced so much and you can be like that makes me wonder which ones the patient". Ruth said angrily.

"Ruth you don't know her so you can hardly comment wait till you do then you may change your mind" Geoff said in retaliation.

Oh whatever happened to compassion Pamela has been through a lot and what do you care". Ruth continued, "Men honestly you think you can all walk over women use and abuse them".

"Do I detect martyrdom here Ruth is it getting

personal because of your relationship" Geoff said looking at Ruth then Kathy.

"You mean because I was treated badly by Malcolm" Replied Ruth "Are you fucking psychoanalyzing me now".

Kathy picked up on Geoff's cue for her to come forward in his defense, she peered at Ruth with a look of superiority "Ruth that's enough lets all be professional I agree Pamela has been through a lot but we need to deal with whatever comes through that door ok?"

Ruth nodded and sat herself down tears rolling down her cheeks.

Geoff put his hand on her shoulder and spoke gently "I am sorry Ruth really I am, but you have so much to learn".

Ruth cursed him under her breath "Sarcastic bastard"

Kathy gave a sympathetic smile and also patted her on the shoulder "Bless you Ruth you really care, we care too but you have to separate yourself from the patients or they will destroy you in the end".

Kathy seemed to be speaking from experience, as her voice seemed to change from a harsh to a more sympathetic tone. Her expression also changed from a sterner to a mellower look. Ruth could see this but never commented.

After a short time had passed with very little conversation and a silent atmosphere, shouting and the slamming of car doors broke the silence. The blue lights from the police van were seen through the ward windows Kathy shouted to the other staff alerting them. "She's here get yourselves ready".

Kathy opened the door and immediately noticed blood on one of the police officers face. The other officer's face looked red and angry. They were dragging a woman between them who looked pale and very angry as she struggled trying to kick them.

She had scraggily wet blond hair with a dirty face she wore a soaked blood stained dress and bare feet. She made no real eye contact with anyone but continued to shout and fight with the police like a wild cat.

"Free me you bastards, get your perverted hands off me". She shouted.

She spat in one of the officer's face and tried to head butt the other.

"Fuck off and leave me or I swear I will fucking kill you". She continued as they pulled her to the floor assisted by the nurses. She was becoming wilder until the doctor approached with a syringe trying to inject her with a sedative. She kicked him in the testicles which angered him he approached her and this time managed to inject her. Kathy then launched forward and pushed Pamela back to the ground, at that moment Ruth shouted "stop!"

No one was actually sure whom she was shouting at but everyone did stop including Pamela who actually gave Ruth eye contact, she was staring at Ruth completely motionless. Pamela began to smile at her tears came trickling from her eyes. Ruth knelt in front of her and smiled back at her placing her hands on her face and catching her tears.

"Pamela your safe now" she said stroking her hair

Ruth turned her head to look at one of the officers "Remove the handcuffs and leave her alone" she instructed.

Pamela rested her head on Ruth's chest and wept.

Kathy warned Ruth "Careful" she advised her and watched everyone move back.

Suddenly Pamela brought her arms forward; everybody hesitated and watched with surprise as she wrapped her arms around Ruth. All were speechless and until the police headed towards the office.

"Good luck with her" the injured officer said.

Kathy and Geoff went to the office with them.

"Get something done about that wound" Kathy advised

"Will do" the officer agreed "And you get something done about her"

Ruth still had staff around her so Kathy felt comfortable escorting the officers to the office and gathering information from them concerning Pamela.

Geoff shook his head "why do I do this job?"

The officers looked at him and said, "Well it can't be easy, but neither is ours"

Geoff came in with a tray of water and dressings "Let's treat your wound for you".

Kathy returned to Ruth who by now was sitting

on a chair next to Pamela.

"She needs cleaning up and admitting there is still a lot to do"

Before Ruth could speak Pamela raised her head and looked at Ruth.

"I want her to help me no one else"

Ruth looked at Kathy and spoke confidently.

"I will see to her" she said.

"You will need help to shower her" Kathy said concerned.

"No she is fine; I will call you if I have any problems". Ruth replied "For some reason I think she likes me".

"Ok but be careful, call us if you need help". Kathy couldn't help being cautious after previous events "She does seem to respond to you, but call us ok?"

Ruth took Pamela to the shower room, she explained how the shower worked and placed a towel and soap near her. Pamela began to take off her damp clothing and place them on the floor; Ruth had picked up some fresh clothes on the way to the shower room.

As Pamela began to shower Ruth noticed scars on her wrists and torso most of which were a result of self-harming. But these scars must have been superficial compared with her inner scars, the deeper wounds that were the result of such trauma in her life. Ruth handed her the shampoo and Pamela deliberately held her hand and just smiled as if to say I know you understand me. Ruth felt as if she could even read her thoughts and returned a smile. Ruth noticed the blood and mud flowing away with the water, drifting away as if it was never there.

When Pamela was drying herself she looked in the mirror and said.

"Am I beautiful now mother"

Ruth replied to her "Yes you are beautiful in every single way" Pamela had a beautiful face with blue eye that sparkled like diamonds, her skin was as soft as peach which glowed in the florescent lights. She hadn't really changed in appearance from her teen years but inside she was damaged from her experiences.

Pamela turned to her and said "Will you comb my hair?"

Pamela was now dressed and looked so much nicer and a true model, her face was soft and glowing, her natural blonde hair was like silk and matching her gorgeous blue eyes. A real angel and Such a contrast from the wild cat that had entered the ward tamed by a nurse who seemed to have an influence on her.

"I have to do your admission now Pamela" Ruth said opening the door to the corridor

"Interrogation you mean" she said smiling

"We can sit and relax in a private room ok?" Ruth said reassuring her.

"Ok sounds good" Although Pamela replied she seemed to have a strange expression on her face, almost detached from the person who spoke seconds before.

Ruth suddenly felt uneasy and walked down the corridor with Pamela. She was aware that Pamela could easily turn on the other staff and attack them. But felt confident that she was safe in Pamela's presence, providing she didn't upset her. Kathy was close by in the office and others were in the vicinity too so Ruth began to relax again. Pamela noticed the other staff and hurried into the private room ahead of Ruth, she obviously knew where she was going as she had been interviewed many times, in the same type of room. Each ward was geographically the same in design making it easy for agency staff to find their way around.

Ruth sat looking out of the glass window glancing at Kathy in the office; Pamela appeared to be very uneasy especially when other patients went passed particularly male ones. Ruth still could not believe the transformation from wildcat to angel, if she hadn't seen the display from the front door with the policemen then she would no doubt feel easier in her presence now.

Kathy came to the door and gave Ruth some papers; she led her out of earshot and began explaining what had happened from the police report. Ruth kept glancing at Pamela checking that she was still calm, while listening intently to Kathy and trying not to show any reaction in case it startled Pamela.

Ruth entered the interview room and sat opposite Pamela someone had made them a drink and Pamela was already drinking hers. Ruth glanced at the panic alarm which was on the wall close to the far wall, the staff often used it in an emergency even Ruth had used it on occasions. Although Pamela appeared relaxed she remained unpredictable and was capable of acts of aggression, Ruth had also been told of Pamela's violent incident in the community that led to her arrest.

"Pamela" Ruth began.

"I am not Pamela" replied in a deep voice.

Ruth hesitated looking at Pamela in disbelief.

"Then who are you?" Ruth said trying to understand her.

"I am James"

"Ok where do you live"

Ruth entered the interview room and sat opposite Pamela someone had made them a drink and Pamela was already drinking hers. Ruth glanced at the panic alarm which was on the wall close to the far wall, the staff often used it in an emergency even Ruth had used it on occasions. Although Pamela appeared relaxed she remained unpredictable and was capable of acts of aggression, Ruth had also been told of Pamela's violent incident in the community that led to her arrest.

"Pamela" Ruth began.

"I am not Pamela" replied in a deep voice.

Ruth hesitated looking at Pamela in disbelief.

"Then who are you?" Ruth said trying to

understand her.

"I am James"

"Ok where do you live"

Ruth was confused by this behaviour and glanced across to the office at Kathy shrugging her shoulders. Kathy was used to Pamela's behaviour and nodded as if to say its normal for her and to persevere.

"Ok who are you?"

"I am Anna" She said in a childlike voice.

"So tell me Anna what happened to you?" Ruth felt awkward talking to this child like personality; she also thought that Pamela was playing games with her. Ruth was not used to this kind of interview and certainly not used to multiple personality conditions such as Pamela had. She could however relate to being maltreated and various types of abuse.

"Do you want to hurt Pamela, or play games in secret" Pamela asked as her Anna identity.

"I want to help you" Ruth said feeling uncomfortable with the voice she heard.

"He plays games with her in secret" The voice continued in an eerie tone.

"What does he do, what games" Ruth asked

dreading the reply.

"I can't tell you its secret" She replied.

"Did you like the games Anna?" Ruth asked.

"No, no they are horrible games" She replied in the child's voice "He hurts me".

Ruth tried to hide her feelings of dread, as she seemed to be listening to her own childhood abuse spoken by Pamela's child identity.

Pamela looked at Ruth and could see the anguish on her face, after displaying a few more personalities the host came forward, this was the real Pamela, a most unusual display and out of character for her to reveal her true self in an interview like this.

"Have I hurt you, I really don't mean to" Pamela said concerned watching Ruth expression change at her identity Anna's remark.

"I just want to help you". Ruth felt as if she had broken down the walls and finally found Pamela, but Ruth herself was feeling the strain of interviewing Pamela and her identities.

Pamela tried to speak of her experiences, but merely broke down and cried allowing her other personalities to take over again. The interview lasted an hour by which time Ruth was exhausted trying to follow a conversation with each personality as Pamela's mind rapidly switched from one to another without a blink of an eye.

Ruth left the interview and excused herself with Kathy as she ran into the bathroom and proceeded to vomit into the toilet. Kathy raced after her and noticed the state she was in, she wet a kitchen towel and handed it to her.

"Are you alright?" Kathy asked.

"I suppose so" Ruth replied.

"Its never easy is it" Kathy said rubbing her back.

"You never forget it" Ruth said wiping her face.

"Forget?" Kathy was confused.

"Christ Kathy I have told you about my childhood". Ruth said shaking.

"Oh my god I am so sorry, I forgot" Kathy realized "Your abuse, and I sent you to interview her".

"Its ok" Ruth said almost smiling "It just gets me sometimes, I relive it especially at night".

"It must be awful, you're some brave lady". Kathy said hugging her.

After this Ruth spent time with Kathy going

over points that were relevant and discarding other remarks. Pamela was so complex it was impossible to know what was true and what was not, Pamela was not lying but possibly fabricating the truth, even her memory was separated into each identity making it difficult to remember anything.

Kathy understood Ruth's dilemma she had interviewed Pamela many times and never got anywhere with her. She often wondered how she ever survived in the community and even kept down a job as a model although she was so beautiful.

"At least you got further than me, I was totally bewildered by these personalities and never spoke to the real Pamela" Kathy said writing Pamela's name on the white board.

"But I thought for a moment that I had broken through"

"Give me by polar any time its more straight forward mania and depression not much else" Kathy laughed and continued writing.

"Trust you Kathy nothing seems to faze you" Ruth said reading Pamela's file.

Ruth read about the events leading to Pamela's

arrest and section, Pamela was working as a model when one of the male models approached her asking for a date according to the male model Pamela went with him but when he led her to his apartment she changed. He made the usual advances but she was reluctant to get involved and became hostile. They were in the kitchen she plunged a kitchen knife into his shoulder and ran out of the apartment. The knife was found near the kitchen door she had obviously dropped it on the way out. The police found her round the corner near a grass bank in mud she fought with the officers they arrested her and put her on a section. The statement seemed to lack detail and was one sided it would seem that she was the assailant and not the victim. The gentleman in question was treated in casualty and refused to press charges.

It is also evident that both Pamela and Ruth had been treated badly by men in the past. Pamela had been raped and her mother murdered by two men who were never caught. Her uncle abused Ruth as a child and Pamela was also abused although Ruth's uncle was imprisoned. Pamela's mother Sarah wanted Pamela to become a child model and encouraged her to perform in front of cameras, she became a model for catalogues later her mother was diagnosed with multiple scleroses (M.S) and reacted badly to the news.

Sarah was a good looking woman and potential model herself, she was also a perfectionist her home was spotless she also had obsessive compulsive disorder (O.C.D) which made it a difficult environment for Pamela to live in everything had to be perfect including Pamela. Sarah collected porcelain and would clean every item of porcelain.

daily not a crack or blemish in anything. Pamela once broke one item and it was glued together Pamela was punished for the deed and made to stay in her room and reflect on her miss deed. Pamela was made to glue the item back together and never forgot it.

As Pamela had been brought up in this perfect world when she was abused she became like the cracked porcelain, her rape and murder of her mother tipped her over the edge and as a result her mind split into many personalities and now at thirty years old she is suffering from multiple personality syndrome and unable to function affectively in society without medication. She has had countless therapy and counseling nothing so far has worked effectively the only way to live a normal life again is to contact the host personality that is the real Pamela and eliminate the other personalities. This is very hard to achieve and can only be done by therapy.

Kath noticed Ruth reading Pamela's psychiatric history and immediately commented, "Well what do you think?"

"It's tragic isn't it" Ruth said tearfully.

"You think?" Kathy said coldly.

"So how do you deal with this?" Ruth said with concerned.

Kathy looked at Ruth and noticed that she was upset, she then shrugged her shoulders and said "We do the best we can with what we have."

"We use the multi disciplinary team such as councilors or psychologists and others, but its not always successful. So you get what Pamela is and that is a revolving door" Kathy was trying to reason with Ruth presenting her with the facts.

"So the revolving doors as we know are those who keep coming back for treatment like those who relapse."

"Yes those who come in go out and return just

as bad as before" Kathy waved her hand as if to dismiss them.

"So we just give up then" Ruth said sharply.

Kathy frowned at Ruth "Its never easy and if you think your going to make a difference forget it, they are revolving doors and always will be" she pointed out to where Pamela was sitting quietly "Pamela is one of them so don't get involved".

"She wanted me to help her". Ruth replied, "To build up a therapeutic relationship"

"Well don't expect a miracle cure or anything, she has been through a lot no doubt about that but as for a way to help her" Kathy was attempting to help Ruth understand the situation.

Ruth felt like she had been shot down in flames, she was confident that she could help Pamela, but needed reassurance that she was doing the right thing.

Kathy pointed to Pamela's file "Look we have to be seen trying to help these people, but we merely go through the motions while society crushes them and sends them back in weaker and more vulnerable".

Ruth stood to her feet and looked at Pamela who was glancing into the office still in the same chair.

"But look at her she has so much going for her beautiful and wise" Ruth then glanced at Kathy.

"Tell me Ruth, why did you choose mental health, why didn't you do modeling your pretty and have a nice figure?"

"I did it to make a difference, to help people". Ruth said sincerely.

"Then you really are delusional" Kathy said in dismay.

Ruth thought about what Kathy had said, in her own mind did she want to become as negative as Kathy. Perhaps the years of working in a mental health environment as a mental health nurse had that effect on people. But then who would help such people if so many had so much negativity. Ruth had been joking with Kathy about the days events on the ward, she was holding a mental health magazine in her hand.

"Here we are" she said confidently "Narcissistic personality disorder".

"Well!" Kathy exclaimed.

"This is Geoff" she insisted.

"A fucking narcissist" Kathy laughed at the thought of doctor Geoffrey as a narcissist "Ruth you kill me" she continued.

"Yes a grandiose of self importance" she read from the magazine "preoccupied with unlimited success, power and brilliance" she read on.

"In other words a cocky fucker" Kathy concluded.

"Shows arrogant and haughty behaviours or attitudes" Ruth laughed after reading this.

"As I said a cocky fucker" Kathy said laughing with her.

"Believes others are envious of him" Ruth went on.

"Hardly" Kathy said "he the last person I would want to be"

"Oh yes!" Ruth shouted.

"What the fuck" Kathy replied.

"Lacks empathy and unwilling to recognise or identify with the feelings of others" Ruth clapped her hands "that's him".

"Yes I do agree there" Kathy said sipping from her glass of larger.

Ruth raised her glass "To Geoff you narcissist bastard" She then drank from it.

"Fancy a Chinese?" Kathy asked Ruth.

"No thanks they are too short and have small dicks" Ruth replied laughing.

"I mean restaurant" Kathy said tutting.

"Know I am in a totally silly mood tonight"

"I can't tell" Kathy replied sarcastically.

"What about an Indian then? Ruth asked.

"Smelly and sweaty" Kath replied, "Yes ok" she agreed.

They left the pub and walked down the street to a nearby Indian restaurant, Ruth sensed that they were being followed and stopped for a moment. She turned and looked around but saw no one. However lurking in a shop doorway was Malcolm, wearing dark clothes and hiding in shadowed areas in order to conceal his identity.

Ruth spent days with Pamela talking to her, attending the ward rounds with other professionals hoping Pamela would speak freely and express the things she needed to, over the months Ruth proved that she was making a difference to Pamela's progress and reversed some of the negativity that had been evident over the years. Pamela's other identities continued to dominate the conversations particularly James who acted as her guardian or superman. Pamela would never freely reveal her feelings to anyone and the other identities often protected Pamela as the host.

Whenever Ruth was off duty from the ward incidences would occur often triggered by a male patient shouting at her or touching her, even smells of cheap after shave or tobacco could cause Pamela to become hostile. Her identities would take over and attack another patient incurring damage and causing her to be restrained and medicated. She even resulted in self harm driven by guilt and shame, people often said that she was suffering from delusional ideations or a persecution complex, but often these were people who had never suffered from any kind of trauma such as rape or child abuse.

Ruth did understand and somehow knew this and felt secure in her presence, in fact as time went on they became very close. Staff had mixed feelings about this, some considered it a good thing as progress was being achieved others thought it was wrong and that the relationship could be damaging. It was thought that transference had taken place causing one or the other to have strong feelings towards the other. Usually the patient experienced this for the professional, in this case the nurse. Others thought that Ruth would jeopardize Pamela's discharge by her friendship causing Pamela to want to stay with her on the ward. It is certainly evident that Pamela was better behaved when Ruth was present as if she could demonstrate behaviour modification to some degree, or have some control on herself or selves. In fact Pamela would search for Ruth on the ward and if she found her she would ask her to sit with her, but Ruth had to be careful not to show Pamela any favoritism.

On one occasion another patient attacked Ruth and Pamela raced to her defense, she hurled herself at the patient like the wild animal she had displayed on admission. Pamela clawed at her like a tiger after its prey and the patient fell to the ground screaming and covered in blood. The staff ran to both restraining both of them, Ruth shouted "Stop" and all was silent. Ruth explained the situation but Pamela's aggressive behaviour was against her as she was seen to cause the more damage. Pamela's last incident was attacking a male member of staff for entering her room, although he admitted he was in the wrong for not having a female escort and Ruth considered that he had an anterior motive. One patient really thought that she was an angel and admired her from afar calling her 'her angel', she often defended her when she is being retrained and shouting 'leave my angel alone'.

Pamela was a strong person when influenced by her other personalities or identities, but Ruth was more able to de escalate situations and normally defused any situation by just calling to Pamela. She eventually helped Pamela and earned respect from the more skeptical members of the team, some staff even called her in when problems occurred. For the first time in eight years Ruth finally felt like part of the team, confident that she had actually made a difference. Pamela is sat watching the music channel Christina Aguilera Beautiful, Pamela never moved until the video finished then waited until it was repeated.

Ruth entered the lounge to see tears rolling down her cheeks.

"This is a beautiful song and video, it has so much meaning, see the underweight girl looking at herself in the mirror how sad?"

Pamela speaks without taking her eyes off the TV screen

"How did you know it was me?" Ruth asked

"I knew" Pamela replied "Look at that skinny boy lifting weights".

"I like this video, it speaks volumes about altered body image" Ruth agreed.

"So many people commit suicide for this very reason" Pamela said sadly.

"Gay men tend to have a greater degree of body dissatisfaction" Ruth said putting her hand on Pamela's shoulder.

"Society can't accept Lesbian, gays or transsexuals because it's not classed as normal" Pamela said, "Well fuck normality"

"I agree fuck normality live and let live" Ruth said watching the video end.

The ward was usually alive with activity a girl with by polar (widely known as manic depression) during her periods of mania would race up and down the ward shouting, then in her depressive period sit and stare at the walls in her room. A schizophrenic would wear headphones playing music to drown out voices when he was experiencing audible hallucinations, sometime only wearing one ear piece. Lunchtime consisted of organizing meals for each patient and hoping that no one actually wore the meal during a fit of temper, or by the fact that they had been fighting. The occasional person needed restraining as they decided to become hostile (kick off) maybe they were experiencing visual hallucinations. Patients were known to listen to voices of command as they experienced audible hallucinations being given instructions by the devil to attack someone.

Pamela had to share a ward with many different patients but seemed to cope most of the time; this was classed as a high dependents unit where people were locked up for their own safety and the safety of others in the community. The presence of psychiatric nurse was not immediately obvious because they didn't wear uniform and wore their own clothes known as muftis. However by observing the activites of patients it soon became clear who were staff and who were patients. Most patients lined up for their medication, these were administered regularly by one of the nurses on duty. Some patients were compliant taking their medication others needed prompting, the occasional patient needed intramuscular injections others ECG (Electric shock treatment) this was mainly used for clinical depression it was like a form of barbaric torture but said to be effective in most cases. Pamela's condition was harder to treat due to the many personalities or identities that some like her created in their mind, averaging fourteen or more and each needing to be eliminating in order to reach the host or the real person.

Pamela's progress was clearly noticeable as she became involved in secular activities with the wards occupational therapists; she was creative and provided evidence of this in art classes, drawing female figures in an array of costumes in connection with her modeling career. Sometimes when she was experiencing a low period or was taken over by another identity she would produce bazaar pictures, for instance drawing barbed wire fences around a child. Sometimes scary eyes that were peeping out of trees or people falling from clouds which all had symbolic meanings usually connected to her past. Ruth was one of the few people who could find meaning in her work through conversations with Pamela or her identities.

As Pamela had showed good signs of recovery, plans could be made to discharge her. Ruth made sure that she would be involved with Pamela's release, she was eager to get her back into the community living a normal life. Normality was probably not what you could say about Pamela's life in modeling as it was based on an hectic lifestyle and sometimes required a lot of self discipline parading the catwalks or working long hours on photo shoots in some exotic location. Life was not all fun and glamour. In fact with Pamela's past and mental health problems it was even harder for her to maintain a position amongst some of the top fashion models.

Ruth was instrument in helping to change all this by supporting her, she seemed to provide her with the confidence to carry on despite her history of abuse. Pamela was actually discussing returning to work and modeling some of the latest fashions. Ruth provided her with the latest fashion magazines so that she could read the latest news on fashion, some of the photographs displayed clothes that Pamela herself had modeled in the past. Ruth could only imagine this type of world although Kathy sometimes suggested that she should venture into modeling, but Ruth merely shrugged off the idea, her life was in helping others not being glamorous like Pamela. Besides Ruth had heard of the bitchy women who went into modeling and she was made to feel very unglamorous by Malcolm who constantly insulted her looks and physique. If people abuse you long enough mentally, you begin to hate yourself and have such a low opinion of who you are in conjunction with society. Your have low self esteem and your confidence goes out of the window leaving you with nothing or a sense of worthlessness.

According to Ruth the object of a hospital is to get people well enough to rejoin society; Psychiatric wards are no exception to this rule. It is just as important to help people to live as normal life as possible in a normal environment. Unlike the old institutions that locked away mad people and threw away the key, this is the 21st century where we are supposed to care about our society and the people who live in it. We are supposed to make a difference today, gone is the stigma regarding mental health or is it, perhaps things are still in the dark ages. Ruth could be considered a pioneer in the field of mental health nursing providing many people like Pamela with hope for the future, maybe she could actually be the voice from the wilderness who cries out to the people. A nurse pleading for reason and understanding of the needs of the mentally ill, offering some glimmer of hope to them while the media just produce negative press about people being attacked by the mentally insane.

Perhaps in helping people like Pamela, Ruth can show the way for others to follow in her footsteps. Ruth believed that people should think positively and make the effort to see the good in people and not dwell on negativity. If Ruth showed that she could make a difference to Pamela's life then perhaps she could this with others.

NEW BEGINNING

After a few months Pamela was due to leave the ward, her discharge was planned centered around her re entering society and continuing her treatment as an outpatient. Her therapy seemed to be a success and she had herself eliminated some of her personalities/ identities and she was a happier person. It was also revealed by Pamela that Ruth actually resembled her mother Sarah and so the initial response to seeing Ruth on admission was based on this. But now the relationship with them was much stronger Kathy was particularly concerned about this advising Ruth to keep the arrangement professional. Kathy was older and more experienced, she had seen so much in her career as a mental health nurse to know when things just didn't feel right and foresaw short comings from such friendship.

The time arrived for Pamela to leave the ward, Ruth was with her discussing a follow up visit. But knew the community psychiatric team (C.P.N) would be taking over, she had to find a way of arranging to see her in between their visit. When Ruth said goodbye she embraced Pamela and slipped a note into her pocket, one of the C.P.N's were present waiting to take Pamela home but was unaware exactly what had happened. Pamela smiled as she put her hand in her pocket and felt the note Ruth returned a smile and said "Good luck and take care".

Once she had gone Kathy led Ruth into the office and threw Pamela's file to one side "That's the end of that one" she said with relief.

"She seemed fine didn't she?" Ruth said sadly trying to conceal her emotions.

"Yes I must admit you did well with this one" Kathy said scrubbing Pamela off the white board "Right all scrubbed off and forgotten" Kathy said coldly.

That very night Ruth went to Pamela's apartment, she knocked on the door then began pacing up and down anxiously. Pamela opened the door she was dressed in a white blouse and blue jeans, her hair was flowing down to her shoulders and her blue eyes sparkled in the light.

"Come in" she said softly as she stepped away from the door.

Ruth entered and after shutting the door followed Pamela to the lounge, the room was tidy with nothing out of place.

Pamela embraced Ruth kissing her on the cheek "Welcome to my home" she greeted "Please take a seat" she offered.

Ruth sat on a soft cream leather settee, she felt a little uneasy as she was unsure whether or not she should be there. If ever anyone found out she was there what would they think and was she doing right by continuing their friendship. At that moment Pamela smiled at her taking Ruth's mind off her own thoughts and instead thinking of Pamela.

"I read your note and so I was expecting you" Pamela said glancing into Ruth's large hazel eyes.

"I was hoping to see you soon after your discharge from the ward" Ruth replied glancing away from Pamela and looking around the room.

Pamela stood to her feet soon after sitting down "Sorry would you like a drink? she asked politely.

"Yes please" Ruth said looking back at her " a

cup of tea would be nice".

As Pamela headed for the kitchen Ruth scanned the room with her eyes she looked at every object in the room. And was attracted to the porcelain cups and saucers on a shelf each one neatly placed in a long line, each ornament was carefully painted with red roses and gold edging. Then she noticed a photograph and walked across the room to view it properly. It was Pamela with an older woman who actually did look like Ruth it was amazing an older version of Ruth no wonder she reacted the way she did on the day of her admission. Pamela's mother Sarah was diagnosed with Multiple sclerosis when Pamela was about nine. Such a stunning woman who could have been a model and walk the catwalk years before her daughter. It was almost like looking at herself in the mirror Ruth had trouble taking her eyes off it, in fact she had been staring at it so long she didn't notice Pamela return.

"That's my mother and me taken a not long before she died" Pamela said sadly.

"Sarah isn't it?" Ruth said nervously "She's beautiful like a model".

"She was my rock and guided me through my

career" Pamela said proudly.

"Help yourself to sugar Ruth" Pamela offered.

"Porcelain cups Pamela" Ruth said admiring the tea set.

"They were my mother's" she replied.

Ruth had noticed a slight crack in the one saucer and tried to cover her one finger over it, but Pamela had seen her and suddenly reacted by fidgeting.

"Oh let me change it for you" she insisted

Pamela had presented it so nicely on a laced tray cloth and on a silver tray as if to impress and now she has one item that shows imperfection cracked porcelain.

Pamela began to rock back and forth as she did on the ward, she had become very anxious and upset. Ruth began to show concern and tried to re assure her, she was worried that Pamela would have a relapse and return to the ward.

"It's ok Pamela really" Ruth said softly.

She thought Pamela had not heard her so spoke louder "Pamela I am here with you speak to me" Ruth felt helpless as she spoke to her.

Then to Ruth's surprise Pamela referred to her as her Mother

Repeating this over and over again "Mother!"

She then held out her trembling hands and continued sobbing, Ruth felt out of her depth but responded, "I am with you".

"I could not save you mother" she shook and continued, "They attacked you and I could not help you".

"But you were only a child" Ruth tried reasoning with her "A helpless child".

"I saw you fall against the cabinet all the porcelain fell cups, saucers plates everything, figures all smashed to the ground".

"Some remain look not all was lost" Ruth explained.

"The masks remain intact all but a small crack in one" Pamela pointed to one of the masks that were painted in a pink design.

Ruth looked at it on the wall it had been hung separately as if it was there for a reason, perhaps to remind Pamela that not everything is perfect and that her life was like the cracked porcelain.

Pamela had returned to that episode in her life that was so painful for her, but this time she was sharing it for the first time with someone else. Ruth sat holding Pamela as she related the full story to her from her own experience. They were at the family home when they heard a noise like the smashing of glass banging wood on wood and then two men appeared scruffily dressed and stinking of cigarettes and beer. The one man spoke in a rough voice "Get em Malcolm" he said wielding a baseball bat hitting some of the porcelain ornaments. They had made such a mess entering the premises and Pamela's mother had tried to protect her daughter by pushing herself forward in the wheelchair blocking the doorway. Pamela was thirteen and a shy, quiet type of girl living in her mother's shadow since she was abused by her uncle. Pamela got to the phone and managed to get the emergency services before Malcolm got to her, the receiver fell under the settee and was not detected for a while Malcolm was too occupied raping Pamela to see it. Meanwhile Roger was attacking Sarah.

Pamela felt him penetrate her in a rough mAnnr his horrible breath over powering her and the contrast of cheap after shave and sweat made the ordeal even worse. Pamela explained in detail how Malcolm had raped her and she felt so dirty afterwards. She was also ashamed and guilt ridden her perfect body had been defiled and her mother's angel was no more, the porcelain doll was cracked beyond repair. But worse than this they battered her mother to death, each blow was heard and the blood spurted onto Pamela's face across the room. Malcolm headed to Pamela as she tried to pull them off her mother, but they stopped at the sound of sirens and lights flashing. Malcolm shouted to her "You're lucky, next time hey".

"Come on" shouted Roger "It's the police.

Malcolm escaped but Roger was hit by a car and killed instantly, there was no trace of Malcolm and he has not been heard of since. The police and ambulance crew found Sarah dead beside her wheelchair and Pamela sat rocking on the floor reciting nursery rhymes.

Pamela was relaxed lying across Ruth reciting nursery rhymes to her a lot calmer and falling asleep, Ruth was also falling asleep exhausted by the whole event but pleased that Pamela had managed to relate the story to her maybe now she could move on in her life.

The next morning both of them were woken by the sound of the phone ringing, the sun shone through a small crack in the curtain and Pamela moved forward to answer the phone.

"Hello" she said calmly.

"Yes this afternoon no problem, see you then bye".

Ruth looked up still sleepy "Who was that?"

"My CPN apparently" Pamela said returning to Ruth and lying across her knees "Coming this afternoon".

Pamela smiled at Ruth "Thank you for helping me last night".

Ruth smiled back at her "Hey its ok, was the least I could do".

Pamela edged closer to Ruth's face with her face, and kissed her tenderly on the right cheek. Ruth returned a kiss pressing her lips softly onto Pamela's cheek, and felt a tingling down her spine Ruth gazed into Pamela's eyes and began to stroke her cheek with her hands whispering, "Cracked porcelain".

As Pamela kissed her tenderly on the lips Ruth's body began to tingle and her heart began to beat faster. Ruth was slightly hesitant and she finally returned a equally passionate kiss Pamela's body was also reacting to the kiss and a feeling of ecstasy over came them both. "I am the cracked porcelain" Pamela said smiling.

"Yes" Ruth replied "

A Perfect ornament cracked by abuse an imperfect world".

"Do you love me?" Pamela asked.

"Of course I do" Ruth replied.

"I mean really love me" Pamela asked stroking Ruth's hair.

"Like as a sister or a lover?" Ruth asked confused.

"As a lover, as in partners or a couple." Pamela said putting her hand on her right breast and stroking her nipple through her blouse and bra.

"Yes" said Ruth undoing the buttons on her blouse so that Pamela could stroke her breast properly. Pamela ran her hand into her bra and played with her nipple with her fingers Ruth sighed as her nipples began to harden. Pamela then kissed her tenderly on the lips once more and licked Ruth's lips as she penetrated her tongue just inside Ruth's mouth gliding it in gently. Pamela then drew back her face and Ruth began to open the buttons of Pamela's blouse, Ruth then moved her hand inside Pamela's bra and began stroking her breast. At this point Ruth could feel Pamela's nipples harden and knew they were both about to become lovers. Pamela stood to her feet and held out her hand in gesture, Ruth held it gently and Pamela led her to her bedroom. The room looked like a dolls house with pastel pink and purple wall paper and white wardrobes, the double bed had a pink flowered bed spread.

Pamela pulled Ruth towards her and they continued kissing on the bed, Pamela was very much the dominant personality in control of the situation. Ruth was willing to be led into submissive state in order for Pamela not to feel threatened. Pamela removed Ruth's blouse and bra then her long skirt and knickers then she took her own clothes off until both of them were lying naked on the bed. Pamela then ran her fingers down Ruth's back until she reached Ruth's buttocks, her hand were stroking her soft tender skin up and down making Ruth sigh. Ruth then did the same to Pamela causing Pamela to groan. Pamela copied Ruth's actions and the two were making love.

The couple embraced and remained entwined for hours reluctant to let go and enjoying the warmth and closeness that they shared. It was a new experience for them both and one that was special for them both, a treasured memory that would be repeated over and over again.

"No one is as tender as you, when you touch me I don't jump or back off with fear". Ruth confessed.

"Have the same problem I hate men touching me, creepy bastards" Pamela said shuddering.

"I thought it was just me who felt that way" Ruth said with a sense of relief in her voice.

After a few hours they both went into the shower together and washed each others body, this became a ritual a kind of cleansing process demonstrating purity and commitment.

Ruth dried herself off and Pamela sat on a chair in the bathroom gazing at the floor, she was crying.

"Pamela what's wrong?" Ruth asked her putting her hands on Pamela's shoulders "Have I upset you?"

"No Ruth I am very happy" Pamela smiled warmly "We are in love".

"Yes it's what you want isn't it?" Ruth asked anticipating the reply.

"Yes more than anything else" Pamela said

kissing Ruth on the lips "That's the power of love".

"I feel the same" she exclaimed "But I have to go before the CPN arrives".

"O.K but come back later" Pamela insisted.

In the meantime Malcolm was contacting Kathy trying to befriend her in order to be back with Ruth. But his attempt to being nice and charming wasn't fooling Kathy and she merely dismissed him from her door. He had caused Ruth so much grief in the past and Kathy was constantly informed of his nasty ways by Ruth and the abuse she had received from him only proved how bad he was. But Malcolm was not going to give up without a fight and went out each night searching for Ruth.

Ruth spent a lot of time with Pamela at her place and rarely went home; she always avoided the CPN and never discussed anything at work. However she did seem to be distracted at times and avoided any conversations about her private life, but Kathy was her friend and she knew there was something wrong. She had not seen Ruth socially and that was certainly out of character for her, Ruth was a very sociable person who liked to go out even when she was with Malcolm. Malcolm tried to control her life and keep her in away from friends and family, but Ruth was a strong person who fought against his abusive behaviour and finally split up with him.

Ruth and Pamela spent quality time together discussing their past lives of abuse and this only increased their bond with each other. The romantic aspect of their relationship grew ever more passionate and now Ruth was fully aware that she had crossed the boundaries of the nurse and the patient relationship. There was no turning back from this situation falling in love with Pamela sent Ruth hurdling into a new direction the consequences of this would be severe.

On Ruth's first day back to work she acted as if nothing had taken place, according to her Pamela had left the ward and she had not seen her since. She hid her clothes in Pamela's wardrobe and there was no other evidence of her being there. Pamela was equally as discreet not wanting to cause any problems for Ruth and seemed to be responding to treatment. Also Pamela had been preparing Ruth for a few photo sessions organized by her female friend Tara, she spent time showing her how to apply makeup and modeling for clothes. Posing was strange for Ruth and so Pamela had to demonstrate positions to be in for each shot, she even had a digital camera and took a few pictures of her own. They both took it in turns using the camera and posing for pictures until Ruth got the idea of modeling. At first it was awkward for Ruth but she soon began learning the moves and became a natural. Pamela also demonstrated the moves that she did on the cat walk so that Ruth could try live shows eventually. Pamela played music such as David Bowies 'Fashion' in order to provide Ruth with atmosphere, soon they were both parading across the lounge in various items of clothing as if on the cat walk.

The months passed and things were very quiet, Kathy finally approached Ruth about not contacting her out of work.

"We haven't gone out for months Ruth"

"No I have been a little tired lately" Ruth replied avoiding eye contact with Kathy.

"So we must arrange something sometime" Kathy continued

"Maybe yes" Ruth said hesitantly.

"You might know who is still contacting me" Kathy said trying to gain eye contact with Ruth.

"Not Malcolm" Ruth said turning to face Kathy

and looking at her in the eye.

"Yes he wants some stuff he left at your apartment but can never find you in" Kathy said puzzled.

"He hasn't got anything there" Ruth replied puzzled.

"Well he thinks he has and he keeps asking me where you are, so where are you?" Kathy said inquisitively.

"Avoiding him if you must know, you know what he's like, do you think I liked being knocked about, abused, tormented and humiliated?" Ruth's tone was hostile and she was raising her voice.

"Ruth calm down I'm your friend and I did help you when he was rough" Kathy said trying to control the situation.

" I'm sorry I know you were my rock" Ruth said putting her hand on Kathy's shoulder then withdrawing it swiftly "But I hate him and don't want anything to do with that man ever again".

"How old is he Ruth?" Kathy inquired .

"Thirty eight, why do you ask?" Ruth asked taking a file from the cabinet.

"Just curious" Kathy said writing on the white board.

"You have been with him for three years" Kathy continued.

Ruth suddenly dropped the file and some of the papers scattered around the floor, she began picking them up one by one and became very nervous.

"What's wrong Ruth?" Kathy enquired in a concerned manner.

"Nothing its ok, I am just tired that's all" Ruth said continuing to pick up the papers.

Ruth was starting to think about Malcolm's age and calculating that he would have been in his early twenties when Pamela and her mother were attacked,. This meant that the name Malcolm and the description could well have been him. The way Pamela described the incident Malcolm could fit the description of one of the men, the surviving rapist and murderer. But was this possible and was he capable of committing such crimes as these, he may be violent but would he rape someone or go as far as to kill someone. She could not discuss it with Kathy or Pamela for separate reasons but she hoped that it wasn't him for everyone's sake.

Ruth finished collecting the paper together and put them back in the file, Kathy finished writing on the board and walked towards the door.

"Let's have a drink" Kathy said looking at Ruth in dismay.

"Yeah Ok Kathy good idea" Ruth replied sighing with relief.

Ruth knew that eventually she would have to tell Kathy about Pamela and then she could discuss her concerns about Malcolm. But for now she was safe with her secrets and just wanted to carry on working and forget about everything that had happened. But Kathy seemed to know that Ruth was hiding something and observed her for the rest of the day. Kathy was discrete and thought she could find out more if she followed her when she left work, she also wanted to make sure Malcolm didn't follow her or harass her in any way.

Ruth stepped into her car and sensed that someone was behind her, she looked back a few times but saw no one. She drove down the street and hesitated wondering whether to go home or to Pamela's apartment. Going home meant that Malcolm might be there waiting for her, alternatively she could lead Malcolm to Pamela's apartment. She drove around for some time before deciding to go to her own apartment then sat outside for a while looking up at her lounge window.

Malcolm had gone to the apartment and was walking down the street hoping to find Ruth there; he crossed the road and seemed to be heading in her direction then disappeared. Suddenly there was a knock on the window on the driver's side where Ruth was sat waiting, Ruth jumped as she saw a figure peering in at her.

"Excuse me" The man commented, "Could you tell me where Wellington Street is?" He said politely.

"Yes" she replied "Just ahead, the next road on the right".

"Thank you" He said and walked on.

At that moment Malcolm appeared "Well Ruth you're a hard one to find I must say" He said in a deep groining voice.

He was unshaven and his hair was wild, his eyes looked blood shot and his thin face was blotchy in places. he was dressed in jeans and a checked shirt.

"So aren't you going to invite me up to your apartment?" He continued.

Ruth was hesitant and said nothing for a while, thinking about the men that attacked Pamela and her Mother.

"Why?" She asked her voice quivering.

"Why, what?" He asked confused.

"Why should I?" she said more confidently.

"For old time sake, let's have a drink and discuss things" He said smiling.

"I don't think so, those times have gone" Ruth said anticipating trouble.

"Now Ruth you have to admit we had good times" Malcolm said trying to touch her shoulder through the open window

"Don't touch me ok" Ruth shouted.

Malcolm suddenly changed his expression to the angry violent person that she once knew, he leaned forward and raised his fist to strike her, and Ruth moved away from the window and screamed. Suddenly a hand appeared and grabbed his shoulder; Malcolm swung around and tried to punch the person who had grabbed him. But the sight of the uniform and the fact that the person had over powered him by pulling his arm up his back deterred him. Two police officers stood at the side of the car the one held Malcolm and the other one was talking to someone. It was Kathy who had been near by and witnessed the entire thing, she was explaining about Malcolm contacting her and wanting to get access to the apartment.

Ruth was relieved to see and stepped out of the car to greet her, she hugged her and then looked at her for a moment

"Wait a moment" she said "Were you following me?"

Kathy was about to reply when Malcolm broke free from one of the police officers and headed for Ruth, the police moved quickly to stop him but not before he hit her in the mouth with his fist.

"Take that you bitch!" He shouted in rage.

The police pulled him down and handcuffed him while he continued shouting at her "I will fucking get you I promise".

He was taken away as he continued to hurl abuse at her.

Ruth wiped away the blood from her lips and stared at Malcolm as he was driven away by the police her eyes filled with tears. "I can't believe he hurt me again the bastard".

"Kathy pulled a tissue from her hand bag and offered to mop the blood from her mouth, Ruth stood trembling while she did so.

"Come Ruth let's get you cleaned up at your apartment" Kathy offered.

"No its ok" Ruth said thinking about Pamela and getting to see her.

"Are you sure you're ok?" Kathy asked continuing to mop the blood away.

"Yes I am now" Ruth replied getting her car keys from the ignition.

"At least let me walk you to your door" Kathy offered.

Ruth knew that she would not get rid of Kathy unless she agreed to allow her to escort her to the door, and so she nodded and after locking the car they both crossed the street. Meanwhile Pamela was also worried about Ruth and was heading towards her apartment walking swiftly down the street on foot. Kathy bathed Ruth's lips and noticed her lower lip was slightly swollen.

"You need to put a cold compress on that lip" She said smiling "What are we going to do with you, getting yourself in such relationships".

Ruth smiled back as much as she was able "I know the things I do".

Kathy then walked towards the door "Well I

will have to go in work tomorrow".

"O.k. thanks Kathy" Ruth said gratefully.

Kathy embraced her and left the apartment heading towards her car, hiding in the shadows was Pamela who noticed them embrace. She walked up to the door and knocked firmly the sound echoed down the corridor. Kathy looked up to the apartment in astonishment as she saw Pamela through the lounge window, she realized why Ruth was acting the way she was and decided to just drive on down the street.

Meanwhile Pamela was questioning Ruth about Kathy.

"Ruth what's going on are you seeing Kathy?" she said not even noticing Ruth's lip.

"No" Ruth replied removing the wet tissue she had used to reduce the swelling on her lip.

"For fuck sake did she hit you?" Pamela asked looking at her mouth.

"No you don't understand" Ruth pleaded.

"Don't I, well fuck you" Pamela said heading towards the front door.

"It was him!" Ruth shouted "My ex Malcolm".

Ruth realized what she had said and covered her mouth with her blood stained tissue, watching

Pamela stop and turn around slowly.

"What" She said in disbelief.

"He came here and caused trouble then hit me" Ruth hoped that Pamela had not heard the name.

"Malcolm?" She inquired.

"Yes he hit me" Ruth said showing Pamela her lip.

"Jesus Ruth I don't believe this" Pamela approached her and gazed into her eyes then looked at her lip.

"The same bastard that raped my mother and me, is that him?"

Ruth interrupted her "Wait it might not be the same man".

"No shit Ruth for god sake he's your ex" Pamela began shaking and collapsed on the settee putting her head in her hands "No it's not real".

"Pamela I was living with him, he couldn't do that its merely coincidence" Ruth said hoping to calm Pamela down and convince her to stop getting upset.

Pamela sat silently while Ruth sat beside her neither spoke for a long time then Pamela put her arms around Ruth and kissed her on the left cheek.

She then held her tight and began to cry, her tears trickled down Ruth's face and she too shed a tear. After a while Pamela looked at Ruth's swollen lip and touched it tenderly with her fingers.

"Anyone who hurts you, hurts me" Pamela said smiling "Its all about us now".

Ruth attempted to return a smile "It's all about us" She agreed.

The next day Ruth went to work she was sat listening to the report given by the night nurse handing over the shift. The night nurse seemed weary and anxious to get the report finished, speaking about each patient in turn describing her night shift and the behaviour of the patients. Although Ruth was there she was not attentive to detail, but rather picked up aspects of the report and thinking about Pamela back at her apartment. She was analyzing her relationship with Pamela, was she making a mistake or was she helping Pamela to rebuild her life by helping to remove those many identities that Pamela had developed. Certainly the identities never emerged when Ruth was present, only when others were present or when Pamela was upset.

Ruth rationalized the relationship by the fact

that she was making a difference and there was a marked improvement in Pamela's behaviour. It was certainly true that by ending the relationship she had the power to destroy all that she had set out to do. Therefore she was now in a dilemma and no one could make the decision for her whether to continue the relationship or end it. What was important to her was her love for Pamela, the need to be close to her and share her experiences as well as her bed. The compassionate side of relationship was only part of what she wanted; being closer than she had ever been with anyone else was another aspect of her relationship. When they kissed it was like Pamela had breathed new life into her, giving her a sense of completion and lasting ecstasy.

Kathy was not on that day so Ruth felt that she could work through the day without feeling guilty about what she was doing. She worked with the other nurses on duty; each one had continually brought her back to reality by discussing the patients and relevant activities of the day. None of the staff knew anything about Pamela or any other problems that she had, although they were curious how she got her facial injury. The day passed so slowly and Ruth was continually looking at the clock hoping that the time would come for her to leave work and see Pamela.

Meanwhile Pamela had left Ruth's apartment and returned to her home, she was equally eager to see Ruth and discuss their future together in modeling. Pamela had found photographs of her childhood as a model for catalogues and more recent photographs of modeling career. She spread the photo albums out and sat listening to music reflecting back to the shows that she had performed at with wonderful backdrops and elaborate scenery.

Ruth left work and headed straight to Pamela's apartment she was delighted to see the dining room table with a white table cloth and two meals plated up so nicely, Pamela had made a real effort to prepare a meal and decorate the table with an array of flowers in vases. Ruth looked across the room at the photo albums.

"Is that you as a child model?" Ruth asked.

"Yes you can have a look after we have eaten" Pamela said pouring some wine into two glasses.

"This is nice" Ruth said sitting down and tasting the wine.

"Cheers lets drink to us" Pamela said holding

her glass up.

"To us" Ruth touched Pamela's glass with hers "All about us".

The evening went well as they looked at the Photographs and listened to music, sitting cozily together on the settee as they had done so many times before. The lights were dimmed and once they had discussed the day's events, Ruth decided to confide in Pamela by discussing her years of child abuse by her so called uncle. In reality he was merely a friend of her fathers who used to visit her when her father was out and threatened to tell her father that she threw herself at him if she said anything. So she kept quiet for years until she was older and wiser, then she exposed him for the pedophile that he was and her father attacked him one night. The man lived but never reported her father for assaulting him; he just left the area and was never seen again.

Pamela's real uncle had assaulted her and although Ruth knew her story listened intently as she related it to her. Her uncle Peter was a short, fat man who wore glasses with thick lenses and a Scottish accent. He insisted on Pamela sharing what he called their secret and visited her room as often as he could when the opportunity presented itself. He used cheap aftershave that lingered around her on her clothes and in the atmosphere.

"These smells are the things that haunt you along with the nightmares or flash backs of previous events" Pamela said bitterly.

"I can understand that, it's awful isn't it" she agreed.

"So called secrets that can never be revealed for fear of being guilty of leading them on".

"Dirty sleazy bastards" Ruth commented.

"My life was a living hell for a while" Pamela said continuing her story.

"At least my father believed me and beat the fucker up" Ruth said.

"Peter lingered around for a while, then disappeared when things got a bit rough" Pamela reflected back to one aspect of the past when Peter was exposed for assaulting another child. He was at his allotment in his shed when a gang of men put petrol on it and burnt him to death. This was rough justice for all the times that he assaulted children, he was screaming as he caught fire and had no way of escaping the inferno.

"No one knew but I saw him burn, I watched

from near the gates to the allotments". Pamela thought for a moment "Whenever I dream of fire I think of him in that shed".

Once Pamela had related her story to Ruth she explained how she wanted Ruth to pursue a career in modeling with her and experience the glamour of stage work, and join the catwalk.

Ruth was a little excited by the thought of modeling in shows but was not prepared to disappoint Pamela by refusing to try it at least once. Pamela had contacted her photographer friend Tara and arranged a session in the studio. Tara was looking forward to meet Ruth and photograph her but was hoping that Pamela behaved herself and not cause her any problems. Pamela reassured her that Ruth would keep her under control and that Ruth was sensible and stable.

Ruth appeared in the studio that week with Pamela and to Tara's surprise Ruth gave a brilliant performance once she had managed to relax. The photo shoot was a success as Ruth had worn many outfits and posed in so many positions with props and scenery just like she had seen on Pamela's photographs.

"Amazing!" Tara said clicking at the shutter to the camera and instructing Ruth to move in various positions.

Pamela was in the background mimicking the movements so that Ruth could see and copy her. Pamela then had a few more photographs taken of her then a few of both of them together. Tara played some music and began to transfer some of the photos on to computer making a decision on what pictures to keep and use for magazines.

"You are very beautiful" Tara said to Ruth "A natural, so photogenic and if you like I can make you a model".

"Really" Ruth said cheerfully "Do you think so?" she said hesitantly.

"Yes really" Tara said confidently.

Ruth took some convincing in order for her to believe she could ever do modeling professionally. Her lack of confidence stemmed from her being abused by Malcolm, and constantly humiliating her. She was made to feel like dirt and constantly insulted by him.

Pamela was convinced that Ruth was capable of modeling and both Tara and her considered that Ruth was photogenic and a beautiful woman.

Ruth had stated that she was a nurse and not a model, she felt that she had the looks, but lacked the confidence to be a model.

"Try it for my sake" Pamela said pleading with her.

"I will consider it" Ruth replied not wanting to disappoint Pamela.

"I can put you in touch with Pamela's agent" Tara said laughing.

"Tara's sister Angela" Pamela said laughing with Tara.

Pamela seemed to have a hold on Ruth; she was strong willed and determined to influence Ruth and keep her by her side. She hated anyone being near Ruth and seemed to protect her as much as she protected Pamela. They were becoming inseparable it was only work that kept them apart, even then Ruth was feeling the strain of being away from Pamela. She had become disillusioned by mental health nursing due to the other staffs negativity. Yes she had made a difference with people like Pamela, but the pressure had become too much and she had to think of her own sanity.

ALL ABOUT US

Since the photo session Ruth had returned to work with new thoughts in her head. The idea of modeling became ever more desirable as the routine of the psychiatric ward become more mundane. Even her best friend Kathy was pushed into the background as her relationship with Pamela became stronger and more intense.

Kathy was on duty and determined to tackle Ruth about her new found relationship and source of distraction from her work. She followed Ruth into the kitchen and made sure that they were alone before she spoke to her.

"Ok what's going on" She said in a superior manner.

"What do you mean" Ruth said surprised at Kathy's bluntness

"When I left you at your apartment, you had a visitor" Kathy continued.

"You were spying on me I knew it, for god sake Kathy" Ruth began getting upset.

Kathy slammed her mug down on the sideboard and pointed her finger at Ruth.

"I told you to be careful and you have been so distracted from work" Kathy said angrily.

Ruth felt herself getting angry but remained in control.

"Kathy I'm sorry if I am not performing that well, but I have a lot on my mind" Ruth said feeling herself getting upset.

"By that you mean Pamela" Kathy added

"What!" Ruth said raising her voice.

Ruth tried to conceal the fact that she was having a relationship with Pamela.

"Pamela, what has she got to do with this?"

But Kathy knew Ruth and could see that she was hiding her true feelings for Pamela.

"Ruth you have always phoned me outside work and we have been out socially as friends, suddenly you don't call me and disappear from your apartment".

"Ok so you spy on me" Ruth said in reply.

"Only because I am concerned about you as a

friend" Kathy said reasoning with her.

A member of staff entering the Kitchen and disturbed them; she had obviously heard the shouting. "Is everything ok?" she asked.

"Yes of course" Kathy said looking at the member of staff and then at Ruth.

Both Kathy and Ruth had the opportunity to calm down, but the member of staff could sense the atmosphere and soon left the kitchen.

Kathy placed her hand on Ruth's shoulder "I want to help you as a friend".

"But I'm ok Kathy, never been happier" Ruth tried to convince Kathy.

Ruth bowed her head almost in shame.

"My god there's more isn't there? Kathy said in dismay.

"I love her" Ruth admitted.

"Oh shit" Kathy said in disbelief.

Ruth glanced at her with tearful eyes "I can't help it" she paused "What am I going to do?"

Kathy shook her head "I don't know, I really don't know".

"The biological time machine people are said to be in an emotional time warp" Ruth said "that's how experts explain it"

"Yes but it could be transference or counter transference" Kathy said "Or the other way around you know what I mean".

"Oh the patient falling in love with the therapist or vice versa" Ruth replied.

"You know how it works and you hardly know Pamela" Kathy tried to reason with Ruth.

"I know about transference and all it entails, but we love each other" Ruth insisted.

"Are you sure about this?" Kathy asked concerned.

"I am honestly Kathy" Ruth said smiling.

"Does anyone else know?"

"Nobody not even my parents". Ruth replied.

"God they will flip" Kathy said concerned.

"I know it worries me" Ruth said her smile turned to a frown "I really don't know how to approach them".

The months passed by, Kathy remained quiet but watchful over Ruth; she was very concerned but was impressed how Ruth had helped Pamela. But she was so concerned about Ruth and convinced it would end in heartache. All she could do was pick up the pieces and be there for Ruth when needed. Kathy found herself in a dilemma either help her friend by keeping quiet or expose the relationship and deal with the consequences. But she had to also think of Pamela and the effects it would have on her mental health condition, by exposing Ruth it would mean risking Pamela having a relapse and returning to the ward.

Kathy felt that she should reserve her opinion and forget about the aspect of crossing the boundaries of patient and professional familiarities hoping that Ruth would eventually come to her senses and distance herself from Pamela for her own sake.

Ruth returned to Tara's studio with Pamela and to their surprise Tara had developed the photographs taken months earlier. The pictures were stunning as both of them appeared glamorous and most of the photographs seemed to come to life.

"See" Pamela said "Now you're a model".

Ruth was amazed "I don't believe it, they are amazing".

Tara smiled and looked at the photographs then the women "You both look good".

"The next step is magazine and catalogue work" Tara said confidently.

"Are you serious" Ruth said surprised.

"Yes of course" Pamela said encouragingly "This is it now, stardom".

Pamela was right Ruth was at the beginning of a promising career and the months progressed so did she, from strength to strength appearing in magazines and catalogues. Two years passed and Ruth had left her job as a nurse and became a professional model with all the training behind her. But it was not all a bed of roses neither was her relationship with Pamela at times. But it was still better than her previous relationships especially Malcolm who had not been seen by anyone since being arrested years ago. Ruth never pressed charges after the last assault due to not wanting to involve Pamela in any of her problems.

Ruth was concerned about her relationship from the perspective of her family and friends and so she discussed this with Pamela. Pamela was mature enough to deal with this and agreed that Ruth should handle it in her own way. Ruth contacted her mother first and explained that she was in a new relationship and that they would visit soon. She led her mother to believe that it was an heterosexual relationship by not explaining the facts on the phone. Ruth concealed the truth until her mother was able to meet Pamela in order for her not to have time to think of the situation and stereotype her.

Driving to her mother's home, Ruth became particularly nervous, with sweating hands could hardly grip the steering wheel. What would she say to her mother, how could she explain to an old fashioned woman that she was in a lesbian relationship. She was already classed as the black sheep of the family without more shocks for the family to cope with. They thought she was odd when she went into psychiatric nursing, the whole family thought that she would psychoanalyze them. The closer she drove to the street the more she dreaded going there, any excuse would have been a good one to avoid going.

Ruth finally arrived outside the house; it was a semi-detached house with a well-kept garden. The drive looked as if it had been recently swept and her sister's car was parked close by. Ruth sat looking into the lounge window and noticed the figure of a middle-aged woman in her fifties with short cropped hair and distinctive sharp features peering out at her.

"Oh god" Ruth gulped nervously.

"Is that your mum?" Pamela asked.

"Yes that's her, her names Diane" Ruth said hesitantly "So let me do the talking and please don't say anything".

They walked up to the door and her mother greeted Ruth, she hugged and kissed Ruth but seemed to pull back quickly as if she had been forced to embrace her. Pamela sensed an atmosphere between them but kept quiet as requested by Ruth.

"How are you Ruth?" Diane asked in a superior tone.

"I'm fine thank you" Ruth replied her voice was tense anticipating a challenging remark.

"Good come in" Diane said waving both her and Pamela in.

She watched as Ruth and Pamela sat down then turned her head away looking towards the kitchen and shouting "Emma your sisters here".

A young voice called back to her "Which one" she shouted

"Ruth and a friend" she replied.

Ruth's mother turned back and immediately looked at Pamela and then at Ruth.

"So where is this man you wanted me to meet, I hope he isn't like the last boyfriend, what a waste of space he was" She said bitterly.

She seemed to be addressing Pamela when she said this expecting a reply.

Pamela remained silent trying to avoid eye contact.

At that moment a man walked in the room and stopped in his tracks when he saw Pamela.

He was a nineteen year old with a thin body, long greasy hair and a bad case of acne.

"Who's this then" He asked staring at her.

"Put your eyes back in David it's your sister's friend" Diane said in disgust.

David hovered round for a while then entered the kitchen to join Emma.

Ruth then turned to face Pamela and introduced her "This is Pamela my girlfriend".

Ruth's mother just nodded at Pamela and she smiled back at her as if Ruth was just introducing a friend to her and not a lover.

"Mother she's my partner, we are together in a relationship" Ruth explained.

Her mother stood with her mouth wide open looking at Ruth then at Pamela and back at Ruth.

"Are you joking with me" Diane finally said.

"No why would I" Ruth said feeling herself getting tense.

"But I really don't understand" Diane said looking at Pamela.

"Oh Christ mother what's to understand that I am gay, a lesbian" Ruth suddenly stood up.

"Oh this is ridiculous Ruth honestly" Ruth's mother was beginning to shout and caused David to enter the room to see what the commotion was all about, he turned to his mother and then Ruth.

"What's all the shouting for" He asked.

"Ask her!" Ruth said pointing at her mother.

"Mom" He said looking at his mother who had become red in the face with anger.

"Is this why I haven't seen you for a long time, because of her" Diane said sharply.

"Her, she has a name, Pamela" Ruth shouted.

David looked bewildered trying to make sense of the arguing "What's wrong?" he asked.

"Pamela and I are lovers and mother is having trouble excepting it" Ruth said addressing David.

"David keep out of this she's obviously gone mad working in that nut house" Diane said in temper.

"Ok that does it, we are leaving" Ruth said gabbing Pamela by the hand "Come on lets go".

"Ruth wait" Diane said "Think about it rationally".

"Mum don't say any more, I've had enough!" Ruth screeched.

At that moment Emma entered the room, she resembled Diane even to the style of dress and hairstyle.

"What on earth is the shouting all about?" she asked.

"Your sister is a lesbian and that's her girl friend apparently" Diane shouted.

"Oh god mum it's a fad she will get over it" Emma said shrugging her shoulders.

Ruth walked out of the room into the hall Emma followed behind her showing concern as her older sister.

"Come back Ruth lets talk" Emma pleaded.

"Christ Emma I thought you would understand" Ruth said turning back at to look at Emma.

"But I do Ruth" Emma continued .

"Oh yes so its one of them fads" Ruth said shaking in temper.

"I only said it to please mum" Emma insisted.

"Well get this we love each other and are in a meaningful relationship" Ruth shouted grabbing Pamela's arm for support.

"Fine" Emma replied with a note of sarcasm in her voice.

"Fine is that it, fucking great, that's your response to our relationship" Ruth was almost spitting her words out and squeezing Pamela's arm.

"Oh Ruth please you drop a bombshell like this and expect us to except things" Emma continued with her sarcastic tone "What about dad do you think he will understand?"

"No I don't but that's him" Ruth said releasing her grip on Pamela's arm and opening the door.

"He would just say my heads fucked up that's all" Ruth continued.

"Oh Ruth be reasonable" Emma said sensing her mother in the background.

"I am but you all have your perfect world with no allowances for something different" Ruth was struggling to open the door.

"Well it is a little odd and hard for us all to accept" Emma continued almost performing for her mothers benefit.

"What a load of fucking crap Emma" Ruth replied managing to get out of the door with Pamela.

"Well lets face it you've always been odd Ruth" Emma jibed

"Well fuck you" she addressed Emma "And the rest of you" Ruth shouted from the drive.

Ruth passed her father as she raced to the car in temper "And before you start you can fuck off too!"

Her father stood and looked blank at her, while Emma shouted from the door "Take no notice of that fowl mouthed bitch Dad, she's a mad lesbian".

Ruth had reached the car and opened the door, she heard her sisters remark and shouted over the roof back at her "Yes well at least I don't live off my parents, you money grabbing bitch".

With that Ruth entered the car and speeded down the road, her father remained on the drive bewildered by the argument that took place.

"You were a great support I must say" Ruth said sarcastically.

"But you asked me not to say anything" Pamela replied.

"Fine so I get all the flack and you just stand there and say nothing" Ruth was so angry that she stalled the engine.

Pamela remained quiet knowing that whatever she said would be wrong; she also wanted to avoid an unnecessary argument. The Journey home was long and Ruth took hours to calm down but eventually she did apologize to Pamela. Pamela also had a mark on her arm where Ruth had clung to her this developed into a bruise later that evening. Ruth cooked tea and made up for her behaviour in as many ways as she could think possible. As for her family she never spoke to them for a long time. She was concentrating on Pamela and her modeling career.

Pamela encouraged Ruth all the way in Ruth's modeling career and Ruth kept Pamela out of trouble. They successfully kept men out of their lives making it obvious they were not interested in male friends in a sexual way. Neither did they want to pursue any female relationships only each other gay males were acceptable, as they felt safe with them. As they were both beautiful both sexes were attracted to them and both often pestered them.

Fashion shoots on location were some of her favorite jobs although some places could be awful and conditions bad. Both Pamela and Ruth traveled together and were inseparable when not being photographed. They were enjoying the places, such as historical settings and tropical beaches but whoever said modeling was easy is mad. According to Pamela it consisted of long hours and hard work performing in front of cameras. Adverts were harder to get into and required self-discipline and good timing to act correctly.

Pamela had demonstrated how to walk like a catwalk model giving her step-by-step guidance; she already knew how to stand like a model.

"Throw your shoulders forward and push your pelvis slightly forward" Pamela instructed.

"Like this" Ruth said practicing.

"Exactly" Pamela replied.

"Ok so far" Ruth said confidently.

"Right toes of your foot down first and most

of your weight on the ball of your foot" Pamela continued "It's almost like walking on tip toes, watch me" she demonstrated the moves.

"I feel clumsy" Ruth said falling back on her heels.

"Let your body move naturally and learn to smile with your eyes" Pamela instructed demonstrating each move even the required look.

Then Pamela demonstrated more footwork and then went on to legwork, visual concentration on an object ahead using a vase on a shelf at eye level, then the body movement. After a while Pamela put music on and they practiced to music, playing old and modern songs.

They practiced and practiced for months until Ruth began to do it naturally, she was now ready to walk the walk as a model. Her first chance to prove that she could perform on the catwalk; she performed in a few small shows with Pamela before trying a bigger challenge in a major fashion show. Initially Pamela was on each of her performances in order to show Ruth how to act in front of an audience. The flashing of cameras and the applauding of audiences was a little daunting at first but even this was accepted as the norm after a while.

Ruth was building her confidence in modeling and eventually performed on a big show on the catwalk dressed in the most amazing fashionable outfits. At first Ruth was very nervous, but Pamela was always there to support her and sometimes performed with her. Ruth could feel the adrenaline rushing through her body each time she entered the stage and it continued until she was back stage. Sometimes she was so nervous she was physically sick before her performance and had to learn to control herself prior to the show. They performed with top models like Sheena Moore among many others.

Sheena Moore was an established model like Pamela who started out as teen model. Sheena had ginger hair, blue eyes and a often seemed to wear green outfits. On one show she wore a maple crown, which was tied into her ponytail and a long green layered dress with various shades of green all around it flowing down in lines. One critic called her a botanical princess, which she hated and actually tore a magazine up because it was displayed inside the center pages.

Sheena was one of the models that

demonstrated her hatred of Pamela and Ruth's relationship showing openly admitting that she was homophobic. One night she was about to go outside after the show and discovering that it was raining took Ruth's coat. She walked for a while and then noticed Ruth's car nearby, she had often seen Pamela and Ruth stepping inside it after shows. She decided to take out her car keys and began scratching it, writing obscene words on the door. Suddenly she heard a voice behind her and was greeted with a fist to her face, followed by a punch to the ribs after receiving a few more injuries she fell to the ground.

A loud noise came from a nearby building, which startled the attacker ran away in great haste. A crowd soon gathered around Sheena one woman knelt down and checked to see if she was breathing. Sheena was conscious but stunned and began to speak "Help me" she said with her arm extended.

The woman nodded then spoke to the crowd "Someone phone an ambulance quickly".

Pamela and Ruth were close by and rushed forward, Ruth noticed her coat that Sheena was wearing but never mentioned it. "Does anybody know her?" the woman asked.

"Yes we do" Pamela said.

"We work with her, she's called Sheena" Ruth added.

The ambulance arrived and Sheena was taken to hospital, Pamela and Ruth joined her and helped to provide information about Sheena. They stayed with Sheena until she was admitted onto a ward, contacting her family for her and making sure that she was comfortable. Pamela and Ruth visited her regularly in hospital after the show ended each night and took a bunch of flowers or other items. Sheena never forgot they're kindness and began thinking differently about their sexuality, she admitted vandalizing Ruth's car and became a loyal friend from this day forward.

Pamela and Ruth eventually reached notoriety when they performed in a fashion show for television called 'City on fire' the costumes ranged from stylish to futuristic and demonstrated so many different ideas from a multitude of fashion designers from all over the world. All kinds of bizarre ideas began to immerged with creations from up and coming artists with fresh ideas. Materials from everywhere were used such as bin liners, crepe bandages even baking foil.

Pamela was dressed as an angel all in white with feather like wings and pearl like sequins on her long flowing dress. She represented good and pure as she stood next to Ruth dressed as a devil woman with a red satin dress and black tights. The concept of good and evil in the show was done as part of the entertainment in preparation for the more serious fashion displays. Unfortunately because of the revealing of Pamela and Ruth's sexuality courtesy of other models, this performance raised concerns by the religious elements of the public. Fashion critics discussed the shows performance and designs some outfits were considered shabby and too casual for the show. Certain items look better on the hangers and some of the models were described as wooden or lifeless. City on fire was said to be a mixture of good and bad ideas rolled into one, although the concept of fire was good some designers were at risk of getting burnt. Clearly some of the bizarre ideas should never have left the drawing board or even the artists mind. The concept of the Angel and the devil was hardly original and demonstrates a lack imagination on the organizer's part.

Kathy was observing the patients in the lounge

when she saw this performance on television. One of the patients saw Pamela and said 'there's my angel' Ann entered the room and also saw the performance.

"Oh my god, Kathy look at your mate" Ann said critically.

"I know" Kathy said in despair.

"She is making a fool out of herself" Ann continued.

"She's just enjoying herself" Kathy replied.

"Well it's her funeral and you know the outcome" Ann said pointing at the television .

"Maybe" Kathy shrugged her shoulders.

"I bet Malcolm is looking at this and going mad" Ann said concerned.

"Well let's hope he isn't for her sake" Kathy replied equally concerned.

It began to attract the media and soon Pamela and Ruth found themselves getting a lot of attention, but not for all the right reasons. One member of the press made a point of exposing them as lesbians prior to this the word was never mentioned. Although people knew of their relationship it was not considered an issue until now. The reporter approached Ruth and started asking her personal questions but Ruth dismissed him with the wave of her hand. Ruth simply said "No comment".

The reporter was so annoyed with not receiving any information so he commented saying 'It's not enough that we get anorexics now we get lesbians on the catwalk' the same reporter was said to have hounded a model to death for being anorexic, she was devastated by his comments as were her family and friends.

Pamela read it and commented "Oh fucking hell lets go to the Land of Oz as we are apparently freaks".

"Shit what are they doing to us?" Ruth said angrily.

"That's the media for you" Pamela said clearly used to the type of news that sells papers.

"So who needs this crap" she continued.

After the show ended some of the models arranged a party to celebrate the show's success. Pamela and Ruth decided to attend and were approached by a group of male models one addressed Ruth saying "How would you like to be with a real man?"

"Why do you know any" Ruth responded

spontaneously.

"Oh I forgot you're a lesbian" he said laughing.

"Listen you little fucker if I had my way all men would be castrated" Pamela said pointing to his groin.

"Yes give me some shears and I will start now" Sheena said laughing.

The men walked away and joined another group of women hoping to have more success with them. Sheena looked at both of the girls and smiled "That's got rid of them for a while" she said laughing.

Meanwhile back in their local area Malcolm had re emerged from wherever he was hiding and saw a billboard in his area. A photograph of Ruth and Pamela posing in glamorous outfits advertising watches stood out causing him to stand still and stare at it. His mouth began to drop and the sight of Ruth in a photograph confused him. But the biggest shock came when he got home and saw the local newspaper near his front door. The article that caught his eye was about Ruth and Pamela's lesbian relationship. Malcolm became furious and began smashing some of his things with a baseball bat that he kept by the front door. He then went out still wielding the bat searching frantically for Ruth, walking the streets hoping to find her at a local pub or club. He was determined to find her staying out all night and becoming more furious when he failed to see her. The more he searched the angrier he was getting bumping into people in the street and grunting under his breath.

Then he saw a figure that resembled Ruth and followed her, he was convinced that it was her. She walked down the street until she reached an alley, and then turned round looking behind her. She proceeded down the alley conscious of someone following her, and then saw Malcolm nearby gazing at her. She continued walking then turned again and noticed that Malcolm had disappeared, so she carried on walking at a faster pace until she reached the end of the alley.

Suddenly she felt a blow to the back of the head followed by a series of hits to the head and neck.

Before long she had fallen to the ground her body limp and covered in blood. Malcolm stood over her and stared at her body satisfied that he had killed Ruth. He then walked away still carrying the baseball bat in his large apelike hand.

Soon the police arrived and examine body confirming that the woman was dead ambulance crew arrived soon after and ag. with the police that the woman was the victim brutal attack. One of the policemen looked at l face and commented "I know her face".

"Who is she?" another policeman asked.

"I don't know but she looks familiar like a TV star or a model" He said trying to remember exactly where he saw her.

Pamela was leaving the stage when she heard about the murder, she immediately ran down the corridor to the changing room. One of the models moved out of the way as if she had a disease looking at her as if she had two heads.

"Where's Ruth? She asked.

"Over there in the corner" She replied pointing to the area where Ruth was getting changed.

As Pamela passed some of the models one of them spoke to another.

"There's the other lesbian" she muttered.

"They are causing us all problems with their sexuality" Another commented.

"Exhibiting their Lesbian behaviour and ruining the show" They continued.

"It's on TV and in all the papers" One said bitterly.

Pamela ignored them and continued to walk towards Ruth who was now in sight. She was watching a television on the wall and failed to notice Pamela walking towards her. Pamela called across to her but she was too engrossed with the program to hear her.

It was not until she sat beside her that she noticed Pamela and then looked at her with her large hazel eyes and spoke to her in a low voice. "There has been a murder in our area" She said sadly.

"A murder?" Pamela said puzzled.

"A young woman our age" Ruth continued concerned.

"Probably a lesbian too" One of the models commented.

"Have you got a fucking problem with lesbians? Ruth shouted to her.

"Yes when they ruin our show" the woman replied.

"Look if it's not Lesbians its anorexics or Muslims" Pamela commented in retaliation.

"Yes but you fucking take the piss flaunting

your sexuality to everyone like we all need to know" said a black woman as she brushed passed them.

"What's it to you, we have rights as much as you do" Ruth shouted.

"Are you being racist?" she replied almost spitting at her as she spoke.

"Far from it I am talking about equality" Ruth continued.

"A lesbian equal to me as a Christian" the woman snarled.

"But we are equal to you, are you condemning us?" Pamela asked.

"No god is, your both evil" she said turning her head away from them.

"What sort of god condemns anyone for their sexuality?" Ruth asked.

"I told you" she said pulling a dress off the hanger and starting to remove her top.

"How dare you quote god to me when you dress like a prostitute" Ruth said pulling at her clothes.

Suddenly the woman pulled away from her and shouted loudly "Filthy slag, keep your hands

off me".

But as the woman pulled away from Ruth the material tore

"You've torn it now you crazy bitch".

Suddenly a fight broke out and the girls began to pull at each other and fell to the floor.

Pamela raced to Ruth's aid and one of the women rushed forward to help the other model.

Before long a few of them were fighting and creating so much noise a few security men came in the room and split them all up.

Both Ruth and the other model were accuse of starting the fight and were reprimanded by the organizers of the show. Both blamed each other and they were warned that if they continued causing trouble that they would be banned from appearing on the show.

Ruth agreed to ignore any comments made about her sexuality and concentrate on modeling, it was hard with all the snide remarks but she did so for the sake of her job. Pamela was less impressed but followed Ruth's lead in order not to bring any more attention to them. One of the organizers made all the models apologies to each other and told their agencies that this must not be

was in their area Pamela and Ruth walked down the street discussing the last show.

Malcolm spotted a couple of women walking along a road near his apartment one blonde and the other brunette and so he followed them. One of them was wearing a fur coat and the other a blue coat with a black skirt. The blonde haired woman in the fur coat separated from the other woman and Malcolm followed her. She headed across the road and was walking into the nearby park and disappeared into the darkness. Malcolm walked slowly behind her trying not to startle her as he too entered the darkness, using the trees for cover. She was almost back on the road again when Malcolm attacked her just as he did with his last victim, using a baseball bat he hit her repeatedly across the head until she fell down. Helpless she was continually battered until she died.

Meanwhile close by Pamela and Ruth were heading to Pamela's apartment.

"What was that!" Ruth said.

"What!" Pamela said in surprise.

"I thought I heard something" Ruth said anxiously.

"Like what?" she said concerned.

"Nothing" she dismissed the fact she heard a noise "But I do think we were being followed".

"Let's get back to my apartment quick" Pamela said leading Ruth by the arm.

They headed for Pamela's apartment both of them expecting someone to jump out of the bushes and attack them. When they finally arrived they raced inside and locked the door behind them, Pamela closed the blinds and they both sat down for a while. Neither spoke for a while just sat in silence with only the lamplight used to lighten the room. They were jumping at shadows and tree branches blowing against the window. They were suddenly disturbed by the sound the phone ringing, it seemed louder than usual and made them both react by jumping simultaneously. Neither answered the phone although it was ringing for quite a while they both just stared at it as if it was a venomous spider or snake waiting to crawl across their body.

After a while things were silent, then a short while after a knock came at the door, which caused them to jump again.

Ruth whispered to Pamela "Don't answer it" she said nervously.

"Who do think it is" Pamela whispered back.

"Could be anyone" Ruth said creeping to the window and opening the blinds slightly.

The door knocked again this time they heard a voice calling "Ruth are you there".

The voice was Kathy's and she sounded troubled.

"It's Kathy come on open up quick".

Ruth rushed to the door followed by Pamela; they both showed concern as Ruth unlocked the door and opened it slowly.

Kathy looked shocked and gazed as she entered the apartment, she saw Pamela first then Ruth.

"Oh thank god your both alive" Kathy said with relief.

"What's wrong Kathy?" Ruth asked concerned.

"My god you mean that you don't know" she said looking out of the window.

"No tell me" Ruth said anxiously.

"The Murder in the park" Kathy said peering through the blinds.

"Oh my god, I knew something was wrong" Ruth said looking at Pamela who never spoke a word.

"How do you know it's a murder?" Ruth asked.

"Because there are police everywhere, ambulances and a blonde woman lying face down on the grass covered in blood". Kathy said distressed.

"A blonde woman" Pamela said concerned.

"Yes I thought it was you" Kathy said looking at Pamela.

Ruth looked at Pamela then at Kathy "The second murder round here then".

"Yes" Kathy agreed.

"Wait did you say second murder" Pamela said in disbelief.

"Yes that's right" Ruth said in reply and agreeing with Kathy.

"Pamela when you were walking into the dressing room the other day, the news was on discussing a murder that took place in an alley close to here".

"Yes and she resembled you Ruth" Kathy said trying to control her feelings.

"Resembled Ruth?" Pamela said bewildered.

"Yes and now this blonde woman" Kathy said "It's too coincidental".

"You mean the murderer is after us?" Ruth said stunned.

"There is one thing you should know" Kathy hesitated "According to the police all the attacks were the same man, except Sheena who survived of course".

"So Sheena was attacked by someone else?" Ruth enquired puzzled.

"Yes either a man or a strong female". Kathy continued.

Pamela headed for the television across the room "Maybe its on here" she said turning on the television.

They all sat down while Pamela tried to find a news channel, eventually she found the correct program and they all watched as the camera showed the park area and the reporter announced the death of a blonde woman found battered to death. Then they showed a photograph of the previous victim who resembled Ruth it became obvious that someone was after them and had mistaken these poor women for them. They were being targeted for some reason; the question was who by and why.

Kathy suggested that Pamela and Ruth go

away for a while out of the public eye and away from danger; Pamela and Ruth agreed and planned a trip to the countryside. They went to a retreat; a cottage near a small village where they considered not many people would know them. They kept in contact with Kathy but no one else in case someone revealed where they were and told someone. They stayed in for a few nights and then ventured out in the car to a nearby public house it was situated right in the village so was not isolated. They used false names to book the holiday and Pamela wore a dark wig when she was in the public eye. They both dressed down with dull clothes and appeared poor in order to avoid drawing attention to themselves.

They kept in touch with the news through television and the newspapers who spoke of a serial killer at large in home town. The media had a field day with this and the fashion show 'city on fire' but no one suspected Malcolm for the murders except Pamela, Ruth and Kathy. They kept quiet because they thought that even if the police arrested him, he could be released with insufficient evidence. This meant that he would eventually realize that Pamela and Ruth were alive and hunt them down.

The one night at the pub the women sat quietly in a corner watching the news, and being surprised at the things they heard about themselves. Both were considered as disappearing from the public eye due to the bad publicity regarding their relationship. As for the murders the police were no further with their investigations and who knows when the killer would strike next. Ruth looked at Pamela who was staring at the television; Pamela then glanced at Ruth and smiled.

"Don't worry we are safe here" she said confidently.

"I know" Ruth replied.

At that moment three women who were sat close by were discussing the fashion show, each in their fifties.

"Don't they make a big deal out of the lesbian thing" the one said.

"Yeah but don't you think they flaunt their sexuality?" said another.

"No wonder they disappeared" one of them said.

Both Pamela and Ruth remained quiet but were annoyed at the comments made by the women. Ruth whispered to Pamela "They obviously don't understand anything that they consider beyond the norm".

"So fuck them" Pamela said "They are obviously homophobic"

Ruth stood up and headed towards the bar, one of the women nudged one of the others "She looks like one of them models".

"No can't be she's too scruffy" said another.

"Yes your right besides the blonde bimbo isn't here" she said sarcastically.

"True they are never apart" another said.

Ruth carried on to the bar feeling upset by their comments, once at the bar she waited to be served standing by two men. One of the men looked her up and down his eyes were scanning her body stopping at various parts of her body that took his fancy. Ruth was aware of his eyes looking at her and the fact that he cut his conversation short with his friend in order to do this. The other man was also looking but was less interested than his friend.

"Hello things are looking up" said the observer.

"Hello" Ruth replied politely.

"Are you and your friend on your own?" He continued.

"Yes we are" she said waiting to be served.

"May we join you?" he continued confidently.

"I don't think so" she said waving to get the bar mans attention.

"We are harmless and only after female company" the other man said.

Ruth thought about the situation Pamela and her were trying to avoid drawing attention to themselves as lesbians, perhaps being with them would distract people from looking at them and thinking of her as one of the lesbian models.

"Yes ok" she agreed.

"So take us to your friend" the one said.

They all headed for the table where Pamela sat bewildered by the sight of two forty year old men dressed in shirts and jeans. The one had receding hair and a moustache the other was fatter with a freshly trimmed beard.

"This is Alan" said the one "and I am Jim" he continued.

"This is Pamela and I am Ruth" she said smiling and feeling a little uneasy in their presence.

"So are you two local?" Pamela asked trying to make conversation.

"Yes we are from the next village" Jim said.

We are farm hands" Alan said looking at Pamela as he did at Ruth at the bar.

Pamela felt more uneasy than Ruth as she avoided eye contact with Alan.

"So where are you two from?" Alan asked inquisitively

Ruth looked at Pamela and replied "South London" she said trying to avoid saying exactly where they were from.

"That's a bit vague" Jim said looking at Alan "Don't you think mate?"

"yeah so what do you do in South London" Jim asked hoping to gain more information from them.

"She's a photographer" Ruth said pointing at Pamela "And I am nurse"

"A nurse, useful to have you around" Alan said smirking.

"Yes if your mentally ill" Ruth said laughing "I am a psychiatric nurse".

Alan and Pamela laughed with Ruth but Jim seemed less amused as if she had insulted him. Ruth detected a look of disappointment in Jims expression and his behaviour appeared a little strange afterwards. Pamela was oblivious of all the activity and leaned towards Ruth "I need the toilet" she said tapping her foot under the table. Ruth realized what she was doing and replied "Yes I will join you"

Once in the toilet Pamela gazed in the mirror "I prefer to be blonde" she announced.

"Yes you look better as a blonde" Ruth agreed.

"Those men are creeps" Pamela said.

"I know especially Alan did you see how he looked at us" Ruth said.

"So why invite them to our table" Pamela said confused.

"Because of them women near us, they thought they recognized me on television" Ruth explained.

"So what if they did, I don't understand" Pamela continued.

"Well they are expecting a couple of lesbian's one blonde and one dark haired".

"I am wearing a wig" Pamela pointed to her hair.

"Yes but if we have men with us that will throw them off the scent" Ruth explained.

"I see your point but you could have gone for

less creepy ones" Pamela said laughing.

"That Alan is creepy but Jim seems ok" Ruth said also laughing.

"Well I think we should move on and ditch them" Pamela said with a more serious tone.

"That Jim seems to be worried about me being a psychiatric nurse like he has something to hide" Ruth said concerned.

"He is probably an escaped patient, a schizophrenic or by polar maybe" Pamela said laughing.

"Just our luck, to get mixed up with a schizophrenic". Ruth said laughing with her.

"So what do we do?" Pamela asked.

"Get rid of them somehow, we don't need complications now" Ruth said.

They both left the toilets and returned to the Alan and Jim at the table, Ruth was worried that one have them may have slipped something in her drink and deliberately knocked it over Pamela looked at what she had done and didn't touch hers. Jim looked at Alan then at the women with a disappointed look in his eyes.

"Let me buy you another" Jim offered.

"No thanks" Ruth replied.

"But I insist" Jim said sternly.

"Well I insist you don't" Ruth replied abruptly.

At that moment one of the women sat opposite shouted across to them "Jimmy Clark behave yourself with those women or I will have to tell your wife".

"Fuck you Janet we are only having fun" Jim replied.

Janet stood up and approached the table followed by the other women who also seemed to know the men.

"I think you women need to know these men are scoundrels" Janet said loudly.

"Why don't you tell the whole pub Janet you slag" Alan said nastily.

"Well at least I'm not a pervert like you" Janet said abruptly.

"We should go" Ruth said picking up her coat.

"Don't go ladies" Jim said disappointed.

"We have to go we are traveling on tomorrow" Pamela said lifting her coat from her seat.

One of the women watched as Alan grabbed her by the arm; Pamela took her drink and poured it over his head. Janet began to laugh which annoyed Alan and he got up quickly as if he was going to hit her instead he grabbed her by the hair and her wig came off. Alan stood shocked and all went silent in the pub. All the women looked at each other and Jim looked directly into Pamela's eyes.

"It's them" Jim said in shock.

"Who" Alan shouted.

"The lesbians" Janet said laughing "You daft fuckers you have been chatting up lesbians".

Pamela and Ruth made a swift exit feeling the eyes of ridicule on their backs, while the men stood embarrassed by their experience. The women kept the men occupied while Pamela and Ruth drove off relieved that they would never see any of them again.

The next morning they moved on traveling further up country to a more excluded spot and spent the remainder of their holiday in quiet seclusion. They stayed at a guest house a few miles from the nearest village. They enjoyed their experiences of nature and even skinny dipping in a lake. Pamela was the first to strip off her clothes and jump into the water, Ruth was reluctant but eventually removed her clothes and joined

Pamela in the lake. Only the birds and other wild life could disturb their peace, as they savored the moments of ecstasy in each other's company. Watching the autumn trees expel their leaves and fall around the couple that were lying on the ground still naked.

"I wish moments like these could last forever" Pamela said holding Ruth's hand.

"I wish time would stop still" Pamela replied.

"I love the quietness and the gentle breeze swaying the trees and blowing the leaves across the fields" Ruth said with a sigh.

"You're such a romantic" Pamela said leaning over to kiss Ruth on the lips.

Ruth moved her head forward and met Pamela's lips with her own; they shared a passionate kiss then lay holding each other closely. Neither of them wanted to move but eventually they had to get dressed and return to their guest house.

There were a few places of interest such as castles and museums. In the towns Pamela and Ruth visited the local pubs and restaurants without being recognized. The small cafes and shops were very inviting with friendly people and interesting items such as pottery, souvenirs and of course porcelain. They felt free as they walked down the streets but always expected someone to recognize them and ruin their holiday together. However nothing did happen and they enjoyed what time they had left without interruption.

FASHION

It was soon time to return to reality facing the world once more and all the prejudice remarks concerning Pamela and Ruth's sexuality. Since their absence a young female model that Pamela knew had committed suicide, she was anorexic and couldn't take any more publicity concerning her condition. Her life had been followed by one reporter after another each wanting their pound of flesh, hounding her for more information about her condition.

This type of thing was not uncommon in the modeling profession, Models were under pressure to look good and stay slim no matter what the cost. And the media would find a story' no matter who they hurt in the process and to hell with the consequences, many victims fell by the wayside as one more statistic. People became objects of ridicule because of daring to be different in the eyes of the general public, even today in the so-called modern world. Anything goes in fashion unless it offends the media or perhaps politicians.

It is also widely known that in the world of fashion models tend to compete for popularity and it becomes a dog eat dog profession. Often in the background of the glitter and glamour of showbiz comes bitchiness and jealousy everybody wants to be in the limelight and outshine the rest. Of course as in any profession a minority of genuine people become trampled on in their effort to establish a career for themselves, as short lived as it is. Although most of the models appeared to be competitive, some of them were enjoying being in front of the audience and cameras, and less interested in being the best. The other problem was the drug addiction and wild parties this caused many models to fall by the way side, it was all about coping with pressure some could and others suffered.

Models had assembled to practice some moves on the catwalk prior to the fashion show,. David Bowie's song 'Fashion' could be heard in the background as well as other classic songs such as Michael Jackson's 'Billy Jean' also Kraftwerk's 'Model'. Many of the organizers were discussing the props and equipment to be used for the show. A few models began to parade up and down, but soon stopped because of the lack of attention that they were receiving. One of the male organizers was extremely camp and began to display his displeasure of one particular model, by dismissing her out of his way. He was also not happy about the lighting suggesting that it was too bright and needing to be dimmed.

The press wanted to get stories about the fashion show, as early as possible in order to bring any relevant news to the public about any latest scandal. The organizers equally wanted publicity but to promote the show and sell the designs to the right people. Some people were very good at stealing ideas from others, so people tried to keep things under wraps. The fashion guru's became nervous just before a show was going to be organized for this reason. Some of the finest artist's were in the fashion industry working hard to perfect the best drawings for the clothes manufacturers to produce properly. The cloth had to be as close to the idea as possible and appeal to the imagination of the public by use of colour, texture and correct material.

Pamela and Ruth were back in the middle of the fashion world, but hiding away from the press for fear of being noticed by unsavory characters like Malcolm who was seeking to harm them. They got hate mail from people who were clearly homophobic, judging by the content of the letters. Threatening to harm them or worse, the details could be quite graphic and sinister.

Ruth discussed mental health nursing with some of the models, demonstrating the type of illnesses she used to nurse. She would never discuss patient's names of course just a few examples of the situations that she encountered, she thought it might help them to understand mental health more easily

"One woman was by polar you know manic depression, they are either high as a kite or down in a deep depression". Ruth took a breath "Well one woman while in her manic state wanted to be a model, she went out and bought loads of clothes with her credit card". Ruth explained. "She got size ten clothes but she was size 20 plus".

"No way" Sheena commented, "She was fat, and wanted to be a model".

"Yes but she was delusional" Ruth said sadly.

"How bad is that" another model commented "Sorry I mean how sad is that".

Pamela always disappeared when Ruth

discussed mental health not wanting to listen to anything that would reminder her of her days spent in hospital. The patient that called her the angel, who claimed she saw a halo over her head, freaked her out. Ruth also remembered the time when Sheena was attacked Pamela went missing and appeared with Ruth when they were by Ruth's car. Perhaps Pamela had experienced one of identities protecting Ruth's car from being damage. James her male identity could have taken control and done this. Ruth was quite concerned about this as Pamela could have moments where an identity would emerge occasionally.

Pamela continued to guide Ruth through the steps of walking the walk on the stage and platforms, showing her how to walk gracefully as Pamela's mother and friends taught her. She demonstrated facial expressions and turning in style. Gloria, a friend of Pamela's who also grew up in modeling, also guided Ruth. A beautiful Asian girl called Leeja demonstrated self-control. She walked the catwalk with discipline as she modeled some very interesting eastern styles. A few Russian girls demonstrated a few ideas from their designers from places like Moscow and other Russian cities.

They were working away from home so that was one blessing; Kathy had contacted Ruth to re assure her that all was well. Malcolm had obviously gone underground lurking beneath the soil with his slimy friends the worms, in other words he was with his friends in the gutter. However although he was hiding away, he was mapping out how he was going to kill them both.

FALLING

Ruth was becoming despondent with the fashion world while Pamela was oblivious to her need to get away from the limelight and continued to perform for the cameras. Pamela had spent most of her life as a model so everything came natural to her; even the bitchy remarks never fazed her.

Ruth could feel herself sinking into some deep boggy mire and was drifting from Pamela's clutches fast. Even the fact that many people continually referred to them as a couple, she didn't feel as close as she did when they were on holiday. Pamela was encouraged to do many solo performances, which boosted her ego, she was chosen because of her blonde hair and outstanding beauty. The sound of David Bowies 'Fashion' boomed out of powerful speakers and the parade continued, with Pamela leading the parade of models onto the catwalk.

Ruth had time to reflect on the past, which wasn't a good thing; she was dwelling on her life with Malcolm and thinking negative thoughts. Pamela had become the stronger person with her sights set on more positive things such as the next job and holidays abroad. As Ruth started to lose her sense of direction she began to shrink into a depressive state, her mind spiraled down in to a dark pit or tunnel. She began to feel lost, alone and sinking as if she were being pulled into a swamp.

Ruth thought back to when she was receiving counseling; she was sat in a room in a room with a middle aged woman who questionably was going by text book terminology and had never experienced being abused in any way. She was a very smart and clean lady who probably had no vices or appeared to be someone from a good family.

She was obviously trained to do her job and that's all it was to her, a job.

She went through a few counselors and each one came out with the immortal words 'How does it make you feel' In which she was dying to say 'How the fuck do you think it make me feel'. Instead she would cry and the councilor would offer her a tissue, that was the extent of her sympathy, Ruth later discovered from her nurse training about keeping a professional distance. Ruth also hated those moments of silence that seemed to last hours although it was a few minutes, how she wanted to scream or swear at this time.

Eventually Ruth was sent to a psychotherapist who she did manage to connect with, She then discussed her nightmares and the aspects of abuse that she felt comfortable telling. It was very painful but she discussed the various physical and mental abuse, the fear of not wanting to go to sleep because of the night terrors. She hated people who hid their face behind masks or wore strong makeup this indicated the need to hide their identity. Then came the flashbacks or reminders of past events, faces reminded her certain people she hated, smells or types of clothing worn by some men played on her mind.

Ruth only had Kathy at one time to talk to about aspects of her past, but even she didn't know the full story, much of Ruth's life was locked inside her head. Pamela knew a little but Ruth always kept things from her for fear of causing Pamela to relapse. So she learned to cope with the burden of knowing just how bad it was, the only time things really returned was when she was feeling low like the present time. Malcolm could never help her when she used to wake up screaming or punching the wall, or self-harming in her sleep finding unexplained scratches on her body, when she would claw at herself. Malcolm just grunted and left the bed; he was discovered in the morning on the settee.

Kathy knew about the abuse from her childhood and from Malcolm who used to abuse her mentally and physically. She would often go to work with marks on her from Malcolm and she would make up some excuse until she finally had enough and threw him out of her apartment. He was also very possessive and jealous going into mood swings if she even spoke to somebody else, often the fights between Malcolm and her were about her going out with Kathy.

Ruth was finding it difficult functioning, she was not able to get up in the mornings to attend the shows and wanted some sort of relief from the stress that she was under. She would do anything to stop the pain from stomach cramps or mental torment. Pamela was on a high with her modeling so Ruth was reluctant to tell her at this point. Although the signs were there Pamela didn't see them.

By the time Pamela realized what was happening to Ruth it was too late, Ruth had cut her wrists and was bleeding badly. Pamela entered the hotel room just in time; she soaked towels and wrapped them around her wrist. She then phoned the emergency services for assistance, hoping that they would arrive in time. They arrived soon after rendering assistance to Ruth and gathering details from Pamela. Ruth entered the ambulance escorted by Pamela who by now was getting very anxious.

Ruth was taken straight into a booth in casualty a sight that Pamela was used to. Rachel had only seen it as a mental health student years ago with the psychiatric liaison team. Pamela sat beside Ruth holding her right hand and talking to her. Casualty was busy that night with staff rushing around and patients filling the cubicles or waiting room.

Pamela thought back to her many admissions the atmosphere was the same, doctors and nurses standing around a desk-discussing patients. Ambulance drivers coming in with newly admitted patients on stretchers or in wheelchairs. The Staff were gathering information from people such as patients, patient relatives and friends.

The whole atmosphere was completely clinical and so impersonal or so it seemed.

"Look at them Pamela rushing about, we are the last ones they want to help" Ruth said bitterly.

"What do you mean?" Pamela asked.

"The fucking self harmers that's what I mean" Ruth said sharply "They think that I have attempted suicide just because I've cut my fucking wrists".

"Calm down Ruth please" Pamela pleaded.

"Don't they realise people self harm to relieve themselves of stress or tension" Ruth continued "Its to reduce physiological and psychological tension rapidly"

"This is casualty they never do understand mental health issues" Pamela said.

"Fuck it hurts" Ruth said holding her wrists.

"They will be here shortly" Pamela said reassuringly.

"Yes they will and cleanse my wounds without anaesthetics and wont care how they dress my arm because I'm a self harmer or mental health patient."

"Come on Ruth this is fucking stupid keep calm or I am off" Pamela shouted.

At that moment a nurse opened the curtains and called into them "Could you please keep the noise down, there are sick people in here you know".

"Sorry" Ruth said looking at Pamela "I am really".

"I know you are" Pamela said smiling.

"Why can't just me and you exist in this world, why all the work and complications" Ruth said sobbing.

Pamela put her arm around her "Life has to go on and I have had set backs too".

"Yes you have sometimes I forget when your up there on the catwalk confidently walking along" Ruth replied.

"I have set backs or as you would say relapses, lose my memory and do all kinds of bizarre things" Pamela said reassuring Ruth.

"I suppose we help each other in many ways" Ruth said in a merrier tone.

"fighting the demons and monster's From our nightmares" Pamela said kissing Ruth on the forehead.

"Make love our goal" Ruth replied confidently.

Once the doctor had seen Ruth and her wounds

cleaned and dressed by the nurse she waited for the psychiatric liaison team for their part of her treatment. It seemed like hours before they came and they didn't disappoint her with their usual questions of why she did it and was it intentional. They then asked more probing questions, such as information about her psychiatric history or personal life.

She spoke to Pamela first apologizing for her actions and letting her down. Pamela understood although she was shocked at her actions, trying to find answers to why she did it. Pamela herself still had mental health issues and kept personalities concealed in her head, like skeletons in a closet. It certainly wouldn't take much to release her demons once more, only her love for Ruth kept them at bay.

A woman approached them dressed in a brown flowered top and plain dark green skirt; her long ginger hair was tied back with a yellow bobble. Her blue eyes concentrated on observing Ruth's face then she looked at the dressings on her arms.

"You must be Ruth" she said in a sickly sweet manner "I am Emma Williams".

"Yes and you are clearly from the psychiatric

liaison team" Ruth said abruptly.

"Do I detect a note of hostility in your voice" Emma replied sarcastically.

"Fuck you" Ruth said scornfully.

"You're a psychiatric nurse are you not?" Emma continued unfazed by Ruth's abusive remark

"Yes and I know the score, you ask me questions and being non judgmental psycho analyze me with your eyes and mind" Ruth said bitterly

"You have been modeling recently haven't you?" Emma said trying to gather more information.

"Yes and I'm a lesbian before you ask" Ruth felt herself getting angry.

"Ruth listen to her she's trying to help you" Pamela interrupted.

"Yes let me help you Ruth" Emma continued glancing at Pamela and back to Ruth.

"Ok but I understand where this is going and just want to go home" Ruth said addressing Emma and Pamela.

"Yes we are but be patient and we can spend time abroad for a while" Pamela said smiling.

"I will go now and visit you in a while Ruth ok?" Emma said moving away from the bedside.

Pamela watched Emma disappear behind the curtains then looked at Ruth who held her head down in shame.

"I suppose you think I'm stupid?" Ruth said in a low voice.

"No you forget I've been there" Pamela said in an understanding tone.

"Yes but I have been looking after you and now I am the weak one" Ruth said ashamed.

"Ruth we have come a long way and experienced so much together, I should have realized that all this glamorous life style is a bit much for you" Pamela said with empathy.

"Yes but I didn't want to let you down, but I was worried about upsetting you and causing you to relapse" Ruth said gripping Pamela's hand.

"I know and I think it's time to think of you and your needs and fuck mine" Pamela said with a smile.

"It's all about us not me and that's what I want" Ruth said tearfully.

"Yes let's deal with that ok?" Pamela agreed.

Ruth was discharged from hospital on antidepressants and pain relief, she was confident that Pamela now understood her limitations as a model and they just worked on modeling for jewelry and clothes with a less demanding schedule away from the lime light. This suited Ruth and although Pamela found it mundane and boring she did it for Ruth's sake. Both of them were supporting each other working through nightmares and low moods together, they shared a common enemy in their past and dealt with it bravely together. The enemy was Pamela and Ruth's past traumas of abuse, this had haunted both women at various times and they both wore the scars beneath their skin.

Occasionally Ruth experienced Pamela's other identities, as she displayed them, but it was less frequent as she felt more secure with Ruth. The identity Anna the child appeared after Pamela had experienced a nightmare or some other sort of trauma. James was a rare identity these days as her angry episodes were few. Ruth experienced low moods and was on anti depressants and dealing with her condition. Pamela's memory was a problem as this was shared by her identities, Pamela, as the host would struggle to remember important events and often used a note pad in order to remember important things. When Ruth was with her she became her memory prompting her about times and dates.

As time went on the media that had criticized them for their open displays of lesbianism and public protests for gay liberation forgot them. The media found new victims to pester and intimidate, carefully avoiding racism, sexism and all kinds of prejudice remarks that caused such problems in the past. They were cunning but clever enough not to get sued by celebrities as they went on one witch-hunt after the other destroying people professional reputations and lives.

One of the worst parts of Pamela and Ruth's mental illness was the nightmares they occurred often and dominated both their lives. The images that the mind was capable of creating could be horrific and so real. Some were directly from experiences of their past, such as abuse from childhood or married life. There were the usual dreams of falling or flying which suggested trauma in their life or escaping from bad situations perhaps. Some interpretations indicated escapism. Often vampires or monsters were involved in their nightmares the figures that emerged from the darkness and terrorized them. These could easily have been their abusers from their childhood, ghosts from their past. Because it was so realistic one or the other would wake up screaming or find scratches on their body.

The dreams of medieval castles, maidens in distress or being carried off by dragons to caves were quite common. So were the vampire nightmares running in fear of their lives. Either Ruth would come to Pamela's rescue or vise versa. Even in the dreams they wore such elaborate costumes, such as a long dress with a high collar and a long sweeping cloak. Or small briefs over dark tights and shapely body Armor with shoulder pads.

One night Pamela dreamt of wearing a porcelain mask and being attacked by someone with a baseball, she is knocked to the ground and the mask is cracked while her head and face is covered with blood. After which a number of images of herself immerge out of her own body all wearing different clothes and some in uniform indicating her many identities. They appeared like ghostly spirits one wearing a black outfit with a veil, she lifts the veil to look at a grave stone of Ruth. Pamela wondered whether this was symbolic of Ruth's death, like a premonition. Sometimes Pamela would kneel beside the grave and place flowers by her grave. Another figure is in a wheelchair obviously Pamela's mother but Pamela is in the wheelchair being pushed about by Ruth.

All the images are her own identities none of them are the host. Even a child in a white night dress is Pamela as a child and often lost in some wood or in a dark room somewhere. A man is another image with her features he is looking down at his own penis or punching a wall. Sometimes a female soldier would appear brandishing a rifle or blade in a threatening manner.

Ruth's dreams were similar with similar outcomes death being one of them, usually her own. Ruth's dreams consisted of rats and spiders invading her personal space. Falling down a pit and dropping onto spiders, or snakes. Falling out of a tower or off a cliff, on a few occasions she was Pamela's mother crying for forgiveness sat in a wheelchair. Ruth's biggest fear was loneliness and so her worst nightmare was being alone in somewhere like a station or bus stop.

Pamela and Ruth would wake up from a dream either screaming or crying. This resulted in comforting each other. A vivid dream tended to make them think it was real and part of their lives after all the characters were there. The people in the dreams portrayed real characters from their past often features were exaggerated like that of cartoons; monsters were always huge and menacing. They always tried to escape but moved in slow motion as if they were stuck to the floor. Some dreams involved walking through many doors but never getting outside; as each door opened they entered another room.

Dreams could be interpreted in many different ways, but for those with a mental illness they become more complex and harder to understand. Most dreams can be related to the day's events known as recalling or recapping moments that mean something to you like flash backs. A series of ideas can induce a combination of thoughts that formed some kind of story whether it is consistent or not. Ruth often dreamt of being in a wardrobe in her dark and secluded place when the doors suddenly opened and a man wearing a porcelain mask appeared. The wardrobe was her protective place that no one was allowed to enter and the man represented abuse.

People interpret dreams in various ways the idea of flying was generally to escape from a situation or place that you don't feel comfortable in. Often Pamela would witness Ruth being attacked and in her dreams and raced to her rescue, but in some dreams she could actually see Ruth in an open casket surrounded with flowers like those they saw in the countryside on holiday. She would then see many familiar faces looking over the coffin some weeping. Then a parade of models walked around the grave just as if they were on the catwalk. This seemed to be all about Pamela's anxiety of losing Ruth and she often spoke to Ruth about this dream. Ruth had similar dreams about Pamela but often it involved a funeral at a crematorium with friends and family looking on.

In one nightmare Ruth had, she was walking on the catwalk when suddenly faced with masks each one falling from above, some smashing on to the ground. Images appeared before her wearing porcelain masks. Ruth pulls the masks off in frustration as she hates masks; behind each one is a person she knows. Behind the first mask was Pamela, the second Sheena, the third was Gloria and the fourth Emma her sister. But as she pulled off the final mask was Malcolm, as she removed his mask he became angry and chased her down the catwalk. Ruth ran and ran until the stage ended, she then jumped off. Malcolm and her fell and landed on the ground amongst masks and the bodies of Malcolm's victims which lay all around them. Malcolm stood up and picked up his baseball bat, Ruth jumped to the left then to the right to avoid the bat. Malcolm hit the masks and bodies in a frenzied attack, his eyes were menacing as he began staring at Ruth. Then he hit another mask and this time the mask shattered and Pamela's face appeared, this changed into Pamela's mothers face Sarah, then disappeared. Ruth ran again but this time felt as if her feet were being weighed down by led, this time Malcolm caught up with her and hit her with his baseball bat, she noticed the blood splash and everything went black. She woke up and was quaking with fear. Pamela was looking at her and Ruth noticed that Pamela had blood on her face.

"Have I hurt you?" Ruth asked concerned

"No take a look at your legs" Pamela said alarmed

Ruth looked at her legs and then her hand which were also covered with blood

"My god I've been scratching myself" Ruth said horrified

"Yes let me help you clean yourself up" Pamela said "just like you did with me on the ward" Pamela actually remembered this.

Pamela got a damp flannel and cleansed Ruth's wounds, she reminded her of Ruth's activities in her sleep which explained how she received her injuries. She actually clung onto Pamela which accounted for why the blood was on Pamela and no wounds were discovered on her body.

Pamela was known for the occasional sleep walking finding herself in odd places around the house, but sometimes returning safely to bed. She also had panic attacks and flash backs triggered by smells, seeing a person who reminds her of people from her past. Pamela was also a person who had compulsions and rituals; sometimes she would have mood swings for no apparent reason. The dreams seemed to enhance these conditions or behaviour escalating events out of all proportion, causing harm to her and sometimes others.

Pamela said although she had never taken drugs she had out of body experiences and sometimes hallucinations affecting one of the six senses usually visual, seeing things that were not there. Ruth has been her rock stabilizing her along with her cocktail of medication and occasional therapy of some description. Ruth just needed to stay out of the limelight and hold on to what sanity she had left. Ruth tended to heal quickly and bounced back from her depressive state with support from Pamela. They were still in love and took their relationship to new heights the so called forbidden love continued.

THE POWER OF LOVE

Early one morning on a baking hot morning in midsummer the phone rang in Pamela's apartment, it rang for a while before Pamela immerged from the bathroom covered in a bath robe and a towel wrapped around her head.

"Hello" Pamela said hesitantly "Oh hello Angela, how's Tara" she continued.

"I'm fine, yes she's good too" Pamela said then nodded as she listened intently.

"I would love to but Ruth may not want to" she said looking at the bedroom door.

Ruth had heard the phone and stood in her dressing gown with a worried look on her face.

"Let me get back to you ok?" Pamela said placing the phone on the receiver.

Pamela began to miss being in the limelight, she loved performing in front of a crowd right from childhood when she was trained to walk the cat walk.

"Tara wants us to model cosmetics" Pamela said watching Ruth head towards the kitchen.

"Really is that for magazines? Ruth asked.

"Yes and for posters in shopping malls" Pamela continued "Not bad money".

"Ok" Ruth said eagerly "We need the money at the moment".

"Oh and she said there is a new fashion show being prepared" Pamela added.

"You know how I feel about shows Pamela" Ruth slammed down her cup "I hate them".

"This is different" Pamela pleaded "It's a love thing and we could be great in this one".

"I am never going back on a cat walk" Ruth insisted.

"Not even to tell the world that we are getting married" Pamela said confidently.

"Married?" Ruth was puzzled "You want to marry me?".

"Yes a civil wedding maybe here and then honeymoon in Lake Garda in Italy" Pamela said positively.

Ruth stood quietly for a while thinking about what she had said "Married".

"I am proposing to you Ruth" Pamela said smiling.

"Well yes ok" Ruth replied smiling back.

"The show is called 'The power of love' it's said to be big" Pamela continued excitedly.

"Where is it?" Ruth asked.

"It's a traveling show being staged in London, New York and Paris" Pamela added.

"Makes me nervous just thinking about it" Ruth admitted.

"Ruth you will be fine, it's going to be amazing, loads of celebrities and top models" Pamela tried hard to persuade Ruth.

"But I am not as confident as you and remember last time?" Ruth said trying to convince Pamela not to let her do it.

"But your stronger now and I will take better care of you this time" Pamela was very convincing.

"You said it's about love?" Ruth asked.

"The power of love" Pamela said holding her arms up dramatically.

"The power of love" Ruth asked "That's a song isn't it?"

"Yes I suppose so" Pamela said grinning.

"So it's a show based on a song then?" Ruth asked.

"Maybe, but what an idea and foundation for the fashion show" Pamela replied.

"Sort of a hippy thing then based on sixties and seventies fashion no doubt" Ruth said with excitement.

"Yes mixed with 21 century fashion" Pamela said equally excited by the thought of an infusion of 20th and 21st fashion ideas.

"Tara and Angela will be in the audience" Pamela announced with delight.

Pamela managed to convince Ruth that it was advantageous to model in the show; it was more of a theatrical event judging by the costumes. Flower power using displays of flowers with hippie costumes performing to the Beatles song 'All you need is love' a fitting opening to the show.

The London show opened in the height of the summer with selection of models some that had performed many time and models that were new to the cat walk. Gloria Thompson, who was a friend of Pamela and Ruth, was at the show.

Gloria was a woman with mixed race parents, her father was a white Englishman and her mother was South African. Gloria had a coffee brown complexion and dazzling white teeth, with long black hair and stunning large brown eyes. Although she was heterosexual she believed in people living their lives as they want to and criticized no one. She lost a friend a few years ago called Kim who lost her battled against anorexia, collapsing on a catwalk during a show. Kim's parents were wealthy and sent her to a private school for her education. Kim could not fulfill her parent's expectations. So she became a model, but lost her life due to the complications of anorexia, her death was so tragic.

Pamela and Ruth faced their usual battle against some of the models who disagreed with their relationship. But they stuck together and had support of Gloria when it came to any disagreement. When they met Gloria she greeted them with open arms making more of a fuss of Ruth because she knew that she was struggling.

Gloria explained about Kim's last days with affection and knew that they would understand. Kim was feeling depressed as the press had hounded her about her condition. Facing Kim with her anorexia was like introducing a spider to someone who feared spiders. She suffered most of her life from this eating disorder, eventually her heart became weak and she died.

Family, friends and colleagues attended Kim's funeral; many models were there dressed in dark clothes looking far different from the outfits that they usually wore. Many of them were crying and some whispering to each other some discussing the funeral while others were more concerned with what people were wearing. The family remained together and refused to associate with the models, blaming them for leading Kim into modeling. The truth was that Kim herself wanted to be a model and chose her own career, she never wanted to follow her parent's lifestyle. Walking in her parents shadow was not option in her eyes, she had her own identity and it wasn't to be a spoilt little rich girl like some of her former friends.

Once the first show was filmed the press rushed to the stage doors to see Pamela and Ruth. One of them was the one who had caused them so many problems in the past. He was lingering around them like a vulture after his prey, hungry for a story he caught hold of Ruth's hand and spoke to her "So the lesbians are back" he said peering into her eyes.

Ruth pulled away and surprisingly Gloria came to her rescue "Let her go you bastard" she shouted for all to hear.

"So the blacks are lesbians this year" he said rudely.

"How dare you insult her you fucking creep" Ruth shouted.

Pamela raced forward in her defense but Ruth had already slapped him and Gloria kicked him between the legs.

The reporter fell to the ground in pain and all three women cheered.

Security guards escorted the reporter out of the building and he immediately hailed a taxi and disappeared down the street. The other reporters moved away from the women and pursued the other models. Hoping to gather stories from them instead, some of the models seemed pleased to provide them with what they needed. Discussing past experiences and enjoyment of appearing in the show.

The fashion critics were very keen to get good seats expecting to see more than fashion, as the title suggested. In fact 'the Power of love' fashion show was about more than fashion, it was a statement or underlying message about the freedom of choice. The object was to get rid of the stigmas surrounding the gay scene, mental health, racism and a whole array of prejudices that we face in the world today. It's all about loving yourself and others, expressing how you truly feel, and speaking out to the world.

Pamela was having her make up applied while Ruth was having her hair styled for her performance. The rooms were full of models being prepared for a magnificent show, their was hardly any conversation as most of the models appeared to be nervous, despite their many appearances on events like this. But this time it was different, because this show had raised more than the usual publicity, thanks to Pamela and Ruth, amongst others. This was the first time transsexual models appeared in a fashion show like this. Rocky horror had come to life making it more than a fashion show, selling more tickets than ever and providing the audience with incredible entertainment.

Some of the designs certainly agreed with the love scene displaying so many outfits from top designers. Some are bizarre and some earthier, with the use of many fabrics and other materials at their disposal. The outrageous were people wearing such things as toilet rolls stuck together on models head painted in silver, and a long dress made from cotton with a net curtain design over it. Alternatively one had a plain blue dress with large smarties all over it, traveling down in a coordinated fashion. The outrageous gave more freedom for ideas, as the models were more skimpily dressed with a more revealing demonstration of promiscuity. This left little to the imagination and the see through suit worn by Pamela was well viewed.

The evening wear was so romantic with evening dresses in all colour and designs, the dark blue off the shoulder look as demonstrated by Ruth, or the white and pink designs worn by Pamela contrasted with Sheena's green emerald dress with a matching emerald necklace and bracelet that seemed almost luminous. If this wasn't enough, there was the swimwear with exotic Hawaiian backdrop. The casual look was well received although it was less casual than last year and seemed to be a mixture of casual and formal so as to please the judges. There was then a cross match of cultures demonstrating the unity of nations, for example a mix of India and Europe, Japanese and German which was confusing at times. The wedding outfits showed that every sort of sexual persuasion was being addressed this demonstrated that the message that Pamela and Ruth were campaigning was finally being recognized and understood. The honeymoon was a little more farcical and almost gave the opposite message; Pamela and Ruth were not involved with this display and never modeled any of the outfits on this occasion.

The idea of mixing ancient history with the modern was not a new concept but effective when it came to fashion design much like tying rags in the hair and wearing sandal type shoes on their feet. The high wedge shoes wear popular and furs seemed a must for some designers. Long flowing skirts and hooded coats were also popular as well as the shades of pastel blending in many colours. Black and white stripes and squares in many patterns were shown in contrast with subtle shades of red or grey.

Ruth had become confident again and found that she was able to walk confidently on the catwalk in various costumes. Models respected her more as they did Pamela the whole idea of lesbians on a catwalk and certainly since the death of Kim, people's ideas of anorexia seemed to change. It was like the whole world had changed overnight although this was not the case, It was however the start of something new.

The backdrops were spectacular especially the love themes giant hearts everywhere, it was like 14th February Valentine's Day. Celebrities from around the globe attended. Pamela and Ruth were becoming very popularly all over the world. A rainbow tunnel was available that lit up as the models traveled under it, while various coloured confetti drifted down from above. The romantic evening showed a wonderful backdrop of a moonlit sky with many stars shining brightly against a black background.

Gloria wore outfits that complimented her beautiful coffee coloured skin tone at one point displaying a leopard style cat suit then contrasting this by wearing an evening gown in beige and cream with matching elegant jewelry. Sheena appeared with her wearing her favorite green velvet gowns. Each designer seemed happy with the way the models were displaying them on the catwalk, looks of contentment appeared on their faces. Smiles made it obvious that they were confident others would approve of their designs too.

Ruth's sister Emma was in the audience watching as Ruth appeared several times on the catwalk. Ruth was never aware that Emma was there until the last night when Emma waited for Ruth to appear back stage. Emma stood waiting watching each model pass her and head for the dressing room.

"Ruth" Emma shouted as she saw her approaching.

Ruth hesitated and looked at Emma; Pamela nodded to her acknowledging her.

"Hi Emma" She said politely.

"Hi Pamela" Emma replied smiling.

"Emma how are you?" Ruth said hesitantly.

Ruth led Emma away to a quiet room.

"Ruth I know its been two years but I have missed you"

"Me too" Ruth replied.

"I do understand about you and Pamela and I am happy for you".

"What about mom and dad?" Ruth asked.

"You know them I tried to explain things" Emma explained.

"But don't hate them for it".

"I hate no one honestly" Ruth insisted.

"Then come and see them please" Emma pleaded.

"I will after the tour is over ok?" Ruth explained.

Ruth embraced her sister they both shed a tear and both sat for a while talking about the show.

"You were brilliant in that show, you and Pamela" Emma said smiling.

"It means a lot hearing that from you" Ruth said smiling back at her.

"I love London's fashion week its always appealed to me, the year they had the Egyptian theme" Emma said excitedly "Elizabeth Taylor portrait of Cleopatra as an idea for fashion and introducing a modern slant on it" She added.

"Yes that year was good" Ruth agreed.

"Pamela looked good in her silver and black outfit" Emma continued, "You make a great couple and perform well on the catwalk together.

After a short while Pamela entered the room and seemed to address them both "Are you hungry?" She asked, "Shall we go for lunch somewhere?"

Ruth looked at Pamela and then at Emma "Shall we?".

Emma nodded "Yes that would be nice" she agreed.

They all left the room and headed to the exit, across the street stood a series of restaurants. They headed across the road "Indian or Chinese?" Ruth asked.

"Chinese if that's ok" Emma said waiting for the others to agree.

They chose a nice quiet cubical area and sat comfortably surrounded by a few people on other tables. An American couple sat in the next cubical and were talking loudly as if they wanted them to here their conversation.

"The fashion show was fine but the god damn Lesbians spoilt it as usual" The woman said spitting venom.

"Well if our daughter was like that I would disown her," The man said dismissively.

Ruth looked at Pamela with an angry expression, but to their amazement Emma responded.

"What a pair of ignorant tossers, don't they understand anything". Emma shouted.

"Leave it Emma, its not worth it" Ruth said trying to prevent trouble.

"We get this crap all the time, we are used to it" Pamela said looking at the menu.

The Americans left the restaurant soon afterwards and the women placed their order.

Emma was still annoyed by their comments and continued to discuss it with Pamela and Ruth.

"I really didn't know what you were going through" Emma said "I feel so bad because I too was negative about you" Emma bowed her head in shame.

"Come on Emma you were driven by other peoples opinion, influenced by their thoughts". Ruth said in an understanding manner.

"Some people can be very persuasive, using pier pressure and all that sort of thing".

"I realize that now but what about mom and dad?" Emma asked.

"They may never understand because of their generation" Ruth replied.

"Anything out of the norm is considered odd, my mother would never understand either" Pamela said sadly.

"Is she dead?" Emma asked.

Pamela looked at Ruth "Yes in a way she is". Pamela said, "She was murdered".

"My god no way" Emma said in an empathetic manner.

"Yes and the killer is still at large" Pamela added.

"The one that has been murdering all them women?" Emma asked.

"Who knows" Ruth answered swiftly.

The food soon arrived and nothing more was said about the murder of Pamela's mother. Instead the conversation changed to more discussion about the fashion show and about holidays. The evening seemed to go quickly Pamela and Ruth took Emma back to her hotel and they both hugged Emma.

"Don't forget my invitation to your wedding" Emma said.

"Of course Emma" Ruth replied, "You will all get one".

"Take care Emma" Pamela said "see you soon".

Emma looked at Pamela strangely when she this as if she would never see her again. Emma thought she could see a strange light around her head almost like a halo. It was odd because

Emma had often had dreams of Angels ever since Pamela visited her parents home all that time ago. It freaked her out then as it did now, something was clearly wrong in her eyes but she was unable to convey it or express why she felt weird.

The show was a great success in London and Paris; audiences were entertained by the 'love theme' although they had mixed feelings about the types of sexual persuasions displayed in the show. The stigma remained with some people who criticized the gay acts who dressed so elegantly on the catwalk. On the last night in of the show in New York Pamela announced the engagement of Ruth and herself to a television reporter. She announced a civil wedding in England on their return, which was frowned upon by the public and media alike. It seemed although they were accepted for who they were marriage was too extreme.

The news reached England and soon became news headlines, many people saw the news and television programs wanted to book them on their show. Once again they were being interviewed and found they were popular again. Pamela was watching the interviewers body language while Ruth was talking

"You speak to us about normality and I say what's normal about the so called Christian society pushing out lesbian, gays and transsexuals like they don't count".

"Yes and what about the media who hound people for stories about anorexia or other illnesses forcing them to take their lives".

The bishop leaned forward already red in the face "Christianity is as it always will be opposed to homosexuality and the media help to display this". He pointed his finger at Pamela and Ruth "Your display of lesbianism only demonstrates the meaning of the bible regarding abstaining from fornication and so banish such wicked behaviour from society".

"Fucking hypercritic bastard" Ruth said angrily "Your sort mess with little boys and call us wicked how dare you".

"Look at the profanities displayed by these women doesn't that say it all" The bishop said addressing the audience.

Ruth rose from her seat and walked towards him, security moved in quickly.

Pamela walked forward pulling Ruth back "Don't let these ignorant fuckers upset you they are not worth it" Pamela said moving her back to her seat.

"Let them have their say" The vicar insisted.

"I speak for all people who are suppressed by the bullies of society".

"So who are the bullies and who are the suppressed?" the interviewer asked.

"The suppressed are anyone who could be deemed as different" Pamela said "But god bod just want these people away out of sight"."Yes and the bullies are people like that wanker over there who thinks he himself is god, a true narcissi full of his own importance". Ruth said trying to remain in her seat despite her mood.

"Clearly you are an example of lower class scum and have no connection with the real world" The bishop said dismissing them with the wave of his hand.

"Oh well Mr Bishop let me tell you that you are the one that is delusional and out of touch with reality" Ruth stood up again and Pamela stood beside her.

"What an arrogant jumped up prick you are, get your head out of your arse and join the real world where people like us do exist". Pamela said pointing at him.

"Centuries ago you people would be burnt at the stake as witches". The bishop said angrily.

"Oh that's a bit extreme" the vicar said laughing.

"There you have it old fashioned methods from old fashioned views" Ruth shouted.

"I am sure the audience think society needs a broom up its arse Pamela shouted.

The audience applauded upsetting the bishop.

"See how the devils children influence his flock, society needs to be rid of such people before society is destroyed". The bishop continued.

"I say get rid of religion and politics and your half way there to having a descent society" Ruth shouted in anger.

"Yes get rid of those who dictate about what we should eat, wear and act in society according to religion". Pamela added.

Again the audience applauded and watched as Pamela and Ruth left the stage they then returned with people with anorexia, transsexuals and people with various deformities.

Pamela then took centre stage and looking at the religious elements across the stage announced,

"These people want to be part of your society with your help they can be". Pamela's words seemed to echo out into the audience as they all stood up and clapped.

"There's your answer bishop Ruth said watching him and the other religious leaders leave the stage.

On another show Pamela and Ruth was invited to a morning show, which was broadcast nationwide and watched, by millions of people. The presenter introduced the program and spoke positively about the power of love fashion show.

"The power of love show proved to be successful in London" The presenter said "How do you think it will go in Paris and the United States?"

"I imagine it will be as successful as it was in London" Pamela said confidently.

"The power of love is about unity and love in many ways be it heterosexual, homosexual transsexual or any other way, across the world" Ruth said.

"So why shouldn't it be a success, fashion is not just about style and elegance its about making a statement" Pamela stated pointing to a poster of Ruth and herself in stylish evening gowns.

A few designers were introduced to discuss the power of love show from the prospective of the designers and their styles and up and coming costumes including imaginative ideas. One of the designers introduced Sheena as she modelled a few outfits on the stage. Other models helped to display other designer's outfits and the show ended with Pamela and Ruth announcing their engagement. The presenter congratulated them and spoke about the show going to Russia, she mentioned a diplomatic reason to visit Moscow and discuss the power of love in order to unite the world.

Ruth realised that Malcolm was a violent psychopath; he had all the signs such as no shame in what he did. Ruth was the only one in his life and she could have no family or friends round her. He displayed acts of selfishness, he was lazy, harmful and immoral acting as if this was normal and acceptable. Ruth began to wonder why she hadn't seen this before in him and recognised the signs of a psychopath. Perhaps she could have acted more swiftly and prevented things happening as they did. It then occurred to her that he was capable of raping and killing Pamela's mother.

Malcolm intentionally and methodically

murdered women and was still free to continue to do so. He roamed the streets at night searching for Ruth hiding in shadows and hoping that one night Ruth would appear.

Malcolm came out of the suburbs into and began to search for the women once more. He was annoyed by the news that Pamela and Ruth were to be married and wanted to discuss this with Ruth. Malcolm had become a serial killer and a psychopath. He went to Ruth's apartment first hoping to find her there, lingering around the corner waiting to follow her into her apartment.

Pamela continued to have nightmares of Ruth being murdered by Malcolm with his baseball bat, killed just like those innocent women who resembled them. The police never found the killer and So the murders remained unsolved.

Malcolm finally caught up with Pamela and Ruth as they entered Pamela's apartment. He had only seen Ruth enter the door and followed her up to the apartment. He was close enough to stop the door from shutting with his foot and then pushed his way inside. Ruth tried to prevent him from entering but he was too strong and forced her away from the door.

Ruth ran across the room and Malcolm caught up with her, punching her in the face, she fell back onto the settee and he raised his baseball bat to hit her. At that moment she screamed blood trickling from her nose. Suddenly he let out a yell as Pamela plunged a knife into his back she was shouting in a deep voice at him, but nothing made sense. Malcolm staggered to the floor trying to get the knife out of his back. The knife eventually dropped onto the floor and landed beside Malcolm who lay bleeding and groaning.

Pamela helped Ruth to her feet and dialed emergency services, as she did so she smelt Malcolm's after-shave and froze on the spot realizing he was her mother's murderer. Memories of her mother's rape and murder came flooding back. Ruth stroked her hair "its ok your safe" she said confidently

At that moment Malcolm rose to his feet and ran at Ruth with the knife firmly in his hand Pamela pushed Ruth out of the way and Malcolm plunged the knife into Pamela's stomach.

Pamela fell back and Ruth shouted "No!"

Ruth grabbed the baseball bat and hit him repeatedly over the head, then Pamela and her leaped forward and pushed Malcolm over the balcony and he fell to his death.

Pamela fell to the ground holding her stomach the blood seeped through her clothes. Ruth grabbed a table cloth and tried to stop the bleeding. The colour drained from Pamela's face as she lay in Ruth's arms tears rolling down her cheeks.

"Don't go, I can't live without you" Ruth said crying.

But Pamela was weak and eventually let go of her hand.

"Stay with me Pamela, I need you" Ruth pleaded.

But Pamela closed her eyes and died.

The police entered the apartment followed by Kathy, who had been contacted by Ruth earlier. Ruth was rocking with holding Pamela firmly in her arms and she was mumbling nursery rhymes.

Kathy knelt beside Ruth with her hand on her shoulder and began talking to her.

"Ruth its Kathy" she said trying to get her attention.

"I am not Ruth, I am Sarah" She announced.

"Come on Ruth lets sort you out" Kathy said

trying to free her from Pamela.

"Stop calling me Ruth" she shouted, "I am Sarah".

One of the policemen tried to help Kathy to free Ruth from Pamela as the ambulance crew arrived, but Ruth held her firmly and continued rocking back and forth.

"Don't touch her, go away" she shouted.

Kathy looked up at the ambulance crew and then the police

"Give us a few minutes please" Kathy said tearfully.

Kathy held onto Ruth as the ambulance crew took Pamela away, Ruth remained silent staring into space with a fixed expression on her face. After Pamela had left Kathy got Ruth ready to leave the apartment, they walked down the stairs and Kathy noticed the tape around the area where Malcolm had fallen. Close to this was a black body bag, which contained Malcolm's dead body.

Ruth didn't seem to be aware of anything not even Kathy who was escorting her into a van. Ruth did turn her head and appear to look up at the apartment but then looked back and returned to her blank expression. Things had happened so fast from their final show to the last moments that Pamela and Ruth shared together. From Pamela's admission to the beginning of their relationship Kathy was trying to rationalize the entire event in order to relay it to the police. She was the one that had to explain everything to them and to Ruth's family. As for Pamela's relatives they needed to know a lot about what went on as Pamela never kept in touch with them.

Kathy went with Ruth to a psychiatric ward close to the one where her and Kathy worked. She was greeted by a nurse there and led to a quiet lounge area near the office. Kathy sat Ruth down and watched as Ruth drew her knees up and grabbed them with her hands and began rocking just as Pamela once did. Ruth then sang nursery rhymes over and over again.

Kathy began speaking to the nurse "Hi Gill, you know Ruth don't you?"

Gill nodded "Yes Kathy, Its very sad to see her like this".

"My best friend reduced to this" Kathy replied.

"I can't believe it poor lady" Gill said looking at her rocking.

"Take care of her for me" Kathy said looking at

Gill then Ruth.

"I will and come here whenever you like Kathy" Gill offered.

"Thank you" Kathy said squeezing Gills hand as she walked away.

Kathy looked back at Ruth in the lounge and then left the door; she walked down the corridor to the main entrance and passed the security officer. As she left the building she looked back at the ward where Ruth was staying her thoughts drifted back to Pamela's admission and the start of Pamela and Ruth's relationship. She couldn't help thinking that maybe Ruth would have been well if it hadn't been for Pamela. But then if it hadn't been Pamela maybe it would have been someone else, perhaps Ruth was just one of those nurses who cared too much. As for the love affair, did that truly exist or was it all one sided. Pamela saw her mother in Ruth and maybe that was all, Ruth on the other hand loved Pamela but this could have been transference and again not true love.

No one but Pamela and Ruth could ever answer to whether or not they were truly in love. They were fighting to be accepted in society as lesbians and began to be finally recognized when Pamela was murdered. Kathy wept as she walked through the car park she took a final look back at the ward and entered her car. After a short spell sitting in the car she drove away out of the hospital and towards her home.

The next day Kathy returned on her day off, she brought with her Ruth's mother Diane and two sisters Emma and Claire. Claire was Ruth's younger sister who was at college, she slim with dark hair and was very smartly dressed. They entered the ward after going through the security checks, Ruth's mother seemed particularly nervous constantly looking around her just like Ruth did when she first entered a ward.

Kathy pointed at a room where Ruth was sat staring into space, she was rocking just as she did when she was at Pamela's apartment. Emma was the first to approach the room she kissed Ruth on the forehead and hugged her, but Ruth did not respond. Then Diane kissed and hugged her and still there was no response. Finally Claire moved forward and kissed her, Ruth stopped rocking and tears began to trickle from her eyes.

"What's wrong with her?" Claire asked.

"She's suffering from depression" Kathy

replied.

"Can I speak to you?" Diane asked.

Kathy led Diane out of the room leaving Emma and Claire who were sitting either side of Ruth. Diane looked at Kathy then into the room where her daughters were sat.

"Have I been so bad that I have to be punished like this?" Diane asked.

"Why do you say this?" Kathy replied.

"What a bloody mess" Diane said touching her forehead with her right hand.

"What do you mean?" Kathy asked

"You know about the abuse?" Diane said in a low voice

"Yes Ruth told me some time ago" Kathy said puzzled

"Well I was told first by Ruth, I thought she was attention seeking and ignored it" Diane stared at Kathy "Me, her own mother, turned her away" she looked back at Ruth "I caused all this because I turned her away again when she needed my support".

"But" Kathy was interrupted by Diane as she continued to explain.

"That's not all" Diane said "She kept a diary every year and wrote about events, its all in there, what he did and the fact that I wouldn't listen."

"She doesn't blame you Diane, I know that."

"So what will happen to her?

"She will get help, but its up to you to support her now ok" Kathy advised her.

"Yes I will, I promise", Diane seemed very positive "Just make her well again".

The ward was particularly busy a by polar (manic depressive) patient was running up and down the ward, a girl was screaming and patients were walking into a smoke filled room. A man was sat staring into space speaking to himself, while a lady walked slowly down the corridor escorted by a member of staff. Diane went back to sit with Ruth Emma moved so that she could sit beside her, Diane held Ruth's hand and was speaking to her.

Kathy knew that there was nothing else that she could do, so she went to the office and spoke to the staff. There was no mention of Ruth's father and it became increasingly obvious that he was no longer with the family. Kathy presumed that there was far more to the abuse story than even she knew, perhaps the diary revealed more than anyone knew. Diane was well aware of the truth, but even now chooses to tell no one. Ruth was the one person who could reveal the facts, but was not in a position to say anything.

Emma left the room searching for the toilet, when she entered the cubical the lavatory bowl was covered with blood. There were blood stained footprints on the floor and as she looked in the mirror she froze on the spot. There in front of her was a reflection of Pamela dressed in white with a shining halo over her head, just like she had seen many times before. Pamela was clutching her stomach and not speaking, blood was oozing from through her fingers. Emma let out a scream and staff rushed into the room, there was no blood around and no evidence of any activity in the area.

Ruth turned to her mother and gazed into her eyes "Mother!" she said clearly, Diane embraced her and wept. Kathy looked on, holding onto Emma who was also weeping. Ruth's brother David had joined them and was sitting next to Claire, they seemed bewildered by all the activity. Emma was trying to make sense of what she saw, it was so real yet there was no evidence of anyone being there in the toilet with her.

THE DARK AND LONELY PLACE

It was a cold winter's day, the wind was blowing and snow drifted along the streets. A solitary figure sat in a room unaware of the blizzard outside, in fact unaware of anything around her. She had been sat for hours without moving, just staring into space her thoughts could have been a million miles away. In reality Ruth was a patient on a psychiatric ward, who was admitted following a traumatic experience suffering from posttraumatic stress syndrome (PTSS). She was in a depressed state and had hardly uttered a word since admission, she had to be encouraged to wash and dress, in fact she needed prompting to do everything. She was diagnosed with clinical depression and treated with antidepressants and psychotherapy, this was a long process and has she had just been admitted it could be months away before progress could be made.

Kathy came onto the ward looking for Ruth, she entered the room where Ruth was sat. Kathy then sat beside her and held her hand. She knew that she would probably not get her to respond but it was worth trying and she may be aware of her presence. Ruth merely shed a few tears, holding her legs, rocking back and forth rhythmically. This was classical of her condition with clinical depression assuming the foetal position as a form of comforting herself. Kathy stayed a while then left to work on her own ward next door, before she left she spoke to one of the nurses who was in the office.

"Hi Janet, how is she doing?" Kathy asked.

"No change yet Kathy" Janet replied.

"Have the family visited? Kathy asked concerned.

"Yes but her mother Diane seemed to distress her although she did keep saying mother and her sister Emma seemed quite nervous". Janet said.

"That's because Emma had a strange experience here in the bathroom" Kathy explained.

A few months passed and Ruth was showing signs of progress, she was communicating with the staff and conversing with other patients. Kathy noticed the changes with her on her many visits. Ruth was now pleased to see Kathy and hugged her each time she visited her, she spent time talking to her about the ward and other patients.

"How are you Ruth?" Kathy asked.

"Ok I think the medication is kicking in" Ruth replied.

"No more nightmares?" Kathy asked concerned.

"A few but less often, but certainly flashbacks" Ruth said.

"About Pamela?" Kathy said watching patients passing Pamela's room.

"Yes about Pamela and Malcolm, sometimes other stuff". Ruth said looking down "Do you think my heads fucked?" Ruth asked looking at Kathy for reassurance.

"Well if your heads fucked mine must be" Kathy smiled at Ruth "Look you have been through a lot and your doing well".

"I am starting therapy soon, you know in order to put things right, you know the score". Ruth said yawning.

"Your tired" Kathy said watching her yawn

again.

"No it's the thought of that therapy, I hate it so fucking irritating" Ruth replied.

"Well you will get there and maybe return to work with me" Kathy said positively.

"I don't know about that".

Kathy smiled "You will get there, give it time".

"I do try you know" Ruth said watching a patient passing by "But I never thought that I would be a patient depending on others".

"Ruth!" Kathy called trying to get Ruth's attention back "Has your mother visited?".

"What?" Ruth said still distracted.

"Has your mother visited?"

"Yes she came yesterday with Emma, its difficult for Emma because of the bathroom experience" Ruth still seemed distracted.

"Are you alright?"

"Yes I thought I saw a light floating around outside" Ruth said looking towards the door.

"Really I don't see anything Ruth". Kathy said also looking towards the door.

"I must be tired, perhaps I should rest". Ruth said.

"I should go" Kathy said.

"You know a patient saw a light around Pamela just like Emma did and Emma saw it when she was at mothers house". Ruth said looking at Kathy.

"Mass hallucinations or something" Kathy said dismissing what Ruth said.

"Piss off Kathy your not taking me seriously" Ruth smiled.

"Now that's the Ruth I know and love" Kathy said hugging Ruth and kissing her on the cheek "See you tomorrow".

"Ok don't work too hard, bye Kathy" Ruth said watching Kathy leave the room.

Ruth was due for her first therapy session; she was nervous and felt the sweat coming down her forehead in tiny droplets, which trickled down her face. She had experienced counselling before and was not impressed with the woman that was counselling her. In her opinion these people were trained to deal with people, but had no real life experience. At least they didn't have the type of life that Ruth had experienced over the years, so how could they understand what was going on in her head. A book can't prepare you for someone sharing their child abuse or the types of abuse she experienced with her ex boyfriend Malcolm. In the words of Ruth 'they were talking out of their arse', so she only attended to get off the ward and to please Kathy. Ruth was dreading the common question they all seem to ask 'How does that make you feel' as Ruth once said when I hear that question I want to slap the councillor or punch him/her in the nose.

Ruth was lead into a room by a nurse and she was asked to sit down on an easy chair. The room was airy and bright; a window was slightly open for ventilation. A woman entered the room, she was a middle aged lady with permed brown hair and a little large in weight. She was carrying a bag with a few papers in; Ruth was looking at her and observing everything. The woman put down the bag, took out a notepad and pen then placed them on a nearby table. She looked a little bit like a teacher Ruth knew at school who came across as a stern woman, who seemed to pick on Ruth.

"I am Sheila and I am your therapist, have you had therapy or counselling before?" Sheila asked looking at Ruth through thick lens glasses.

"Yes I have" Ruth replied in a defensive manner.

"So you know how it works then?" Sheila said in a formal manner.

Sheila seemed to be going through the motions of being a therapist, but Ruth was concerned that she never really cared or understood her. She had the head knowledge but had not experienced life like she had. Ruth explained a little about the abuse she got from Malcolm and the relationship with Pamela. Sheila raised an eyebrow when Ruth mentioned her lesbian relationship and so Ruth assumed that Sheila was homophobic, a heterosexual who didn't understand other types of relationships. Ruth thought to herself to say you have to be none judgemental in this profession is a bloody joke. But then she remembered that if she wants to recover and get off the ward she needed to cooperate. As she knew from working as a psychiatric nurse part of getting well was to comply with treatment.

"So I do know a little about you from watching television, seeing you on the catwalk as a model and through advertisements in magazines". Sheila said pointing to a magazine on a small coffee table between them.

"Yes" Ruth said warily.

"So your friend Pamela" Sheila said being interrupted by Ruth.

"My lover you mean?" Ruth said defensively.

"Yes Pamela wasn't it" Sheila said noticing Ruth's defensive reaction.

"What about her, I suppose your going to ask if we had sex" Ruth turned her body away from Sheila and folded her arms to protect her body in a defensive posture.

"Well it was passionate and meaningful unlike heterosexual relationships". Ruth continued sharply.

Sheila looked up at the clock and then at Ruth noticing the tension in her face.

"You were obviously very fond of Pamela" Sheila said.

Ruth turned to face Sheila in a more open posture, she leaning forward to speak to her.

"Do you know what its like to have a lesbian relationship?" Ruth asked.

"No I am afraid I don't" Sheila said "Do you want to tell me about it?"

"Well everybody should try it, until they do how can they judge us?" Ruth asked.

"Us" Sheila picked up on Ruth's use of words.

"Yes Pamela and me, everyone is so fucking judgemental". Ruth continued.

"Do you think that I am judging you?" Sheila asked.

"Yes, people do it all the time, they live in their perfect world with their nuclear family husband, wife and two children and nothing else is normal well fuck that" Ruth said waving her arms about.

"I am not here to judge you only to try and understand you and help you as much as I can. Sheila was trying to reason with Ruth.

Ruth sat back in the chair for a while and remained silent, she resumed the defensive posture not giving Sheila eye contact. And then Sheila asking Ruth another question, which eventually broke the silence.

"Tell me Ruth how do you get on with your mother?" Sheila asked.

"I wondered when we would get to her" Ruth said abruptly

"How do you get on?" Sheila asked.

"She's ok" Ruth was trying to hold back the tears, then continued "She never understood me, I was the one in the middle who always made mistakes and brought trouble home" Ruth stopped talking for a moment then continued "Emma was always the favourite and my younger sister Claire until David came along".

"So you were the middle child for a while" Sheila said trying to understand her family unit.

"What about your father?" Sheila asked wondering why he wasn't mentioned.

"What's he like?" Sheila continued anticipating a bad reaction.

"He's a bastard, so don't even go there". Ruth looked at the clock not wanting to continue with the session at the mention of her father.

But then she decided to continue again sitting on the edge of the seat.

"Let me tell you about my fucking father, let me tell you how he stood and let me get abused by my so called uncle Ron, that's how much that bastard loved me".

Sheila looked a little uneasy as Ruth was getting angry "My father beat him up, half killed him when he eventually realised what this man was doing" Ruth took a breath and continued "He wasn't even my real uncle just some friend of my fathers, who dared to abuse me and befriend the family, what a sick bastard".

Ruth could no longer hold the tears back, then suddenly vomited in the waste paper basket. She heaved and retched. Sheila reached for the panic button but changed her mind and picked up a box of tissues and passed it to Ruth.

"I'm sorry" Ruth said wiping her mouth with a tissue.

"It's ok" Sheila replied "Is this how you normally react to this abuse?"

"You mean vomiting, shouting and swearing?" Ruth asked.

"Yes it must be very distressing for you" Sheila said empathising.

"If I didn't puke, I don't know what I would do" Ruth said tearfully.

Sheila's eyes appeared tearful and Ruth was able to see the compassion in her face. Maybe she did understand her and that's why she didn't press the alarm.

"The puking is me reacting to the abuse isn't it" Ruth said looking at Sheila and sitting with a more open posture.

"Do you want a drink of water?" Sheila asked.

"Yes please" Ruth replied.

"Do you want to continue?" Sheila asked looking at the time.

"Yes I do" Ruth said composing herself.

"I see" Sheila said.

"Well its that or thump the wall or slap the therapist". Ruth said smiling .

"Well thump the wall, not me" Sheila replied smiling.

Although Ruth found it difficult discussing her passed she decided to persevere, knowing that she needed to get things out of her system. She was vomiting as a reaction to the thought of her abuse, along with her inner feelings coming out in bursts of anger. She was experiencing many pent up feelings that were occasionally released like someone unscrewing a bottle of pop that had been shuck up. Ruth needed to find a coping mechanism that would help her deal with anger and she knew that the psychotherapy would help her and unscramble all her negative from her positive thoughts.

Sheila handed Ruth a beaker of water, which Ruth took from her and sipped.

"That's nice, I feel better for that" Ruth said wiping the excess water from her mouth with a tissue.

"Listen Ruth, you know how it works, you're a professional psychiatric nurse for goodness sake". Sheila smiled and continued, "You're a good nurse by all accounts and a caring person, and you helped many people including Pamela".

"Yes I was responsible for her death" Ruth said putting the beaker on the table.

"Do you really believe that?" Sheila asked.

"Sheila, she ran in front of me when Malcolm came at me with a knife, then Pamela got stabbed in the abdomen". Ruth said pointing to her own stomach.

"So she was defending you". Sheila said.

"Yes she was the stronger person in the end". Ruth said sadly

"But you helped her when she was admitted didn't you?" Sheila asked.

"Yes she was suffering from multiple personality syndrome or disassociated identity disorder, she had fourteen identities each one would emerge at times". Ruth looked towards the door and back. "She was able to switch rapidly from one to the other, one was a man called James he was protecting her, then a child who seemed so vulnerable". Ruth paused "Her voice would change according to the identities, James was a deep voice and the child was a much higher pitched sound".

"I bet that was confusing at times" Sheila said.

"Yes the rapid shift from identity to identity was and in the early stages of her admission, Pamela rarely used her own identity as the host". Ruth explained, "She was hard to interview for this reason alone".

"What about when you lived together as partners?" Sheila asked glancing at the time.

"I occasionally noticed some of these identities when she was sleeping having nightmares, I would here her talking or yelling in these voices, that was scary at times fucking freaked me out". Ruth said looking at Sheila's reaction.

"Must have been" Sheila agreed.

"The child voice was eyrie when she asked for a drink in the night" Ruth said watching Sheila's reaction.

"Were you always close to each other?" She asked.

"Yes most of the time, we rowed just like most couples do, Pamela would get jealous of my friendships with other models, but then I did sometimes after all we were surrounded by beautiful girls it was normal wasn't it?" Ruth was trying to get a reaction from Sheila.

"It must have been difficult coping with her mental health problems and modelling" Sheila said not reacting to Ruth's remarks.

"Yes it could be, but I had trouble coping with modelling being in the public eye, it was a strain because Pamela was brought up in modelling where as I wasn't".

"So how did you cope? Sheila asked.

"I didn't I soon fucked up, I got depressed withdrew while Pamela was high up in her career and I cut my wrists". Ruth again looked for a reaction "I was stressed and wanted a release mechanism in order to relieve the tension, self-harming did it for me".

"And how did that make you feel" Sheila asked.

"Relieved, less tense and relaxed for a while" Ruth said "Not that the hospital understood, general nurses haven't got a fucking clue about mental health".

Ruth showed Sheila the scars on her wrists "Anything beyond physical illness is beyond them".

"So what happened then?" Sheila asked.

"The mental health liaison team visited me in casualty and discuss with me why I did it, I was then given Prozac by the doctor to deal with my depression and fucked off or discharged" Ruth explained.

"And then what happened?". Sheila asked.

"Everything went well I got back on my feet and started work in modelling again, we did a major fashion show called 'The power of love' and all went well until Pamela was killed".

"Did you find that people still couldn't except your relationship?" Sheila asked.

"Some of the models were ok about it others still couldn't accept it and the media were awful, my family could deal with it".

"You said your family couldn't deal with it?"

"No my mother was awful, honestly you would of thought I had committed a fucking murder, she fucking freaked out, my father was a fucking waste of space and my sister sided with my mother when I visited my mothers house".

"It must have been hard for you?"

"Yes like fighting the world, we had everyone

against us from family to clergymen and what with that and a violent psycho of an ex boyfriend after us we got away from it all for a while". Ruth said.

"So what happened after you went away?" Sheila said noticing Ruth tense up.

"That when I became depressed doing fashion shows, Pamela was absorbed with modelling, I then came back to fashion shows with the 'power of love project which was a great success".

"Did you feel abandoned like you were as a child?" Sheila asked.

"Yes I did, I suppose I felt I had served my purpose, just like when I was cast aside after my abuse as a child". Ruth said, "Lonely depressed in that solitude of darkness in the wardrobe".

"You needed to get rid of the stress that you were under so you self harmed" Sheila said reflecting back to Ruth's explanation earlier in the session.

"And sat in casualty abandoned again by the hospital who just thought that I had attempted fucking suicide, you get treated like shit if you cut yourself, they have no time for that sort of thing". Ruth felt herself getting angry again.

Ruth thought for a moment "I miss her you know, she was fun and such good company, yes we had our rows but we were good for each other".

"I can tell you miss her, she was obviously special" Sheila said in an understanding manner.

"Yes people think lesbian relationships are a fad and don't last, just women being silly, but if you've never tried it why knock it". Ruth paused "We understood each other, we may have been hormonal at times but the deep rooted love that we shared could never be compared to a heterosexual relationship, even the sex is different".

Ruth smiled and continued, "It's about kissing passionately and the warmth of two naked bodies entwined together, I really can't explain the rest but believe me its good".

Sheila gave a heavy shy and replied "Well we have certainly covered a lot of ground haven't we, you have discussed Pamela to some depth, your parents and other issues". Sheila put her pad back in her bag "Next time we can move on a bit further".

Ruth nodded "Yes okay".

"So next week then same time and place ok?" Sheila said standing up and opened the door.

Ruth also stood up and they both left the room.

The following weeks went well and Ruth was actually looking forward to the sessions feeling far more positive and forming a therapeutic relationship with Sheila. She was moving forward in this way but still had issues to deal with. Ruth had managed to discuss subjects with Sheila but felt she was still in this dark and lonely place in her mind. She described it as a long dark tunnel with a small light in the distance.

Ruth entered the therapy session as she had done several times before, she was relaxed and prepared to discuss her deepest feelings such as her estranged relationship with her family. She considered that her mother had tried to get closer to her but barriers were still present and she needed to know how to knock them down.

Although her father apparently disappeared when Ruth's diary was discovered, Ruth still required answers as to how it was discovered. Kathy had mentioned the diary on one of her visits, but her mother had not said anything just left it with Kathy. Also Ruth had not seen the diary for years and was dubious about reading it in case she had flashbacks of previous events concerning her abuse.

Sheila sat opposite Ruth as she had done so often before in previous sessions, but she seemed different, she was less relaxed and a little agitated. Ruth could sense something was wrong, but remained silent while Sheila spoke to her.

Sheila gave a cough to clear her throat and then began "So Ruth when we spoke you were telling me about Pamela and that special holiday you had together"

"Yes I would say it was the best holiday that I had ever had, she used to wear a dark wig so that we were never recognised, because we were famous". Ruth replied.

"You spent a lot of time in the public eye?" Sheila said fidgeting with her pen.

"Yes with fashion shows and magazine advertisements, not to mention the media and their antics". Ruth said watching Sheila tapping her pen.

"The power of love show seemed particularly popular and raised a lot of publicity, good and bad I thought, how did you feel about that?" Sheila asked.

"I felt on top of the world like a Princess in a

castle and it was so personal, all about us, Pamela and I". Ruth suddenly stood to her feet and demonstrated the moves on the catwalk "Pamela taught me how to walk the walk and smile or use the correct facial expressions, we practiced to music". Ruth said sitting back down.

"And the costumes were too". Sheila said putting down her pen.

"Yes the top designers were present offering such glamorous outfits and some quite bizarre ideas too".

"What about your family, what did they feel about your modelling?" Sheila asked.

"Oh they hated it, in fact they hated everything I did, he didn't want me around" Ruth replied.

"Who do you mean, your father?" Sheila asked biting her lip

"Yes him!" Ruth said sharply "I hate him"

There was a short silence during which time Ruth began thinking about her painful past, then she continued "He hurt me, he really hurt me and I swore that no fucker would do that to me again both him and my uncle can both go to fucking hell".

"How did they hurt you?" Sheila asked.

"With what they did, touching me, messing with my body thinking they could do this to me and not be caught, but my father got scared and decided to beat my uncle up covering his own tracks". Ruth paused for a moment to think again. "But the evidence was there, all written down".

"Evidence?" Sheila asked.

"Yes too bloody right I kept a diary that no one knew about, placed in a brown envelope in a draw hidden under other items". Ruth said looking at Sheila's reaction.

"I wrote everything down, times and such when he came to me", Ruth suddenly went pale "I feel sick, sorry I need to stop"

Sheila went to touch her to reassure her that she was fine, but Ruth suddenly jumped.

"Sorry, did I make you jump? Sheila asked.

"It's ok, I just fucking freak out sometimes when anyone touches me, it just the way I am sorry," Ruth said.

"I understand" Sheila said smiling.

"Pamela understood me, she went through the same type of things, she was very beautiful with blonde hair and blue eyes with a lovely complexion and figure". Ruth stopped again to collect her thoughts. "Her mother Sarah brought her up as a single parent and introduced her to modelling from an early age, she was so perfect until she was abused by her uncle, her real uncle".

"She was special" Sheila commented.

"Very special like her mothers porcelain ornaments, that was before she was abused then she became damaged like cracked porcelain, imperfect, broken irreparable". Ruth said in dismay "She was never the same after that, she was a happy girl turned sad by her abuser".

"Would you say that you were like her?" Sheila asked

"Cracked porcelain you mean?" Ruth said hesitating she thought about what Sheila had said and became tearful. "Yes I suppose so".

Ruth sobbed and repeated herself "Cracked porcelain".

Sheila looked at Ruth trying to hold back her own tears; she wanted to hug her just as she would her own child. Ruth was sat crying and all she could do was offer her a tissue, Sheila felt helpless at this point. Then she watched as Ruth started to vomit in the waste paper basket as she did on previous occasions. Sheila poured water into a beaker and offered it to her.

"I'm sorry" Ruth said tearfully.

"Its ok Ruth honestly just let it out" Sheila said smiling.

"But I feel so fucking stupid, I'm a nurse for god sake, I should be harder" Ruth said disappointed with her own actions.

"We all have to cry sometimes as you know it's a release mechanism, getting rid of locked up emotions". Sheila gave her a reassuring smile.

"Well I feel like I been through fucking hell" Ruth said looking down and noticing a magazine on a coffee table.

The magazine had a photograph of a oriental mask on the front cover, Ruth turned it over onto the back cover. Sheila noticed her do this but never commented just kept looking at the magazine wondering why she did it. Ruth realised this and explained why she did it.

"There was a photograph of a mask on the front of it" Ruth said.

"You don't like masks?" Sheila deduced from the way Ruth reacted.

"I hate masks they are so fucking freaky I have nightmares of them" Ruth said shuddering.

"I once had a nightmare when I was living with Pamela, I was walking along a catwalk when I was suddenly surrounded by loads of people wearing masks". Ruth simulated a mask over her face with the use of her hands.

"They were all coming at me, so I pulled off their masks one by one, behind each mask was a person I knew" Ruth began to mimic the movements "Then behind the last mask was my ex boyfriend Malcolm, he was holding a baseball bat, I ran and fell off the stage I was falling and falling and dropped into a ditch surrounded by dead bodies and masks".

Ruth stopped for a moment "But then he caught up with me and hit me with the baseball bat, all went dark and I awoke covered in blood".

"My word that must have been scary?" Sheila commented.

"Fucking too right" Ruth said staring into space.

"As a child I saw programs with masks in and movies such as the 'The man in the iron mask', I also hate people wearing sun glasses, I don't like people hiding their eyes or their face it disturbs me for some reason".

"So how do you feel when you see the masks?" Sheila asked fidgeting again and looking at the clock.

"Uncomfortable, frightened it sometimes depends on the mask and how it is decorated, I could never tell Pamela this because she loved her masks".

"So you said you don't like masks because you can't see people's eyes?" Sheila asked.

"Eyes are the mirrors of our souls, you can read peoples thoughts through body language, and you can analyse people and determine what is actually going on beneath". Ruth said confidently.

"So can you look in a mirror and read your own thoughts, or when you look in a mirror what do you see?" Sheila asked seeming more agitated than earlier.

"Yes a plain and boring thirty three year old woman". Ruth replied.

Sheila grinned at Ruth and gave a brief reply "You know better than that Ruth".

Ruth suddenly shouted, "Of course how could I be so stupid!"

Sheila jumped and held her chest "My goodness Ruth" she said patting her chest.

"Sorry Sheila but I had a sudden thought, the masks represent deception, and people try to hide themselves behind masks in order to disguise their identity, a way of hiding from the truth, a visual lie".

Sheila looked at her knowing that she had finally realised what had happened to her as a child, blaming herself for the abuse and trying to hide in dark corners. She was also aware of her father's deceit and the way he behaved when his friend was exposed in the diary. Even the dreams of death surrounded her abuse and her own mortality, losing people you trust and love while hateful people survive. But one mystery remained the vision that Emma saw when she was in the bathroom, the image of Pamela with the light behind her head like a halo shining brightly. Also the question arose what about the halo that surrounded Pamela's head, seen by Emma at their family home and the patient who saw this on the ward? Such things had never been explained or maybe could never be explained, such things remain a mystery to all those experiencing them.

"Well Ruth we have covered a lot of ground, so how do you feel now?" Sheila asked.

"Like a weights been lifted off my shoulders, I feel like I have come out of that dark and lonely place and into the light".

"Good is there anything else you need to talk about?" Sheila said looking at the clock.

"An observation of you, if I may" Ruth said with an odd expression on her face.

"Yes of course" Sheila said hesitantly.

"Throughout this session you have been fidgeting and acting really oddly, is there something troubling you?" Ruth asked concerned.

Sheila looked away and then back she then looked to the right and thought for a moment "Yes how perceptive of you, why didn't you say earlier?"

"Because I thought you might tell me" Ruth said waiting for a reply.

"Kathy told me about the diary, she also showed it to me" she paused for a moment "I thought you might be upset that I read it".

"I am surprised that you did and that Kathy showed you" Ruth replied.

"Kathy is a good friend of yours she thought it might help if I saw it". Sheila explained.

"My mother must have given it to her, she obviously found it". Ruth said, "I feeling you knew something about this".

"It is evidence as you said earlier" Sheila said embarrassed

"So can I have it back?" Ruth asked.

"Kathy has it, you would need to ask her".

"Wait a moment you mentioned a blue silk dressing gown, so you must have read all the details, I only mentioned that once".

" I am afraid I did, I wanted to know exactly what your uncle did to hurt you".

"I would have told you, I have nothing to hide". Ruth said feeling hurt by Kathy showing Sheila the diary.

Suddenly Sheila let out a yelp and held the back of her head, she then looked behind her, over her left shoulder then her right. Then began staring behind Ruth without speaking, she then began packing her things together.

"What's wrong Sheila?" Ruth asked watching Sheila looking around her.

"Nothing, I am sorry if I upset you Ruth" Sheila said looking round her.

"You can feel her presence cant you?" Ruth also looked around her "Can you see her".

"I think its time to finish for today" Sheila said opening the door.

"I will make sure you get your diary back" Sheila continued.

Kathy was waiting in the office and saw Sheila heading towards her; she anticipated trouble as she noticed the expression on Sheila's face.

"Kathy she knows about the diary and she is not pleased" Sheila said.

"Oh god, so needless to ask how it went". Kathy said.

"But listen I know this sounds mad but I swear I saw Pamela in the room behind Ruth and she hit me on the back of the head". Sheila said concerned.

"I don't know what to say Sheila". Kathy said confused.

"Felt something at the start of the session today, but I thought it was my imagination" Sheila looked behind her nervously.

"So what about Ruth's therapy?" Kathy said concerned.

"Oh I will continue don't worry".

Sheila left the ward without seeing Ruth, while Kathy continued looking at some paper work.

Ruth appeared at the door looking at Kathy but not conversing, she was brushing her hair and holding a bobble in her teeth.

Kathy saw her in the corner of her eye "Go on say it I know you want to".

"God Kathy what the fuck were you thinking of, you didn't need to show her my diary, it was personal". Ruth said angrily

"Ruth I was thinking of you and I wanted to help Sheila understand you better" Kathy said defending herself.

"Kathy I love you to bits but you should have asked me first". Ruth said calming down.

"Sorry your right I should have asked I will give you your diary back ok" Kathy said.

"There's no hurry Kathy just don't show anyone else". Ruth said smiling.

"No of course not no problem" Kathy smiled back at Ruth and hugged her.

They sat talking for a while and then Kathy left the ward, Ruth went to her room and rested on the bed. She reflected back to her therapy sessions, thinking about the diary and what could have been read. Her mind drifted back to some of the events, but then became too painful to think about so she got up and walked back onto the ward.

It was getting quite busy as teatime was approaching and the patients were assembling into the dining room for lunch. Ruth wasn't very hungry, especially the thought of hospital food. But she forced herself to eat taking a tray from one of the staff and sitting down near another female patient. She was a young girl in her twenties who had lost a child through a car accident and was suffering from post traumatic stress syndrome (PTSS) it was such a shame as she related her story to Ruth. It happened a few months ago the girl was in a car and a young teenage racer drove right across her cutting her up. Her car hit the curb with one of the wheels and her car rolled then hit a tree killing her three year old child instantly. Ruth seemed to be able to comfort her and she discussed many things with from that time on.

Ruth's next therapy session seemed to go well as she discussed her past once more. She spoke about Pamela and even aspects of the diary. Ruth seemed to be in more control and a lot more agreeable, she was less anxious, not as nauseous and her language less colourful. Ruth was on the road to recovery and she even recognised it herself as she commented about coming out of the dark and lonely place and into the light. The dark and lonely place was her wardrobe, which she sat inside if she wanted to hide away from everyone. The future looked good and she could make plans for discharge with her psychiatrist and mental health nurse.

However her past would still be present in her mind, this was something that she had to live, with like her ex boyfriend Malcolm who abused her and made her life a living hell. Malcolm was a violent psychopath who had no conscience and suffered the consequences of his actions by falling to his death from the balcony in Pamela's apartment. His brother Frank was not much better as a sociopath who failed to understand what his brother had done and wanted to avenge his brother's killers as he said to his family at Malcolm's funeral. Who knows how he plAnnd to do this but like his brother he had no conscience and would harm anyone without a second thought.

CRACKED PORCELAIN
ACTS OF ABUSE PART ONE

RECOVERY

It was a cold morning; the snow had been falling heavily on the ground. Cars were struggling to get along and some were left abandoned, to add to the problems visibility was poor. But Ruth's mother Diane had made the effort to conquer the weather as she drove through the snow and ice, sliding along and gingerly applying the breaks. She was travelling to visit Ruth at the hospital; she didn't want to disappoint her so made the effort to go. In her haste she forgot to put on her seat belt and seeing a hazard decided to break fast, she lost control of the car and began to spin across the road into another vehicle.

Diane had hit her head on the window near the door; her head was bleeding as she sat unconscious in her seat. Before long people started to gather round the car, in order to observe the activities, some people were trying to look into the car but no one opened the door. The police and ambulance crew arrived followed by a fire engine; men came forward to rescue her from the car. At that time the crew helped people from the other vehicle. The whole accident seemed to go in slow motion for Diane while her brain tried to interpret the events.

Diane was only just starting to build bridges between Ruth and herself, partly because Diane was fighting with her own guilt and wanting to repair the damage that she felt she had caused over the years. But the years of abuse meant that it would take a lot of word to solve all their problems. The problem now was that Ruth certainly didn't expect such an accident to occur and will probably be shocked by the turn in events.

Ruth was waiting on the ward for her mother's arrival; she had mixed feelings about the visit. Although she was glad to see her mother their was always a tense atmosphere with her. She knew that words of apology was not good enough but Diane was willing to try and resolve certain issues such as not believing Ruth when she said that her fathers friend was abusing her. Ruth was also annoyed about her mother finding the diary and taking it to Kathy. Diane had found the diary when she was tidying Ruth's old wardrobe it was beneath old towels and bedding. The fact that her mother had passed it on and Kathy had shown Sheila was a betrayal of trust with all parties. No one but Ruth should have discovered it and it was confidential. Ruth often kept a diary but never as secret as this one, it was concealed in an envelope for that reason and sealed. Often a girls diary was personal and kept the most closely guarded secrets of her life, containing boyfriends names or personal messages.

But the real truth was more simple to understand like did she really want her abuse to be kept secret, maybe because of the shame and humiliate she would face by exposing the abuser. Or did she want the truth revealed and have the man punished for such a despicable crime. She wrote one entry about her blue silk dressing gown that she burned due to the fact that her abuser had removed it from her in her bedroom one night. When she described the aftershave worn by her abuser and the smell of stale tobacco that lingered on his clothes. The things that make her vomit when she smells them on other people amongst other reminders of her past. She was thinking about the dark and lonely place in her wardrobe, where she hid from her parents. Another entry was where she spoke about his visits meaning her dads friend dreading him visiting because he would harm her and no one would know. Not until today when someone read the diary and found all the contents, her father's friend was in prison having got caught abusing other girls.

Kathy entered the ward and searched frantically for Ruth, she managed to find a nurse who pointed to the shower room. Kathy rushed to the door, but then stopped and realising that Ruth would be out and need to get dressed. So she returned to the nurse and explained about Diane's accident, the nurse asked Kathy to sit down, then sat down herself.

"June" Kathy said beginning to explain everything "I need to take Ruth to see her mother".

"Is Diane stable?" June asked.

"Yes she was lucky she sustained a few cuts and bruises" Kathy replied.

"But I hope this don't set Ruth back, she's doing well at present I don't want her discharge ruined by this". June said concerned.

"Yes I know but imagine if she knows and doesn't see her" Kathy replied.

"Yes true" June said in agreement.

"Don't you think she will worry then?" Kathy continued.

"Yes well you had better take her, but don't leave her side ok" June insisted watching Ruth head back to her room.

"She's just gone back to her room Kathy" June said looking back at Kathy.

"Ok I will go and see her".

Kathy knocked the door and waited, Ruth was dressing and heard the knock.

"Who is it?" Ruth asked suspiciously.

"Its Kathy shall I wait here?" Kathy asked.

Ruth opened the door slowly and peeped round at Kathy wearing a pink dressing gown.

Ruth could see the anxiety on Kathy's face "What's wrong?" she asked.

"Its your mother, she's been in an accident" Kathy said.

Kathy had rushed the sentence so that she could tell her all was well.

But she's going to be fine".

"Oh bloody hell when was this?" Ruth said disturbed.

"A few hours ago" Kathy continued "she was going to see you when she skidded and crashed".

"So has she been admitted?" Ruth asked.

"Yes she is on a ward, she's got a few cuts and bruises that's all" Kathy said reassuring her.

"I have had permission to take you to the ward". Kathy said smiling.

"Ok I will get dressed" Ruth said grabbing her clothes and putting them on her bed.

Kathy left the room and waited for Ruth in the office, during which time she was conversing with June. Kathy had been updated with Ruth's progress.

As soon as Ruth was ready they headed off the ward, and out of the psychiatric block to the medical wards. When they arrived on the ward Emma was already there and greeted Ruth with a hug, she then kissed her on the cheek.

"I am so glad that you could come" She said happily.

"Me too" Ruth said with a smile.

Emma went back to sit at her mother's side while Ruth walked round to the other side of the bed. Emma alerted her mother and watched as her eyes opened and she saw Ruth.

"Mum Ruth's here" She said delighted.

"Hi mum" Ruth said kissing her mom on the cheek.

"Ruth" Diane said in a weak voice.

"How are you feeling?" Ruth asked.

"Oh like a fool, trying to battle with the elements you know with the snow and ice" Diane said smiling.

"Why did you risk your life like that Mother?" Ruth asked concerned.

"Well I didn't want to disappoint you" Diane said.

As they continued talking Emma noticed her father coming down the corridor and slipped away from the bedside to see him. She certainly wasn't very happy knowing he was there and met him at the entrance of the ward.

"What are you doing here?" She asked him.

"I have come to see your mother, where is she?" Her father replied.

"No your not" She replied "Your not welcome here".

"What do you mean" He said then noticed Ruth "Oh I see what you mean". He said.

Disappointed.

"Yes and your not welcome here, so go please". Emma said bluntly.

"Ok I'm going but please give her these flowers" He said turning to walk away.

Emma took the flowers from him and walked away, then she turned around and watched him walk through the door, he walked outside and disappeared.

Emma gave the flowers to a nearby patient, smiled and walked back to her mother's bed. Nobody had noticed Emma disappear or come back except Kathy who saw Ruth's father. She also noticed her give the flowers away and couldn't help smiling, thinking it was a wonderful gesture.

Diane sat talking to Ruth for a while; it was most unlike them to converse properly. Diane still found it hard to accept Ruth's sexuality, she considered Ruth to be odd in this way. But then Diane tried to come to terms with it hoping that she would change and provide her with grandchildren. But as Ruth explained you can't turn your sexuality on and off like a tap, either you gay, straight or both in some cases. Besides it wasn't as if Ruth was her only child, her other daughters could provide her with granddaughters.

Diane spent a few days in hospital before being discharged making a full recovery. Ruth took longer to recover and spent time in recreational activities with other patients. It was strange seeing life from the inside as a patient, but oddly enough Ruth was pleased to have the experience. She was able to view things from a different perspective as a patient, being given treatment and medication. Life was so different living on a mental health ward.

Meanwhile in another area of the hospital Malcolm's brother Frank was admitted for acute abdominal pains. He noticed Ruth pass him as she was heading back to the psychiatric unit, but she didn't notice him. He was unable to follow her or even see where she was heading, but he was determined to find out, as he wanted to avenge his brother. He made enquiries during his stay in hospital someone must have known her.

Ruth had a short time left as a patient and had almost finished her therapy sessions. She had more visits from her family and began to build up strength fighting the demons within. Diane had begun to get close to Ruth and asked her to stay with her until she was better. Ruth agreed and plans were going ahead for her discharge, Ruth's sights were set to return to nursing and maybe do some modelling, but she had to contact Tara her photographer when she left the ward.

Ruth had been taken to Pamela's funeral at the local crematorium but couldn't remember much about it as she was suffering from depression at the time. Modelling friends Sheena and Gloria were present along with photographer Tara and their modelling agent Tara's Sister Angela. Others people attended from Pamela's family and other models that were involved in the 'power of love fashion show'.

Ruth always reacted the same about funerals she considered them hypocritical, people were usually false pretending to like the diseased and trying to be nice with people they would normally ignore. But in this case Ruth was too ill to realise who was attending and just remained in her own little world, which was totally out of character for her. She never held back from expressing her views on religion or politics, after all what kind of god stands back while other people suffer, especially his own kind. She was opposed to any god who let children suffer from abuse, if he was a god of justice whether his name was Mohammed or Jehovah he should at least protect them.

Ruth had many arguments with clergymen who pompously criticised Pamela and her for their sexuality, yet within their own faith people in position of office abused children and were protected by their flock. Ruth was more outspoken than Pamela and would not hold anything back, cursing and swearing at them as she expressed her opinion openly to one and all. Another problem that Ruth found was that people would do anything for their religion or god even kill, which was in conflict with her ideals or philosophy of live to love and love to live. Alternatively do what you want to do as long as it doesn't harm your self or others; this is probably more accurate in Ruth's case.

Ruth once dreamt about an argument that Pamela and her had with a clerical group about the so-called abomination of homosexuality. Ruth shouted at them cursing their religion and their slant on the bible.

"You load of fucking hypercritic" She began

"Bad mouthing our sexuality while you sexually attack children" Ruth scolded.

"Have you read the bible on homosexuality?" One of them said pointing at her.

"Christ man you think the bible is everything, do you think you rule the world with your religion" Ruth said pointing at a cross on the wall.

"No, but god rules the heavens and the earth and you are acting against god by your sexual promiscuity". He continued "vile acts of sin and debauchery with you two leading the way".

"Well fuck you and your flock, we are in love and not shagging around thank you" Pamela added

"Listen to them cursing and swearing isn't that proof of how evil they are" Another clergymen said

"Your enough to make a fucking saint swear with your idealist world and grandiose ideations, you would be happy in fascist society run by fascist leader as occurred in history". Ruth said

"Yeah the type of society that excluded anything, out of the norm". Pamela added

"Well we know what the bible says about you" a clergymen shouted

"The fucking bible is ok, but its people who miss quote it, they twist words round, that's what you lot do" Pamela said pointing at them.

After Pamela commented the religious leaders looked at each other and when the audience applauded they left disgusted by what they heard. This was quite common when Pamela and Ruth were together on stage amongst opposing parties such as religious leaders and politicians. They were used to being publicly attacked and criticized for their sexuality. When Ruth woke up she felt stronger as if Pamela had visited her in her sleep and instilled a sense of purpose into her. This was probably one reason that Ruth was on the road to recovery.

CONSCIENCE AND CONSEQUENCES

Ruth had settled into her family's home trying not to think about her past, although reminders of her childhood days were all around her. Her mother Diane had redecorated the bedroom a few times but the old wardrobe was still there which was her refuge, the dark and lonely place that she remembered so well. Hiding inside the wardrobe hoping not to be discovered.

Ruth was a strong believer that what somebody does to others eventually happens to them; she didn't believe in revenge but did think that justice should be done. The idea that you should do unto others as you would have done to yourself fit her ideals. But in order to recover fully she needed to forget her past and move on to a brighter future, she always considered that Pamela was less fortunate than herself. Pamela had witnessed the rape and murder of her mother, which made her own problems a little small in comparison. Ruth was a strong-minded person as a rule and could cope with any given situation and fight for the rights of the oppressed.

Ruth tried to make sense of the visions that Emma had seen of Pamela, the thought of Emma either seeing a ghost or hallucinating was a strange thought. Either Emma had seen an apparition or she was going mad and possibly suffering from schizophrenia. But then what happened in Ruth's therapy session with Sheila when she saw Pamela and felt a hand slap her on the head, it could be argued that Sheila imagined such an event, as Ruth never witnessed anything. The whole situation was bizarre and a little hard for Ruth to take in, even though Emma seemed rational the rest of the time. Paranormal activity for Ruth was a thing that never occurs only with people with either psychiatric or psychological problems. Everything could be explained away and no one could present evidence to the contrary, Ruth believed in simple facts based on hard evidence. All can be explained the ideas of ghosts or guardian angels were a complete myth made up by very eccentric people.

Ruth believed that Malcolm died for a reason

and he deserved to die because he was so evil, Ruth's body was covered in bruises through this mans abuse. If he didn't hit her he used to humiliate her in public or throw her cooked dinners up the wall. He had no respect for anyone neither did does his brother Frank who also abused women.

Frank was busy sorting out his brother's belongings when he found an address book. He scanned through the pages with his eyes when he finally found Ruth's mothers address and phone number and smiled to himself. He through the book onto a table then began pacing up and down in an aggravated manner. Whatever he was plotting could only be sinister and harmful, but being a sociopath that didn't bother him.

Ruth was unaware of Frank being around and so had no idea she was in danger. She thought the death of Malcolm would end all her problems at least she could feel safe after he had plunged to his death from Pamela's balcony at her apartment. But Ruth had other people to worry about such as her father who although didn't pose as a threat to her. But he did worse by allowing her to be abused and not standing by her, considering his friend was more important than her. But one day he must face what he has done and answer to Ruth and the rest of the family for his transgressions.

Ruth was sat watching television when a knock came at the door; she was hesitant but answered it eventually. To her horror it was her father who brushed passed her and entered the kitchen, he seemed angry and started shouting.

"What's wrong George" Diane said concerned.

"It's being branded round at work that I am a paedophile, me that's a laugh" George said.

"So you fucking well are" Ruth shouted.

"It was you wasn't it, trying to get at me". George shouted

"No but I wish I had" Ruth said angrily.

"You nasty bitch I could kill you" George lifted his fist at her

Emma heard the shouting and entered the room, seeing her father she became angry but Ruth had already slapped him around the face and was fighting him.

"You bastard pretending to be so innocent, letting me suffer all that time in the hands of your fucking friend" Ruth shouted punching him in the face.

Emma pulled her off and tried to calm her down.

"The mad bitch should be still locked up why is she here?" George asked.

"Why are you fucking here you pervert" Ruth said trying to get to him.

"Dad just go you've caused enough damage" Emma shouted

"She's caused the bloody damage slandering my name" George shouted being held back by Diane

"She didn't, I did" Emma confessed "I wanted you away from here and locked away for what you did to Ruth".

"You bitch my special Emma, how could you" George was confused by Emma's confession

He pushed Diane away and she fell to the ground hitting her head on the floor, in the confusion Emma saw a figure with a bright light around her brandishing a knife in her hand. The figure then thrust the knife into his chest and he fell to the ground in agony. They all ran to him except for Ruth who stood still staring at George lying on the floor. Emma ran to her mother who was dazed but not injured, Ruth walked forward almost in slow motion. She knelt by his side and saw his eyes staring up at the ceiling he was holding his chest.

"Is he dead?" Emma asked.

"Yes" Ruth replied.

"Did you see what happened?" Emma asked.

"Yes He must have had a heart attack" Ruth said her mind was detached from the situation as if she was having an outer body experience.

"No that's not what happened it was Pamela" Emma paused for breath then continued "She stabbed him in the chest I saw it happen" Emma insisted.

"What?" Diane said holding her head. "She's dead".

"No honest I saw her as clear as I see you now" Emma continued "She stabbed him in the chest with a knife.

"Emma there's no knife and certainly no blood" Ruth said searching round the floor.

"I know what I saw, just like on the ward where you were". Emma was almost hysterical.

Claire appeared at the moment her father had collapsed and was found sat at the foot of the stairs almost oblivious to the whole event almost as if she was detached from the situation. Whether or not she was in shock was not clear at this point, but she sat there even when the paramedics and police appeared in the hallway.

They all attended his funeral but no one mentioned any events that took place at the house. The fact was he was dead and could no longer cause the family any harm.

The family stayed together and hardly spoke to anyone else; they had found it difficult to trust anyone else because of the family abuse. In fact the abuser their father's friend was at the back of the crematorium acting like nothing had happened. Ruth had turned around to look at the people who had attended; there he stood in a suit smirking. Ruth whispered to Emma.

"What the fuck is he doing here" she said annoyed.

Emma nudged her mother and whispered to her, then whispered to Ruth.

"Let mum and I deal with him ok" Emma patted Ruth on the hand.

"Just don't let the bastard near me, or I will castrate the fucker" Ruth said angrily.

"In fact all men should be castrated" Ruth continued.

"Leave me at least one man for reproduction

purposes" Emma said sniggering.

Once the service was over everyone left the crematorium each shuck the vicar's hand but Ruth who just waved in an odd fashion. They looked at flowers outside and walked past George's friend Ron, he smiled at them as they passed and tried to speak to Diane. Diane turned and faced him then spat in his face watching him wipe his face with a handkerchief looking so surprised at her.

"You dare touch my children again" she said angrily.

"She came on to me, I am the innocent party". He said covering his fat stomach with his coat and adjusting his glasses.

Ruth heard what he said and was being held back by Emma who also heard him.

"How dare you even say that you fat bastard" Ruth said trying to get to him.

Claire became very upset and grabbed hold of her mother, while Emma pulled Ruth away from trying to attack the man.

"Come on Ruth he's not worth it" Emma said.

"He's just shit under my foot" Ruth shouted, "Go on piss off pervert".

"Let him go Ruth please your upsetting Claire"

Emma pleaded.

Ruth walked on with the family and had almost got in the car when the man passed by her smirking.

"To think that I got arrested because of you and that other daft bitch" He shouted.

Ruth launched at him scratching his face and kicking him between the legs, suddenly by complete surprise Claire joined in kicking him in the head. Diane pulled Claire off and Emma jumped in Ruth's way. The police soon arrived and began to split everyone up Ruth was still swearing at the Ron.

"I hope you rot in hell you fucking pervert" Ruth shouted watching the police approach her. "It's him you want" Ruth said as one of them held her.

"Why did you let him go, you thick bastards".

A policewoman was holding her "Now come on calm down" she insisted.

"Let me go he's a paedophile and he needs punishing not me" Ruth said struggling.

"Let her go" Claire shouted hysterically.

Diane had never seen Claire reacting like this before and didn't know how to control her. Claire was trying to reason with the police, explaining that Ruth was being provoked by her abusers presence. Diane agreed with her and demanded that the police arrested him.

"He's the trouble causer, he abused my daughter". Diane shouted.

Ron looked at the family then the police, "The bitch deserved it, come on let me have all of you" Ron shouted approaching Ruth.

The police realised what was happening and two of the officers started to walk towards Ron who by this time was laughing and teasing the family with vulgar gestures. The police officers were taken by surprise seeing Ron's antics and stopped in their tracks.

Suddenly a van swerved out of control in the car park and headed straight towards the family, then it changed direction and drove towards Ron. Ron moved backward to avoid the van, tripped over the curb and landed in the road. No one was close enough to move him out of the way and he was hit directly in the head by the bumper of the van. He had no chance of surviving as his head smashed like a melon and blood splashed right across the road. Emma once again witnessed a glow of light coming from the van, which disappeared as fast as it came. She remained silent and just looked across at Ruth who was being held by a police woman, she then looked at Claire who was bent over by the pavement vomiting. Ruth was released by the police during the time the van hit Ron and ran to comfort Claire.

When the police reached the van they found the driver unconscious and appearing very pale with blue lips. It was later discovered that he had suffered a heart attack at the wheel and he died in hospital. Therefore it was questionable whether or not Pamela was actually involved in this incident as Emma thought at the time. Although she could have steered the van away from the family and towards Ron, no one will ever know for sure. It is also questionable whether or not they would even believe her. But again it was another case of a man with no conscience who had suffered the consequences of his actions.

WHO AM I

Ruth was sat talking to Kathy in a local bar; she was dressed very trendy and was amused by her male and female admirers across the room. She was interested to see which one would approach her first; after all she had been chatted up by both sexes. During this time Kathy was trying to have a serious conversation with her, but Ruth was in a silly mood and not interested in any intellectual discussion.

Kathy really wanted Ruth to make up her mind about her sexuality and feel comfortable with her life. But Ruth had to be sure of herself and her true feelings.

"I suppose that I have been attracted to women from an early age, I don't think that I am bisexual, men are weak specimens like Geoff, fucking egotistic fools" Ruth laughed.

"Geoff's just a fucking knob" Kathy said laughing with Ruth

"The men I knew were never kind, generous,

gentle or kind" Ruth said looking at two men at the bar.

"You never met the right men Ruth" Kathy said also looking at the men.

"No I think that I had a lack of self-awareness right back to my early years" Ruth said analysing herself.

"So are you saying that you have subconsciously known all your life?" Kathy asked.

"I don't know it was clouded by my abuse so who knows". Ruth was serious for a second.

"So that confused you?" Kathy said puzzled.

"Yes and no" Ruth said smiling "Stop fucking with my head bitch that's my job" Ruth said laughing.

"Anyway from meeting Pamela I got a label 'femme type lesbian' as apposed to butch" She laughed and knocked her drink off the table. "I belong in the lesbian community now close to the edge I might add walking with my own kind".

"You're a fucking head case Ruth and no mistake" Kathy laughed out loud.

"When I was with Pamela god bless I used to hold her hand walking down the street in order to give me street cred" Ruth was becoming very drunk.

"Its exciting, fun and romantic and I love it, so kiss me Kathy" Ruth was leaning across at Kathy.

"Bugger off Ruth no woman kisses me, I'm true heterosexual" Kathy said pushing her away in fun.

"Fuck that I want a woman, I fantasise about women kissing them loving them". Ruth fell off the chair.

Kathy was still laughing and hadn't noticed her disappear onto the floor.

The next day Ruth got up with a severe headache and bruises on her arms and legs, she got in the shower and looked at her injuries counting the bruises. Her head felt that heavy it was as if it was made of lead. In addition to that she felt quite sick afraid to eat in case she vomited. The words rang in her head never again, she vowed and declared that she was never ever drinking again. Every sound in the house seemed to echo and vibrate in her head; even the quietest of sounds seemed loud.

Emma had visited that day and when she realised that Ruth had been drinking tip toed across the landing past the bathroom. Then put the radio on for a bit of background sound. When

Ruth came out of the bathroom she walked past her younger sisters room where the radio was playing.

"For fuck sake who is playing that music" She said holding her head.

Emma emerged out of the room then saw Ruth heading for her bedroom.

"Oh shit sorry Ruth" Emma said trying to keep a straight face.

"Emma really my head is splitting" Ruth said frowning.

"You must have got pissed last night" Emma said watching Ruth ease herself onto the bed.

"I really don't remember anything" Ruth confessed. "Except for announcing that I am a lesbian to the entire pub". Ruth admitted "That was fun seeing the reaction on peoples faces, it was like who let the fucking lesbian out" Ruth laughed then yelled "ouch!" as her head hurt.

Emma laughed, "Well you seem happier now".

"You think?" Ruth said smiling "Well I feel as if I know who I am".

"Meaning?" Emma asked.

"I have given it a lot of thought and I am sure that I am a lesbian, I feel comfortable with it and see my way forward" Ruth said confidently.

"I am pleased for you, I want you to be happy" Emma said smiling.

"The problem is convincing mother" Ruth said sighing.

"She will come round eventually, she's old school with an old head on" Emma said tapping her head.

"Maybe you're right, I hope so" Ruth said.

At that moment Diane was coming up the stairs, "Time for lunch girls" Diane said heading for the bathroom.

Frank was standing outside the house trying to peer inside from the roadside; he seemed agitated and began pacing up and down the pavement. Suddenly a car screeched around the corner and startled him, which caused him to miss his footing. He fell backwards into the edge and then balanced stopping himself from going further back. At that moment Emma came out of the front door and proceeded to walk down the drive. Frank decided to follow her keeping a safe distance so he wouldn't startle her, but Emma had already started looking around sensing someone was following her. She walked down by the park where one of Malcolm's victims was violently murdered, Frank began to breath heavily and thumped a nearby wall with his fist. He continued to follow her through the park but seemed to want Emma to see him. All he wanted to do was scare her and nothing more at present; eventually he left her alone and walked back the way he came.

Ruth was at the height of her modelling profession when she came in contact with so many organisations and causes. She wanted to help people even though she was so involved in her relationship with Pamela and her career new career in modelling. She loved to be with people who were dependant on others or 'street people' who required help in some way. She was also interested in getting involved with gay rights and fighting for justice, helping the suppressed, finding her own sexuality during this time.

Ruth was contacted by Gay pride International when she was in the public eye modelling on the catwalk with Pamela. They wanted Ruth to be spokes person for their cause when they were being interviewed by the media. They were very supportive when Pamela and Ruth were being victimised and bullied by the press and society in general. Ruth felt free in their company part of the parade dressed as Susan storm from the fantastic four-action heroes wonder woman or cat woman.

Ruth had finally found herself thinking seriously about her sexuality, she joined her friends from the modelling world Sheena Moore, Gloria Thompson and her modelling agent Angela at a local bar in Manchester's gay village. They could guarantee the atmosphere was going to be warm and friendly, as there was hardly any trouble within the gay community. People could relax whether they were gay or straight, as the locals were often seen as non-judgemental and unlike most communities they accepted most people in bisexuals, heterosexuals, transsexuals and others. But the highlight of Manchester was the gay pride festival, a colourful parade seen by thousands of spectators from across the country. Gay pride was an international concern and went on for a week in Manchester with little trouble, the object was to recognise the rights of gay people and let people know that they had just as much right to be in society as everyone else.

Ruth had sleepless nights reflecting back to her past, her therapy did help but the rest was up to her to deal with issues and move on for her own sake. Ruth knew that if she lived a hundred years she would still carry the inner scars of her past, but she needed to introduce her own coping strategies to deal with the occasional reminders of her former trauma. She had dealt with the shame, humiliation, self-disgust and embarrassment of the abuse. Also of the feelings of being contaminated, dirty and defiled, she spoke of guilt, blame and a debased self-image. So she had come a long way to recovery in this sense but she will never be separated by her night terrors or nightmares. Her years of avoidance and isolation had ended with the burning of the wardrobe and improved relationship with her mother Diane, but what also remained were those occasional feelings of anxiety and helplessness when she was reminded of her predator. The smell of aftershave, deodorant or people who resembled him, often music or the smell of nicotine made her physically sick.

Ruth also thought about her femininity such as playing with dolls, make up, wearing dresses or having long hair platted or tied in a pigtail. Her first indication of being different was being attracted to girls and disliking boys but she thought that was abnormal, as her mother tried to introduce the idea of girl meets boy and they get married. She would avoid discussing religion or politics and never speak of same sex relationships and the thought of swearing in public was turned Diane's stomach. According to society, Ruth was a girl and she fitted the stereotype nicely, girls were gentle while boys were masculine. Boys played rugby and football while girls played hockey and netball; Girls who played football were classed as butch and not normal.

Society have a way of casting out those who fail to conform to the ideals of their perfect world, according to mans interpretation of the bible homosexuality is condemned. Mankind has taken out sections of the bible that they are interested in and quoted them to believers encouraging them to act on what they have heard. People have also formed their own religions based on bible teachings and or other books such as the Koran. Most of the laws in society throughout the world is based on the Ten Commandments, this is a way to maintain order others are more extreme such as the Nazi parties way of exterminating the Jews in gas chambers. Hitler wanted a perfect race of people therefore killing all those who failed to conform to society. The gay element of society would have no doubt been killed in some way.

Ruth was aware of the gay scene but until recently had never took an active part in it. As it was never spoken about in her household, she never even thought about it. When she was at university studying to become a nurse, she would mean gay people but not really engage in conversation. She never went to church or participated in religious activates, and did not attend Sunday school. Although some of her friends were religious so she did here about Christianity and cerebrated Christmas, Easter and other westernised traditions. She was also aware of the Ten Commandments and other well-known areas of the bible, but mainly through the media or school. Ruth's opinion about religion was that it was like politics it caused arguments, also in World War 2 catholic fought catholic so where was the sense in that. Ruth was confused by the religions of the world participating in politics and that people lived in fear of god. She was confused by the fact that people dedicated their lives for god or chose to take their lives for the sake of their god.

Ruth had decided that she was lying to herself about her sexuality in order to conform to society; she was living a lie and hiding her true feelings as a lesbian. Therefore in the gay village she could be herself and be accepted for who she truly was a femme lesbian who desired the love of females. Her friends understood the way she felt and respected Pamela and herself for their sexuality, both Sheena and Gloria fought to protect them from homophobic members of society and the media.

Ruth often spoke to lesbians in bars more recently and tried to understand more about herself, she established where she fitted in within the gay community. During her time of discovery she met Samantha Clarke who liked to be called Sammy, she was a very liberated woman in her late twenties with short dark hair, who wore no make up and a slim figure. Sammy was classed as streetwise and seemed pleasant; she appeared to be like Kathy but had a strange idea of morality as Ruth soon found out. Sammy made a point of sitting beside Ruth by the bar, her body language told Ruth that she was attracted to Ruth's beautiful face. She began with an open posture smiling at her then brushed her leg against Ruth's leg and then put her hand on her knee.

"Can I buy you a drink?" she offered.

"A sweet wine please" Ruth replied blushing.

"Oh I am Samantha but you can call me Sammy" Sammy said trying to attract the bar maids attention.

"My names Ruth" Ruth said struggling to get her words out.

"Nice to meet you Ruth" Sammy said gazing into her eyes.

Ruth was taken by surprise at Sammy's confident manner and the way she seemed to charm her better than any man had done with her. They had a few drinks then left the pub heading to Sammy's apartment just across the street. They drank a full bottle of wine and then before Ruth realised Sammy was seducing her.

She began by stroking her hair gently then kissing her neck on the left side, she used her tongue to lick at her ear lobe and made a journey from her ear down her neck. Ruth gave a heavy sigh, opening the buttons on her blouse. Sammy sent her hand inside her blouse, stoking her breast through her bra, she then lifting the bra to reveal her firm breast. Her nipple hardened and she did the same with her other breast, then began fondling them. She then began to kiss her tender body until she reached her nipples. Sammy was clearly turning her on as she lay back and removed the rest of her clothes and lay on the bed. Sammy then removed her clothes and they both began making love, Ruth could feel her insides shaking as she reached an orgasmic climax.

After making love they both lay on the bed, Sammy was acting a little strange as she looked at Ruth admiring her body. She began staring at her as if she was afraid of something.

"What's wrong Sammy?" Ruth asked concerned.

"You have a freaky light behind you, what is it?" Sammy said nervously.

"Really" Ruth said looking behind her.

"Honestly its fucking my head up" Sammy said moving away from her on the bed.

"It's not harmful" Ruth said laughing

"Its not fucking funny I'm telling you" Sammy said shaking.

"It's probably the ghost of my ex girl friend" Ruth said laughing.

"Piss off Ruth I'm serious" Sammy said angrily.

Sammy put on her dressing gown and Ruth got dressed, they went into the lounge and Sammy offered Ruth a drink.

"I have to go Sammy" Ruth said walking towards the door.

"But if you wait we could have a threesome with charlotte" Sammy said smiling.

"Not for me Sammy" Ruth replied opening the door.

"Or Gary he might be keen" Sammy went on.

"No thanks" Ruth said walking through the door.

"No he probably draws the line at making it with ghosts" Sammy said disappointedly.

Ruth waved and shut the door then headed down the stairs, although she had heard Sammy she ignored her last remark. Ruth regretted her one nightstand with Sammy because all she wanted was a relationship like Pamela, she hated the idea of threesomes and mixed sex. She had the feeling that Sammy was only interested in a one nightstand and she had an idea that Gary might have been married and into kinky sex. Besides she was not interested in males just a steady relationship with a woman, Sammy was not the woman for her although she had good sex.

As for the light behind Ruth's head, she was

starting to get fed up with people seeing this light and wanted an answer for the constant sightings. So she booked in at a local clairvoyant's house. She spoke about past relationships, but discussed male relationships and didn't mention any light, vision or ghost. Ruth never mentioned anything in case she made something up, or thought that she was mad.

A week later she went to the same bar in Manchester and saw Sammy, this time a butch lesbian was with her and she noticed Sammy making advances to Ruth just like the last time. She raced forward angrily and began shouting at Ruth, Sammy tried to stop her and the woman punched her in the face. She continued to head towards Ruth ranting and raving at her like a wild bull.

"What are you doing with my girl friend you fucking slag" She shouted.

"Hey she came on to me bitch" Ruth said angrily.

She took one swing and hit Ruth under the chin; she then grabbed her by the hair and punched her in the nose. Ruth slapped her but couldn't get hold of her hair as she had a skinhead. Suddenly a glass was smashed into the woman's face and she fell down to the ground bleeding, while Sammy screamed and knelt down beside her.

"The ghost did that" Sammy shouted "Your freaky fucking ghost".

Ruth stood confused at the activity and was suddenly pulled away as the police appeared, she couldn't see who was pulling her but was led outside the door.

"Holy shit what's happening?" Ruth asked.

"It's ok your safe lets go" a woman shouted.

She looked at her, she was in her thirties, she had fair hair slim and fairly attractive, she had long hair and wearing a t-shirt and jeans. She led Ruth to another pub and sat her down, making sure she was sat comfortably and looking out of the window. She then headed for the bar and soon returned with a damp cloth and wiped Ruth's face.

"Shit you were lucky that butch lesbian bitch could have killed you" She said calmly.

"I don't get it why didn't she?" Ruth asked.

"You are fucking kidding" She said with surprise.

"What tell me" Ruth insisted.

"You have a guardian angel watching over you"

She said smiling.

"I don't understand" Ruth said confused.

"Christ woman a light appeared and then a blonde angel, she smashed a glass into that bitch's face". She suddenly got excited telling the tale "You should have seen the blood spurt out of her face".

"I'm Ruth" Ruth said putting her hand out for the woman to shake it.

"I'm Cheryl and yes I am gay" Cheryl said shaking her hand.

"Thanks for rescuing me" Ruth said holding the cloth on her face.

"That's ok I only did half the job, thank your angel" Cheryl said modestly.

"I thought people were hallucinating about her" Ruth said.

"She's as fucking real as me" Cheryl said laughing "But seriously you need to watch who you mix with and what your doing" Cheryl said warning Ruth about some of the people in the area.

"I gathered that" Ruth said smiling.

They had a few drinks and Cheryl took Ruth to her house and introduced her to her family. She then found some sheets and a blanket and asked her to sleep on the settee. Ruth made a bed out of the linen and lay down to rest on the settee; she was soon asleep and woke up the next morning to the sound of a dog barking. Cheryl was already up and stroking a large saint Bernard's dog-admiring Ruth lying on the settee.

"You're very pretty" Cheryl said smiling.

"Thank you, not all lesbians are butch you know" Ruth said trying to smile "I feel awful".

"Well you have got a sore nose and a bruised chin Ruth" Cheryl said pointing at her chin "And as for the lesbian thing I know because I am one".

"Oh fuck no" Ruth said shocked "I mean my nose and chin, not the fact you're a lesbian too that's good".

"Yes she really hit you and she nearly broke your nose" Cheryl said concerned.

"And your definitely not street wise are you" Cheryl continued "I mean going with Sammy honestly she's notorious for playing around with both sexes, she's probably got all sorts of diseases, she's a right slag".

"Fucking hell Cheryl you know how to cheer me up" Ruth said cursing.

"So do you know your guardian angel?" Cheryl asked curiously.

"She's an ex girl friend who died" Ruth replied.

"Oh I'm sorry Ruth" Cheryl said looking at Ruth's sad face.

"We were engaged when she was murdered" Ruth looked down.

"Jesus I'm sorry, how did it happen?" Cheryl asked.

"Killed by my ex boy friend" Ruth explained.

"Oh god how awful" Cheryl said a little bewildered. "Did you say boy friend".

"Yes I was confused about my sexuality back then" Ruth admitted.

"But now you know?" Cheryl asked.

"Yes I am a lesbian no doubt about that, but not a butch lesbian" Ruth said confidently.

"You have a certain feeling that comes from within, I had that feeling from childhood, it was so confusing because my mother encouraged me to be with boys". Ruth continued.

"Like from a kiss or seeing women naked" Cheryl said looking into her eyes.

"Yes partly and from looking at the female

form in a desirable way, I fancied the arse off Girls aloud and as for actresses like Demi Moore god she gave me an orgasm". Ruth said smiling.

"Do you find me attractive" Cheryl asked edging closer to her.

"Yes I do" Ruth replied bringing her face closer to Cheryl's.

Cheryl kissed Ruth on the lips and Ruth returned a kiss, Cheryl embraced her and then followed with a more compassionate kiss. Cheryl then led Ruth to her room where they made love all afternoon, and then lay naked in the bed cuddled together. Ruth felt as if she had began to love again for the first time since her relationship with Pamela.

"Why do these moments never last" Ruth said looking up at the ceiling.

"I know we should just lye here forever and forget the world around us" Cheryl said with a shy.

"But we have so much to do" Ruth said.

"Yes you have your family to go back to and I have to deal with my own problems" Cheryl explained.

Ruth kissed Cheryl and stood to her feet, moving gracefully to the bathroom.

"You move so well Ruth" Cheryl said admiring her naked body.

"Well I have performed on the catwalk as a model" Ruth said shaking her bottom.

"I would love to have seen that" Cheryl said walking past and slapping her on the behind.

"I will perform for you sometime" Ruth said laughing.

"I think you have done that already" Cheryl said joining in the laughter.

They both entered the shower together covering each other in shower gel and washing each other. Ruth then got dressed and let Cheryl dry her hair and comb it into place, Ruth then did the same with Cheryl's hair and then she too got dressed. Ruth said goodbye to Cheryl and left her house for her mothers home.

Ruth returned home and discovered all the family sitting in the lounge, they all looked at her and then each other.

"Ok what have I done now?" Ruth asked suspiciously.

"Nothing" Emma replied.

"It Malcolm's Brother Frank" Claire said concerned.

"He's after you" David added.

"David!" Diane shouted.

"We have had nuisance phone calls and letters from him with sick comments" Emma said looking at Diane.

"This is my fault I brought all this trouble to you" Ruth said regrettably.

"No don't say that" Emma said hugging her "It's not your fault that you got involved with a psychopath".

"So how long has this been going on for?" Ruth asked.

"Since you were ill" Claire said looking at her mother "Right mum?"

"Yes we have been followed, contacted by phone and had letters sent to us" Diane said worried.

"So have you contacted the police?" Ruth asked.

"Yes we have but they say he hasn't threatened us in any way so they can't do anything" Emma replied.

"Perhaps I should see him and sort this out" Ruth offered.

"No way Ruth, he might kill you" Claire said concerned.

"So what the fuck can I do?" Ruth shouted, "Let my family suffer?"

"We all need to stick together, never be on our own anywhere ok" Diane advised.

"Good idea" Ruth agreed "Lets have a plan of action, going out in twos and all that".

The phone was ringing everyone looked at each other for a while interrupted them. Then Ruth being the closest picked up the receiver and spoke.

"Hello" She said but no one answered "Why don't you fucking answer you sick bastard" She shouted.

Again there was silence "Go fuck yourself" Ruth said slamming down the phone.

She looked at the family sat staring at her and realised what she had said.

"I'm sorry I got carried away" Ruth admitted.

The weeks went by and the family did stick together, the phone calls continued and more non-threatening letters arrived. Each letter read similarly 'why did you kill him' was written every time but other things were added like 'have a nice life'. The handwriting indicated a lack of education and that it had been written in anger. No one quite new how dangerous he could be, however it was clear that he had the opportunity to harm any of the family but never did. Was this an indication that he was only capable of intimidating people or was he waiting for the right time to kill Ruth. Whatever his intentions were the family had to act to protect themselves from impending danger. Emma contacted her boy friend and asked him to come round for male support, he was joined by a few friends who offered to help them.

That night Ruth stayed at her mother's house, she lay on the bed with her mind drifting back to the years of abuse living with Malcolm. She was remembering the punches he gave her and kicking her when she was on the ground. She thought about the mental torture and humiliation, both at home and when she went out with him. She could still hear his voice shouting abuse at her and speaking to her in a sarcastic tone.

She soon drifted off to sleep and awoke in a daze, she crossed the landing and all was quiet. She went into the bathroom and used the toilet, then proceeded down the stairs for a drink. Something seemed wrong as she walked down the hallway to the kitchen, suddenly treading on broken glass and cutting the bottoms of her feet. Once she was in the kitchen she noticed the back door window was smashed and the door was ajar. Then to her horror she noticed blood stained footprints and a spray of blood up the wall. She walked into the lounge and to her horror she saw bodies everywhere.

Her mother was lying on the ground with blood all over her head. Some of it was now on Ruth's hands. She almost tripped over the next body that was Claire with the same head injury. Then on the settee was David again with the same injuries, with his eyes staring up at the ceiling. Ruth followed the footprints up the stairs until she arrived back in the bathroom; on the floor was Emma's half naked body lying in a pool of blood. The bathroom looked a mess with blood on a towel on the toilet and over the floor.

At that moment she heard a noise behind her, she turned and saw a large shadow appearing on the wall by the stairs. She ran into her bedroom and barricaded the door with her set of drawers and walked back towards her bed. She heard the sound of wood on wood as a heavy object was hitting the door over and over again. Pieces of wood were splintering off as the attacker began to form a gap in the door. Ruth stood helpless as the large figure entered the room and came towards her. He was wearing a white porcelain mask just like Pamela used to have on her wall with black eyes and a decorative design all over it.

The attacker swung at her trying to hit her head, Ruth fell backwards onto the bed and just as he attempted to administer the fatal blow a bright light appeared. Pamela was stood with a large knife in her hand and stabbed him repeatedly in the back. Then Ruth his removed his mask and revealed the identity of her attacker, it was her Father George. Ruth screamed hysterically and fell back onto the bed hiding her face.

Eventually she passed out and awoke to find Emma beside her, she was shaking her and trying to calm her down "Ruth" she shouted.

Ruth began to respond to Emma, as she opened her eyes and clung hold of her.

"What happened?" Ruth asked.

"Jesus Ruth you scared me" Emma said trying to comfort her.

"What a fucking nightmare" Ruth said realising by seeing Emma alive that she had been dreaming.

Then Ruth looked at her blood stained hands "Oh my god what happened to me?"

"Christ Ruth don't you know?" Emma asked "You obviously had a period last night and didn't expect it, you must have gone to the bathroom and made a mess in there and in the kitchen".

"What a fucking mess, I am so sorry" Ruth said ashamed.

"You must have had a nightmare probably about Frank" Emma said "He was obviously on your mind from our conversation last night".

"I am sorry I thought I was getting better" Ruth said.

"You are but that crap about Frank evidently brought it all back" Emma explained.

"Hey I'm supposed to be the bloody expert" Ruth said smiling

"So it must be rubbing off on me" Emma said returning the smile.

Ruth wrapped her arms around Emma and kissed her tenderly on the cheek.

"I love you big sister" she said.

"Hey lets not go too far" Emma said laughing.

"You know what I mean" Ruth said tapping her on the arm.

"You daft bitch of course I do" Emma replied.

At that moment Claire entered the room "Is she ok?" she asked.

"Yes she's fine" Emma replied.

Claire walked over to the bed to hug Ruth, then noticed the blood on the sheets and on Ruth's body "Christ Ruth what's happened?"

"Time of the month, you know period" Ruth explained.

"Oh god" Claire replied shocked.

"It was kind of unexpected this time, caught me on the hop" Ruth said ashamed.

"It was an accident Claire we all have them" Emma said sharply.

"Sorry I wasn't criticizing honestly" Claire said in her own defence.

Emma was about to speak when she saw a bright light crossing the room and caught a glimpse of Pamela, as she seemed to vanish into the wall. She never mentioned this due to the situation at the time and not wanting to distress anyone any further although she knew that Pamela was only there to protect Ruth.

Diane had followed Claire into the bedroom "Well the bathroom is clean now".

"Good I need a shower" Ruth said pointing to her nightclothes.

Emma passed her a bath towel then realised that Ruth was too weak to walk on her own and helped her to her feet. "God I feel light headed" Ruth admitted.

Both Emma and Claire escorted Ruth to the shower in case she collapsed. They helped shower Ruth but they were both shocked at the scars on her body from Malcolm's abuse and self-harm injuries. Ruth had noticed her expression change.

"Claire what is it?" She asked.

"Nothing" Claire replied abruptly.

Emma looked at Ruth in surprise and appeared bewildered at Ruth and Claire. Ruth decided to say nothing at this point, but knew Claire was hiding something. Her whole mannerisms seemed to indicate some sort of concealment, as if something had happened to her at some point in her life. She had obviously kept it locked up inside but Ruth needed to help her or at least seek advice from other professionals.

Later that day Claire was sat on a settee in the

lounge; she appeared very insular, agitated and withdrawn. Ruth sat beside her and was quiet for a while, Claire was nervous and jumpy reluctant to converse with Ruth. Her bottom lip was a little scabby as if she had been biting it in a agitated moment just has she had done this biting her nails.

"Claire what's wrong" Ruth said using the direct approach.

"Nothing" Claire replied.

"You can tell me I will understand" Ruth pleaded.

"Just leave me" Claire shouted.

"Something is hurting you inside isn't it" Ruth continued.

"No, no, no" Claire repeated suddenly crying

Ruth pulled her close to her and found it difficult to hold back the tears herself.

"My god, he had you too" Ruth said beginning to cry realising exactly what had happened.

"He told me to say nothing or he would blame me, he also said I would have to go away like you did". Claire explained.

"So it was Dad I knew it" Ruth said angrily.

"Yes it began after you left home" Claire said sadly.

"Well the bastards dead now, we have to move on" Ruth said stroking Claire's hair.

Diane was standing in the doorway joined by Emma "When will it end, this family is cursed" She said bitterly.

"Take my pain away Ruth" Claire insisted.

"You hold on Claire we will fight this one together, survived this and so will you" Ruth looking into the eyes of another victim, it was like looking into a mirror at her own soul.

"We are all here for you Claire" Emma added.

"Whatever it takes we are close by to help you" Ruth said.

"Yes you have us close by we are supporting each other remember" Emma said stroking her arm and hugging her.

Diane finally walked over and joined them, a look of guilt evident in her eyes for not stopping Ruth from getting abuse. Diane could have prevented both daughters being harmed if only she had acted faster and believed Ruth when she approached her all those years ago. If only she could have turned back the clock and repair all that damage or preventing it ever occurring in the first place.

Ruth spent a lot of time with Claire encouraging her to talk to her and sharing the awful experience with her. She also took Claire for counselling and waited for her outside the room in case she needed her. Ruth became so close to Claire and for filled her promise in looking after her and protecting her from harm. Claire needed Ruth strong personality to help her cope with her trauma; Ruth was ideal providing sisterly love and professional help. Claire was very grateful to Ruth, as she knew how much trouble Ruth had been in and what she had been through herself. She knew that with Ruth's help she would be stronger and able to move on confident that she could survive her past history of abuse.

COPING OUTSIDE THE SOLITUDE OF SAFETY

Ruth was now back at work on her old ward, some of the staff resented the fact she was back expecting problems from her or because of her behaviour outside work. But Ruth was strong enough to deal with the staff and ignored all the gossip about her; she just wanted to continue with her work.

She entered the ward looking all around her, as she approached the office she saw a young man about twenty sitting alone looking very anxious, and constantly turning around as if someone was after him. Ruth carried on to the office and found Kathy sat at the desk, she smiled at her, Kathy stood to her feet and hugged her.

"Welcome back Ruth, I knew you could do it" Kathy said.

"Well I had to make the effort" Ruth replied.

At that moment Ann came in she was less

enthusiastic about Ruth returning, she just said hello put some papers down and left the office.

"She has been a bit funny about you coming back, but ignore her, we do" Kathy said patting her on the shoulder. "Come on lets go into handover".

They went into a small room and were joined by the other afternoon staff; they had come to relieve the morning staff and needed to know about the activities of the morning. All about patient care and doctors ward round, discussing any problems and patients progress. Each one was discussed systematically in room order so that the staff could follow the report easily and understand exactly what to expect for the afternoon, even though some were a little unpredictable.

Ruth listened intently and when the nurse reached the young man that she had seen near the office she questioned the nurse.

"Did you say he is suffering from clinical depression?"

"Yes that's right" the nurse replied.

Ruth looked at Kathy and frowned, Kathy immediately picked up on the reaction on her face and smiled. She knew that Ruth had possibly psycho analysed him picking up on other more deep rooted problems. But kept quiet until after the handover, not wishing to draw Ruth into an awkward situation. Kathy was protecting Ruth and didn't want her being criticise especially on her first day back at work. However she did discuss the young man with Ruth after the meeting, partly because she knew that Ruth was very perceptive and could probably see additional problems.

They both stayed behind after the handover had finished, Ruth was eager to discuss the young man with Kathy.

"David Hughes has more issues than clinical depression doesn't he?" Ruth asked.

"Yes I think so" Kathy said waiting for a reaction from Ruth.

"I knew it" Ruth said confidently.

"So what do you see?" Kathy asked.

"Nervousness, anxiety possibly agitated, constantly looking around him" Ruth replied

"Yes which means?" Kathy prompted Ruth for a reply.

"Possibly abuse or even rape" Ruth replied.

"Yes and I have observed diminished alertness, disorganised thought content, acute sensitivity and he does seem to jump a lot".

"So what are they doing with him?" Ruth asked concerned.

"He won't discuss it so what can we do?"

"Can I try and get through please?" Ruth asked.

"Do you think your up to it Ruth" Kathy asked.

"Fucking hell Kathy I am not likely to screw up am I" Ruth replied.

"I know just looking out for you". Kathy replied reassuringly.

"Ok sorry I know and yes I will cope" Ruth touching Kathy's shoulder.

Ruth went to see David who was sat in the same area by the office, he noticed her coming over but continued to look around him.

"David I am Ruth do you want to come with me please" Ruth asked.

David got up and followed her into the interview room; it was much like the one that Ruth had her therapy session in on another ward. But this one was better equipped with a sink and plastic beakers on a sideboard. David walked in and sat down facing the door with his back to the wall, he was focusing on the exit, but felt relaxed in her presence. However he looked at her strangely and at times appeared to be looking over her left shoulder.

"Are you ok" Ruth asked as she too looked over her left shoulder.

"What's wrong?" Ruth asked.

"Nothing I thought I could see something, but no must be a trick of the light" David said looking away.

Ruth didn't question him further just in case it caused him further agitation, perhaps she may have thought he was hallucinating. So she changed the subject, hoping that he would reveal what had happened to him.

"Do you want to talk about what's bothering you?" Ruth asked.

"Christ you're direct aren't you" David replied.

"No point being otherwise" Ruth replied "Shall I tell you what I see?"

"Go on" David said looking at her like someone with a deep-rooted secret.

"Your anxious, bewildered, your thoughts are all over the place, suppressed not wanting discuss the trauma that you have experience, probably because your ashamed or feel guilty as if its your fault, yet it isn't".

Ruth watched as his whole expression changed

from anxiety to sorrow, tears appeared in his eyes, but he remained silent.

"David I know most of us have been there, don't lock it away or it will destroy you". Ruth pleaded with him.

"My god" He finally said "Are you a clairvoyant?"

"No of course not, I have just known people who have". Ruth replied.

Ruth watched his every movement; she could see a male version of Pamela displaying all the emotions that she had done. The acute sensitivity and diminished alertness and the suppressed state even though Pamela had multiple personality and her identities spoke for her the patterns were the same.

"Do you want to keep this trauma locked inside forever, hurting you?" Ruth said prompting him.

"No I don't" He suddenly said.

"Then tell me I am here to help you" Ruth insisted.

"I can't" He replied "It's so painful".

"Share the pain, don't be ashamed". Ruth said knowing that she was reaching his inner thoughts.

"I was attacked" David said tears began to flow from his eyes down his cheeks.

"Attacked?" Ruth asked.

"Yes by a gang of men" David began to tell his story about how he was attacked, beaten and raped.

He eventually revealed all the details, describing the rape in detail. Ruth could see that he had gone from the suppressive state to dramatization. But he was explaining exactly how he felt; Ruth was feeling his emotion and could relate to some of his experiences. At one point he said that he felt nauseous at that point Ruth looked at the empty bin thinking about when she had used it in her session.

"David let out your feelings cry, scream punch the wall if necessary but let it out" Ruth said watching him cry in front of her eyes.

"Whatever makes you feel better" Ruth continued "Curse, swear go mad curse the fuckers who did this to you".

There was a long pause while he tried to control his emotions, Ruth knew about these long silences and not to fill them with stupid questions like 'how does that make you feel'. Instead she put her hand on his shoulder and comforted him, again thinking of Pamela and the hurt she felt when she related her rape to her.

Again David looked over his shoulder this time he commented "Angel".

Still Ruth could not see anything but never questioned David about what he saw.

"When did this happen David?" Ruth asked.

"About five years ago, when I was fifteen" David replied.

"So you have kept this inside all this time and told no one?" Ruth asked.

"Yes, I was too ashamed and considered it was my fault" David said looking at Ruth.

"Well it wasn't your fault, you are not to blame ok" Ruth insisted.

"Went into the toilet and they came at me" David said looking down at his feet.

"Well now you have told me, I think you need counselling" Ruth said standing up.

"You know David I must trust you because you have not displayed violence or shouted or anything else" Ruth opened the door to let him out.

"That's because you're being protected by an angel" David said leaving the room.

Ruth looked back in the room confused, then

left for the office.

She passed the staff room and heard Ann talking to a colleague "She's a fucking liability, why have they had her back".

"I don't know but I don't think she's safe" the woman replied.

"She was always a bit odd, but when she went into modelling with her girl friend and did all lesbian stuff".

Ruth entered the staff room and they stopped talking, both looking at each other.

"Have you seen Kathy?" Ruth asked.

"She's in the office" Ann replied.

Ruth walked away and headed towards the office and found Kathy

"Well what happened?" Kathy asked eagerly.

"He was raped" Ruth replied.

"My god poor man" Kathy said shaking her head.

"Yes five years ago" Ruth said "He described the event and his feelings also his nightmares and terrors".

"So counselling and suicide watch because you

have opened a can of worms". Kathy explained.

"Do you think he is suicidal?" Ruth asked.

"We can't take any chances, it's happened before". Kathy insisted.

"He had no suicidal ideations" Ruth said confused.

"You may well have brought it to his attention subconsciously". Kathy explained.

"He spoke about an angel behind me". Ruth recollected.

"We need to check on him" Kathy said rushing out of the room.

When they reached the lounge area David was sat in the lounge, he looked at Ruth and smiled. Kathy sighed with relief and they both re entered the office.

Later that day Ann spoke to Kathy alone.

"Honestly Kathy do you think Ruth is up to the job?" She said bitterly.

"Of course she is she knows exactly what she is doing" Kathy said confidently.

"I'm glad you think so". Ann replied.

"Well look how she was with Pamela that

ended in tragedy".

Kathy looked at her in disbelief "So you have never made a mistake then?"

"Not like she has" Ann said waving her arms about.

"She caused so much trouble and you let her back here".

"I am not prepared to discuss her so stop going on Ann" Kathy said putting her hand up to wave her away.

"Well she is bound to fuck up at some point". Ann said upset by Kathy's response.

"Well lets hope not Ann, I would hate to see that happen". Kathy said sarcastically.

Although Kathy didn't agree with Ann about Ruth's returning to work, she was concerned about Ruth getting too involved with the patients and making the mistake of falling in love again. Ruth would probably never survive another set back and would never return to nursing. Despite the criticism Ruth was a good nurse with a caring disposition unlike some of the other nurses or support workers.

Following Ann's attitude towards Ruth, she fell down the stairs at home and broke her arm. She said that she felt as if someone was pushing her and swore she saw a light behind her in the mirror. Not that anyone believed her of course, she was known for being a troublemaker, gossiping about everybody in sight. If ever justice was done then it was on the day that Ann fell down the stairs Ruth said 'it's a pity that she didn't hit her chin and bite of her fucking tongue'.

David followed Ruth around at times so he could talk to her; he was on the ward for some time and was finally discharged home safely into the community. He was grateful to Ruth for her help and for getting rid of his demons; he still had flashbacks about his rape and sometimes had things that reminded him of his ordeal such as smells and people's faces that resembled his attackers. He was put on one to one for a while as suicide watch, but was taken off when he was showing positive signs of getting well. Unfortunately when he returned home to his family he relapsed and was found on a railway line, where he had jumped off the bridge to his death. As Kathy said some people you can help but if they are set on killing themselves they will. Naturally Ruth was upset because she thought that she had got through to him, he had plans to change his life and progress. But the night terrors beat him and he couldn't face the rest of his life being afraid or running from crowds. He had panic attacks; startle responses, hyper vigilance and dissociation (a feeling of not being attached to his body). Perhaps by the time Ruth got to him it was too late and he had already decided to end his life, unable to face the future with such memories in his mind. How sad that such victims try to live their lives with such memories locked inside their minds.

People fail to realise when they attack people and violate them that they not only cause trauma then, but it has a lasting effect on them that can last for the rest of their life. Both rape and abuse of every description causes a lifetime of harm to the victim, the scars beneath the skin remain just as the scars on the surface of the skin. They may not be seen but they do exist. The effects on the victim's lives are devastating as they are reminded of the events in nightmares and flashbacks; some people relive the trauma over and over again in this way. Ruth recognised this and made it her job to help such people and cared for them as best she could and as she would want to be cared for herself in this situation.

Judith was a lady with by polar disorder (manic depression) she had an average figure and presented with a very high or low mood. When she was high she was almost incontrollable, however in her depressed state she would sit speechless in the lounge. Ruth tried to get through to her using various techniques at her disposal, these varied by just talking to her or using various stimulating therapies. She was faced with the usual negativity from some members of staff, these were the staff that apposed Ruth returning to the ward so it was no surprise when she was not getting the help that she required. Judith in her high manic state would run up and down the ward in a frantic state, talking fast and sometimes incoherent.

Ruth found herself taking Judith out to her apartment for clothes and then shopping as a break from the ward on leave. She was getting used to being out in society once more having had countless admissions, being released into the community and finding that she couldn't cope effectively outside the ward environment. Ruth discussed this with Kathy in length and made a point of demonstrating how she could make a difference without getting too involved. The general census on the ward was that Ruth was doomed to fail and her achievements would be short lived, using Pamela as an example. But Ruth was very perceptive and picked up on their negativity suggesting to them that they should not think of her as a 'lesbian nymphomaniac who only wants to fuck patients'. This generally shut them up and they continued to badmouth someone else a little weaker than herself. Judith did start to respond to treatment leaving the ward having regular treatment at depot clinic on depot injections. She had regular visits from the community psychiatric nurse (CPN).

Ruth had done her part and continued to help others on the ward like Judith, those who just needed the proper guidance and support to move on in society and live relatively normal lives. That at least is the theory putting it into practice is another matter, which requires careful monitoring and supervision. CPN'S were good at observing patients in the community whether it be in their own homes or in a group community setting supervised by staff in order to make sure they were compliant with their medication.

Problems only occurred when they cried for help and were ignored such as the schizophrenic who told the police that she was going to kill someone; she was ignored and did kill someone. Some people with depression who threatened to commit suicide and followed through with the threat jumping off a bridge onto a railway track. It was time for radical changes in dealing with the mentally ill and good leadership was necessary.

Frank continued to send messages to Ruth's family each letter was more menacing than the last. He had started to make actual threats against Ruth stating that he would hunt her down, find her and kill her avenging his brother Malcolm. Then he would decapitate her and play football with her head. As for her family he had plans to torture and kill them one by one until all were dead. He continued to watch the house from a distance hoping to find one of the members of the family walking alone in the park or in some quiet area. He also phoned the family and made similar threats against each one that answered the phone. His voice was more menacing each time he phoned hoping to send a chill down their spine and make them know that he was serious about causing them harm. He finally spoke to Ruth making his purpose plain to her spoke to her in a deep snarling voice.

"I am going to get you Ruth and unlike my

brother I won't fail" Frank said angrily.

"Go for it you creepy bastard, I 'm not afraid of you" Ruth shouted down the receiver.

"Oh so brave of you, I wonder if you are so brave in person" Frank continued.

"Why don't you fucking find out for yourself" Ruth shouted and slammed the receiver down.

Ruth took Claire to her counselling session, she was as nervous as Claire realising just how vulnerable Claire was and whether she could cope with telling a stranger all about her past. But Ruth knew that sometimes it was easier to speak to someone you don't know than family members or friends, after all these were the experts. On arrival to the clinic Ruth asked for the councillor and then sat waiting with Claire in the waiting area. Ruth placed her hand on Claire's and smiled, in an effort to reassure her that all would be well. Claire returned a smile and began looking around her at people passing by and at the magazines in front of her.

Before long a woman approached them in her thirties she wore glasses short fair hair and medium build.

"Claire" She said looking at Claire "I am

Angela".

Angela put her hand out in gesture and Claire shaking her by the hand. She then put her hand out to Ruth who immediately responded by shaking her hand.

"My names Ruth I am Claire's sister" Ruth said psycho analysing her as she looked into her eyes and watched her body language.

Angela led Claire into an interview room while Ruth stayed behind in the waiting area. She found a magazine to look at and noticed a photograph of Pamela and herself on the front leading to an article inside about same sex relationships. This reminded her of her therapy session with Sheila when she was discussing her nightmare experience when she was walking the catwalk with masks all around her. Then being attacked by Malcolm with a baseball bat, only to wake up covered in blood.

Ruth thought about Claire in that interview room relaying her ordeal as a child. Ruth just wanted to burst into the room and hug her sister, she wanted to tell the councillor to be nice to her, but then that wouldn't help Claire. Ruth knew that Claire needed to speak to someone who was not emotionally attached to her, rather than conversing with family or friends. She had to get rid of her demons, unlock all her freaky images that tormented her mind.

Claire was quieter than Ruth and not street wise; she was less likely to divulge information to a complete stranger. She was a private person and would die if she had to do any of the things that Ruth did, such as perform in public or care for mentally ill patients. She would lose her temper but never curse and swear like Ruth, she would hide and sulk rather than have open displays of moods or emotions. But Ruth always wondered what was worse being quiet and letting feelings out gently or bouncing off the walls like she did.

Ruth could only be patient and hope that Claire would make it through the session, without feeling too bad. Ruth wondered what it would be like for Claire to come out of her solitude of safety like she did. Coming into the light from the dark and lonely place although it was never clear whether or not she used the wardrobe as a hiding place like she did.

An hour passed that seemed much longer for Ruth; the door to the interview room opened and Claire came out first. It was clearly obvious that she had been crying, but by the way she was saying goodbye, she was willing to see her again. Ruth walked over to her hesitantly she wanted to ask Angela a few questions but felt that this would not be appropriate due to patient confidentiality. Ruth also considered that if Claire wanted her to know anything she would tell her without Ruth interfering.

Claire began to smile at Ruth as if she knew what she intended to do, but appreciated her not getting involved. As they walked outside Claire looked at Ruth and began to speak.

"Can we walk through the park?" she asked putting her arm inside Ruth's and linking her.

"Yes ok" Ruth said in agreement.

As they headed for the park Claire began to talk to Ruth in a positive manner.

"Ruth you had counselling didn't you?" Claire asked exquisitely.

"Yes I did but it was more like therapy quite in-depth" Ruth replied.

"Did it help you?" Claire asked.

"Yes but you have to get to know Angela build up trust in her, then you will find it easier". Ruth explained.

"Oh I see" Claire said seemingly happy with Ruth's reply.

"So did you say much to her?" Ruth asked concerned.

"A little but like you said I can't discuss it comfortably at the moment". Claire said in a low voice.

"I just started giving my therapist grief cursing and swearing at her, like the mad bitch I am" Ruth said laughing.

"I can imagine" Claire replied.

"It's not always the answer but it helps me". Ruth explained.

"Sometimes I wish I was more like you" Claire said leaning her head on Ruth's shoulder.

"Christ don't say that, I often wish I was more like you or Emma" Ruth said smiling.

"Can I ask you something?" Claire said stopping Ruth in her tracks.

"What is it? Ruth asked inquisitively.

"What's it like being a lesbian?" Claire asked looking around her for anyone listening in.

"Wow Claire that's a pretty loaded question"

Ruth said surprised.

"I am only curious, its not like I am gay" Claire said laughing.

"Two gay daughters would be a bit much for Mum to take don't you think?" Ruth laughed at the thought of breaking the news to her mother.

"But what I mean is fancying women" Claire said with a confused look on her face.

"You just like women and not men that's all, men mean nothing to me". Ruth explained "I hate men looking at me and I am attracted to women in say bikinis or skimpily dressed, where as men do that for you".

"Oh yes I like to see men in shorts with six packs." Claire admitted.

"So that's where we are different but that's life my little one." Ruth said encouraging Claire to walk on.

Ruth was glad that Claire was thinking positively about her therapy and had accepted that Ruth was a living in her home. She was unperturbed by Ruth's sexuality and felt comfortable in her presence. Ruth was all about changing people's beliefs in society and wanted more people to become voices and not hide in 'solitude of safety'.

THE WAY FORWARD

The ward was due for some radical changes; some of the staff had to move and new legislation was coming into place. Something called ward dynamics, which involved a person centred approach to patient care, focusing on individual care and unique care plans catering for each patients needs according to their illness. This was partly devised by Ruth who had been promoted to a new nursing rank, based on a caring environment conducive to each person's requirements while on the ward.

This also meant a move around of staff and new staff involved in the ward dynamics.

Meetings were held in order to solve problems and discuss strategies to continue running the ward effectively. Ruth was now in a position to discuss about who comes and goes on the ward, Kathy was also there to support her in her decision making. Kathy had confidence in Ruth although she had strayed away from her nursing responsibilities at one point; she was a good nurse and was forward thinking with a caring disposition.

Ruth had sorted her personal life out and needed to gain credibility on the ward to be respected by the staff and make a difference to the patients. Kathy couldn't be more proud of Ruth as she had fought her way back from all her problems. It was just as if she had never left the ward and she was even more confident than ever before. Even Geoff never argued with the new assertive Ruth and looked forward to seeing her on ward round, providing him with information about the patients, which he knew would be accurate. He also knew from experience that Ruth spoke her mind and expressed her feelings about the patients.

As for the International gay pride organisation Ruth carried a permanent banner for them in a symbolic way. Ruth attended the parades and supported them whenever she could get to see some of the colourful marches in various countries. Some places remembered her from her modelling career and looked forward to meeting her. Cheryl managed to travel with Ruth on most of her journey's. She went to some of the best places with her such as Manchester, New York, San Francisco and Toronto. Cheryl took many photographs of the event and wanted to do a painting of it and display it in her local gallery. The parades consisted of people dressed up such as transsexuals or action heroes; many people were making a statement of freedom for all suppressed people. Gay pride was becoming more popular and even heterosexual people were joining in on the campaign for freedom.

Ruth was recognised in San Francisco and interviewed by the media, Cheryl stepped back and watched as Ruth performed in front of the cameras.

"All I have to say is" Ruth said confidently "It is all about us, as gay people we have a voice and will use it".

"What does that mean?" Asked one reporter.

"It's all about freedom of speech, freedom to love without being condemned" Ruth continued "Whether you are straight, gay, transsexual, and we should be free to love as we want to, providing we don't hurt others in the process".

Frank was watching the news in England the world news turned to U.S.A looking at the gay pride movement, which was about to continue in England. He acted exactly the same as his brother Malcolm did when he saw Pamela and Ruth on television. Frank started to throw things around the room ranting and raving at the television, continuing to throw ornaments around the room.

Claire travelled with them to New York just to experience the atmosphere there. Although she enjoyed her time there she looked forward to get back to her home in England. Emma took care of Claire at other times and ensured that she went to her counselling sessions in Ruth's absence. Emma was less protective but still showed that she was just as concerned and loving towards her sister.

Ruth and Cheryl spent a lot of time in the park, as Cheryl wanted to paint the scenery using watercolours. Her pictures seemed to be so alive and in depth, she managed to attract the attention of many passers by. People were admiring her art; even Ruth couldn't believe the attention that Cheryl was getting, in fact it was a bit like the attention that Ruth got on the catwalk but to a lesser degree.

Cheryl was so different from Pamela, Ruth had to get used to someone a little quieter than herself.

Someone who could do without the pressure of fame and fortune, just live a simple life away from the limelight. She loved art and worked as a design artist for various companies as a freelance artist. She was a good portrait artist who often had her pictures exhibited in a local art gallery. Ruth and Cheryl went to many functions together being seen as a couple, Ruth was still recognised in some places as a model from the 'power of love fashion show'.

Ruth and Cheryl were staying in a hotel in Manchester during the gay pride festival; they had seen the parade and spent time in the gay village walking in and out of the local bars. Drinking and conversing with the local people, discussing issues about sexual equality and diversity. Cheryl had taken many photographs, which she loaded onto her laptop, eager to show them to friends at home.

Later that evening Ruth was lying in bed with Cheryl enjoying each other's company; Ruth was admiring a sketch that Cheryl had drawn of Ruth's naked body.

"This is really good, you are an amazing fucking artist Cheryl" Ruth said smiling.

"You think?" Cheryl said modestly.

"My ex girlfriend took most of my artwork when she left" Cheryl continued.

"She was bisexual left me for a bloke" Cheryl said shrugging her shoulders.

"Oh bisexual I don't understand them" Ruth admitted.

"They are greedy they like both sexes" Cheryl laughed.

"I thought maybe they couldn't decide which they wanted". Ruth said confused.

"No just greedy" Cheryl said kissing Ruth "Like you".

"Bitch!" Ruth shouted jumping on top of her.

Cheryl and Ruth laughed as they started to fight, they rolled from the bed onto the floor, then starting a pillow fight jumping on and off Claire's bed. No one else was in the house so they would not be disturbing anyone else. They were free to do exactly what they wanted to do, without causing any damage. Eventually they relaxed and ended up having a bath together locking the door before they did so in case they got disturbed. Using bubbles in the bath, drinking sparkling wine a box of chocolates with soft centres.

"Now this is living in style" Cheryl said sinking into the water.

"Too fucking right" Ruth said laughing and pushing her legs on either side of Cheryl.

"At least we are safe here" Cheryl said reaching for her drink.

"My family are all together today so I know they are safe" Ruth said taking a sip from her drink.

"Well here's to our future" Cheryl said raising her glass.

"Cheers Cheryl" Ruth said as they touched glasses. "I am the happiest woman alive".

Frank had been plotting how he was going to avenge his brother's death and was waiting for the opportunity to catch Ruth in a convenient place preferably alone. He had followed the family at various times but could never catch any of them alone. He was more determined to avenge his brother now and searched for Ruth. Frank's every waking hour was spent either thinking about Ruth or actually looking for her, nothing else in his life mattered anymore.

Frank finally saw Ruth walking to her car with Cheryl, they were laughing together unaware that they were being watched. Frank ducked down behind his own car. He knew he could get his revenge at last, but it required careful planning on his behalf in order to make it look like an accident. He watched them leave the car park driving towards the main road close to the sea. Ruth noticed the car following behind, through her rear view mirror and asked Cheryl to phone Kathy quickly. Ruth knew they were in danger and were calling for help hoping Kathy could alert the police.

Kathy was very concerned about Ruth after hearing about the many incidents that had occurred and fearing for her life. She went to the police station and explained about the past with Malcolm the violent psychopath. Of course they were familiar with Malcolm's history of crime and abuse. Now his brother was performing his antics but to a lesser degree as a sociopath, but the problem was that the police didn't take him seriously and considered him no real threat to society. Kathy was angry by the police due to their negativity and lack of response to her urgent request. However when Cheryl contacted Kathy the police grasped the urgency of the situation and responded immediately.

Meanwhile Frank starts to catch up with Ruth in his car on a hillside by the sea. He overtakes her car and proceeds to ram her car trying to knock her off the road. Ruth went faster to avoid him ramming her further, but he also accelerated and soon caught up with her. He rammed into the back of her causing her to swerve and almost spin over the cliff edge. Both Ruth and Cheryl feared for their lives as Frank made another attempt to knock them off the road. This time Ruth lost control of the car for a moment and one of her wheels spun off the road and left the ground. Cheryl screamed as Frank hit the car again and Ruth hit her head trying to swerve out of his way. Her head was bleeding and she was dazed, she had swerved to a halt stamping on the brake and causing the car to balance on the edge of a cliff. Frank turned his car around and was heading straight towards Ruth's car building up speed with the look of rage on his face. As Cheryl tries to help Ruth stay awake by shaking and shouting at her Frank comes very close to Ruth's car and she is suddenly alerted to move the car, not by Cheryl but by Pamela who appeared behind them. Pamela made sure that Ruth put her foot down on her accelerator by applying pressure on her leg, all Ruth could feel was pressure like a heavy weight on her foot. Cheryl shouted at Ruth in order to make her respond.

"Ruth put your fucking foot down". Cheryl screamed at her hysterically "Ruth!"

Ruth was still trying to focus feeling dazed and confused, everything was going in slow motion as her brain was responding to the traumatic event. Suddenly Ruth's car moved forward slowly at first, then built up speed. Frank's car just skimmed the bumper of Ruth's car and he flew over the cliff and plunged down onto the rocks below. The car hits the rocks below and exploded into a ball of flames that rose up in the air with a mushroom of smoke.

Ruth shook herself in order to bring herself round properly and for the first time actually catches sight of Pamela who was standing by the cliff edge. She noticed the glow around her that so many people had described with so much detail. She turned and smiled at Ruth just as she used to do when they were together, it was a moment that Ruth wanted to remember for the rest of her life. But she was not the only one seeing this, Cheryl sat beside her and watched as Pamela faded and disappeared in front of their eyes. Some would call this a mass hallucination others a ghost, whatever the explanation it was real to them at the time and something saved them from a near death experience.

"Jesus Ruth did you see that?" Cheryl said shaking.

"I saw it" Ruth replied with tears in her eyes.

"Was it an angel?" Cheryl asked nervously.

"No that was Pamela" Ruth said with a smile "And all this time she was protecting me".

"A guardian angel" Cheryl said searching around the area with her eyes.

"She's gone hasn't she?" Ruth said disappointed.

"Yes I think so" Cheryl said still looking round.

They were about to leave when the police and ambulance crew arrived; they all parked up around Ruth's car and approached in one large group. Kathy was with them by this time Cheryl had helped Ruth out of the car and they were supporting each other walking towards the rescuers. Diane Emma and Claire were there too they had travelled with Kathy, Claire ran up to Ruth and embraced her each one of them turned to look at a fading light that vanished into the distance and was never seen again. No one could explain this image or could prove that it ever existed, but whatever it may have been a guardian angel, a ghost or some other phenomenon it was real to those who saw it. If it was Pamela she for filled her purpose by protecting Ruth whenever it was really necessary when Ruth was in the most danger she never let her down.

SHOUT

Two years later Ruth was as confident as ever and finding each patient a challenge, she has successfully won over the respect of most of the staff trying out new methods of therapy on patients. Her confidence grew as patients seemed to respond to treatment and other wards began to adopt these methods. Kathy remained on the ward as a support for Ruth offering advice even when it wasn't required, trying to protect Ruth as if she had been assigned as her guardian angel.

Socially Ruth had learned to cope with crowds and tried not to feel intimidated, she began to realise not everyone was her enemy or abuser. The days of hiding in the wardrobe were over there was no longer a dark and solitary place for her, The place where no one could find her or harm her in any way.

Cheryl remained the love of her life, she was out going and bubbly just what Ruth needed in her life and they were very happy together. But Ruth couldn't help thinking of her past and Pamela featured greatly in her life she would often think of her beautiful long golden blonde hair and radiant smile, her blue eyes and peachy complexion. Cheryl was pleasant and attractive but not like Pamela. Pamela did have a wild side that made Cheryl look like a kitten in comparison with the tiger that she was used to.

Ruth woke up one dark and cold morning rushing around the bedroom trying to find her clothes for work; Cheryl covered her face with the sheets as Ruth switched on the bedside lamp.

"For god sake Ruth what are you doing" Cheryl shouted.

"Sorry but I can't find my clothes" Ruth explained.

"Well you were drunk last night" Cheryl replied "Telling everybody where you worked".

"God did I really, tell me I didn't make an idiot of myself?" Ruth said ashamed.

"You mean when you danced on the tables?" Cheryl said showing her face.

"Was Kathy there?" Ruth said worried.

"No she left because of being due to start work

this morning" Cheryl said reminding Ruth to hurry.

"Ok I am nearly ready" Ruth said grumpily.

"Someone did show interest in you?" Cheryl said smiling.

"Who?" Ruth stopped in her tracks and threw down her brush "Damn hair".

"No time sorry" Cheryl teased her.

Ruth raced to the bed and jumped on top of her "Tell me" she said grabbing her.

"A black woman tall and slim" Cheryl said laughing.

"What did she want to know?" Ruth asked curiously.

"Who you were and you told her about your job" Cheryl replied "Ouch you scratched me under the arms with your talons".

"Sorry Cheryl but you know I play rough" Ruth replied holding her hands out like claws.

"So why didn't you stop me talking about work?" Ruth said still sitting on Cheryl.

"Me stop you are you kidding, motor mouth in action" Cheryl used her hands to mimic talking mouths Ruth when you start you never stop, god knows what you are like at work.

"Speaking of which I have to go to work" Ruth leaned over Cheryl and kissed her tenderly on the lips "love you see you later".

"Love you too you're my bitch" Cheryl replied.

Ruth raced out of the door and towards the car, she stopped for a moment and looked up at the apartment, then she felt uncomfortable as if she was being watched. She hadn't experienced this for a long time not since her experience with Malcolm or his brother Frank She could almost feel their presence. But they were dead one was stabbed to death and fell from a balcony the other was in a truck and plunged to his death. Could their ghosts haunt her or was her vivid imagination playing tricks with her, whatever the situation she was concerned this. Oddly enough it had only affected her recently. Ruth arrived at work meeting the usual patients the one that considered Pamela an angel who always asked Ruth if she had seen her recently. Ruth not wanting to upset her merely said that she was fine and watching over her. All seemed well at work although Ann still considered Ruth a threat to her as she had not agreed to Ruth returning on the ward, despite all efforts on Ruth's behalf to befriend her. All Kath heard from Ann was 'That bitch is on today and shouldn't be here with us' Kath ignored her remarks and continued to support Ruth in her work.

The shift went reasonably well, but Ruth did convey what Cheryl had said about her night out and how she was talking about work at times, then she spoke of a black woman close by taking interest in their conversation.

Later that evening Ruth and Kathy were leaving work together and stepped out into the cold air their feet walking in the freshly laid snow, looking up Ruth noticed the snowflakes falling from the sky.

"I love the winter" she commented.

"You are joking Ruth" Kathy said shivering.

"No honestly I do love it, I want to make a snowman" Ruth said laughing.

"Your on your own there" Kathy replied laughing back.

"Don't spoil my fun" Ruth said with her hands on her hips.

"Hope my car starts" Kathy continued.

"Have a lift with me we are both on in the morning" Ruth offered.

"I suppose it makes sense" Kathy agreed.

Meanwhile in the darkness the figure of a woman dressed in black was walking in the park close to Ruth's mother's house. The woman was black and had mean eyes and frowned as she looked across to the park gate onto the main road, she watched a few people passing by before she responded. A blonde haired girl in her thirties walked close by then out of the darkness came the black woman she was brandishing a knife and screeching the words "Satan's demon" then raising the knife above her head continued shouting "Die fallen angel die".

She was that loud that she attracted the attention from quite a few passers by, some who screamed at seeing this knife wielding maniac.

The victim screamed and tried to cover her face with her arms while the assailant continued to gash at her arms. Blood appeared everywhere spraying into the air and dropping onto the snow making tiny holes. More blood splashed onto a gang that were close by and some of the men attempted to disarm the woman. The frenzied attack lasted a few minutes but must of seemed longer for the poor victim who by now had become hysterical. Her arms and face were covered in blood, fortunately her clothes protected her from receiving any fatal injuries she had padded herself up for the winters weather. Despite the clothes some items were torn and the woman had managed to cut parts of her face, neck and hands.

Ruth had been driving past when she noticed the attack both her and Kathy raced out of the car to the woman's aid, Ruth dashed across the road not even looking and was just missed by a car cruising by. Ruth knelt beside the victim and spoke calmly "Your safe now" then touched her arm gently saying "Let me help you".

The victim wiped the blood from her face with one swooped, she was trying to focus on Ruth.

"Who are you?" she muttered.

"I am Ruth a nurse" Ruth explained.

"Is she ok?" Kathy asked.

"Yes when we can get help for her, no thanks to that woman" Ruth shouted.

Looking at the black woman being held down by the youths.

Both the police and ambulance crew were soon on the scene, sirens blaring and blue lights flashing. A crowd had gathered and formed a circle around the victim and helpers, while the police had handcuffed the assailant and threw her in the back of a police van. The youths were being questioned while Ruth continued to help the victim.

I am Sharon" the victim said in a quivering voice, she was in shock and cold from lying in the snow.

"Sharon the ambulance crew are here now" Ruth said standing up "They will take you to the hospital".

One of the police officers had left the youths and was talking to Kathy.

"Did you see what happened?" He asked abruptly.

Kathy looked at him with disbelief and replied "Yes we both did".

"Well what happened?" He asked impatiently.

The officer had dark hair with a reseeding hairline; he had a large hook shaped nose and a small moustache growing beneath his nose.

"A black woman attacked her with a knife" Kathy replied.

"Yes she attacked her calling her a demon" Ruth added.

The officer bent down to Sharon who was being helped by the ambulance crew.

"Ok love can you tell me what happened and did you know the woman?" He said bluntly.

"Oh for fuck sake" Ruth shouted "can't you see the state she is in?"

"Don't shout at me who do you think you are?" The officer shouted back.

"I am a psychiatric nurse who know exactly what I am talking about unlike you" Ruth shouted furiously.

"Come on Ruth leave him to it" Kathy said pulling at Ruth's arm.

"But this fucking prick thinks he can cause this poor woman more trauma" Ruth continued.

"Do you want me to arrest you?" The officer asked.

"Bring it on you thick bastard" Ruth continued.

"Ruth!" Kathy shouted "stop it now!"

"Sensible woman" the officer went on.

At this moment other officers came forward and pulled the officer to one side.

The officers seemed to support what Ruth said but not the way she said it, the officer seemed disgruntled and began pacing up and down until the ambulance crew took Sharon away to the hospital.

Kathy led Ruth back to the car; Ruth was still seething with temper at the thought that the officer wanted to interview a distressed victim. Sharon could have been killed by a frenzied attack by a woman who was obviously insane calling Sharon a demon or fallen angel.

The next morning Ruth was getting ready to go to work, she had related the experience to Cheryl the night before then went to bed. Ruth went into the shower and as she began to wash her legs she noticed the odd scratches on her legs that indicated she must have caused herself self-harm during the night. This was something that had not happened for a while; she had evidently had a nightmare as she used to do probably induced by the incident near the park last night.

"Ruth are you ok" Cheryl asked concerned.

"Yes of course" Ruth replied getting dressed.

"Well you had a nightmare last night and began tossing and turning in your sleep". Cheryl explained.

"I was having a nightmare about Sharon,

empathising imagining that it was me being attacked and fighting for my life" Ruth said examining the scratches on her legs.

"Did you do that?" Cheryl asked "All those scratches".

"Yes but I am used to doing that, I dreamt about Malcolm and Frank it seemed so real" Ruth became tearful.

Cheryl raced over to comfort her "My love I am here for you, I won't let you be harmed" She said with a smile.

Cheryl was a very sincere person confident and level headed who really cared for Ruth, but Ruth held up a wall of protection which didn't allow for sentiment or getting too close to anyone since Pamela. After all she lost Pamela and she was frightened of losing anyone else, Ruth was protecting her own feelings.

Cheryl didn't understand this and felt pushed out at times, the sexual aspect of their relationship was good, but as for a deeper more meaningful relationship this wasn't to be at the present time.

Cheryl kissed Ruth on the lips "You know I love you and hate to see you upset?"

"I know" Ruth replied, "I will be fine".

"The black woman who attacked the white woman, was she the one we saw in the pub?" Cheryl asked.

"Are you serious, how do you expect me to remember anything I was drunk" Ruth replied with a frown.

"I just wondered" Cheryl said playing with Ruth's long hair.

"Too much of a coincidence don't you think and how many black women live around here?" Ruth said keeping perfectly still while Cheryl platted her hair.

"That's true we are close to a Afro Caribbean area so perhaps it could be anyone" Cheryl agreed.

Later that morning Ruth picked Kathy up for work; she stopped the car outside Kathy's house and waited for her to appear. While she was waiting she looked up at the sky a group of black clouds gathered above her the ground was already slushy underfoot and the snow had turned to ice making it slippery under foot. Kathy came out of her apartment building walking gingerly across the ice frightened of slipping, occasionally sliding as she walked. She eventually reached the car and opened the door cussing.

"What awful weather" Kathy commented.

"Oh morning Kathy" Ruth said smiling.

"Sorry morning Ruth" Kathy said smiling back.

"Well we are going to have a storm today by the look of them clouds" Ruth said pointing up at.

"Well we may get a storm at work if that woman turns up" Kathy said.

"Do you think that she will come to us?" Ruth asked.

"Somehow I do" Kathy replied regrettably.

"They arrived at work with an atmosphere that could be clearly cut with a knife, it was obvious that Ann was on duty and feeding negativity to the other staff. If she was nothing else, she was a good trouble causer and knew how to ruin anyone's day by instilling all wrong messages into an otherwise happy staff. Her theme for the day was Ruth's approach to the patients and her therapeutic therapies, being positive in the approach to caring for each one as individuals and not thinking the worst of them. The need to see the good in them and look for promising signs of recovery was Ruth's prime directive, She was determined to see this in operation and expected the staff to follow her in her approach. Ann never liked Ruth and would sabotage any of her projects just because it was her leading them. Ruth tried to reason with her and offer her extra training but Ann was homophobic and always hated Pamela and Ruth's relationship openly criticizing them and finding a way to destroy Ruth's reputation. She amongst others were shocked when Ruth came back to work as a nurse and disapproved at anything she said and done. Her idea of Lesbianism was to burn them at the stake as people once did to heretics or those accused of being witches.

The time went by quite uneventful until the ward was alerted about an admission Sure enough from the information received a black woman was being admitted called Rachel Hutchinson calling herself the Raven. Raven was reported to be diagnosed as schizophrenic and had been arrested for the forensic attack of a blonde white woman who Ruth and Kathy knew as Sharon. All the ward staff was alerted even the other wards close by just in case they needed support. The doctor was alerted so that he could be present when she arrived. Ruth drifted back to the time Pamela came in it was the same time in the evening, the weather was stormy then and the police brought Pamela in handcuffed and fighting. To see Raven arrive in the same way shocked her one of the officers was also the one that Ruth was arguing with which didn't help the situation, he was just as obnoxious and used what Ruth considered as unnecessary force. She didn't agree with what Raven had done to Sharon but considered it her state of mind and nothing to do with her own personality. The fact that Raven was subjected to audible and visual hallucinations influenced her own judgement and she was unable to function clearly without these voices of command telling her to do things. She believed that God was telling her to hurt people and that he wanted to cleanse the earth from evil, demons or fallen angels had to be destroyed. She was led to believe that some angels were deceptive they were wolves in sheep's clothing, they were usually blonde and wore virginal white gowns and spoke softly. Raven sounded quite credible too as she related her story to the police, community psychiatric team and other professional bodies, she presented as a frightening woman even her voice sounded chilling as she spoke low and gravely.

"Let me go you bastards!" Raven shouted.

Ruth looked into her eyes, then stared at the police officer with disapproval.

"Remove those handcuffs right now!" She insisted.

The officer looked at her in disbelief.

"You are joking of course" He replied.

"Do I look as if I am joking, I mean it take them off now!" Ruth shouted.

Even Kathy looked surprised at behaviour, but then thought back to when Pamela came onto the ward; Kathy remembered how well Ruth handled the situation.

"Remove the handcuffs" Kathy said looking at Raven in an untrusting manner.

Ruth approached Raven who appeared calmer and began to relax after the handcuffs were removed.

Ruth took Raven into the interview room, Kathy followed close behind her and sat in the office close by, she was in view of the room in case their were any problems. While she was in the office the police explained what had happened.

"This woman is dangerous" one of the officers explained.

"Try telling them that especially that daft bitch talking to her". The other officer said angrily.

"Gentlemen we are quite often in these

situations and Ruth knows what she is doing" Kathy said and under her breath she added, "I hope" She felt really uncomfortable about Raven.

"Well good luck with this one" He said.

"So has she been in your cells all night?" Kathy asked.

"Yes and shouting out all night about demons, a little scary really" The officer admitted.

"So did she mention the incident with Sharon? Kathy asked intrigued.

"Only that she thought Sharon was possessed by demons and used by Satan to for fill his mission on earth" the officer looked at Kathy "If that makes sense".

"She should be put down" the other officer said.

"Officer it's a well known fact that most schizophrenic patients pose more of a threat to themselves than others" Kathy explained.

"Well known to who the public who get attacked" the officer replied.

"I am referring to the mental health nursing profession, Its mainly alcohol and drug abuse that can increase the incidents of violence, such people with a brain disease like this should be encouraged to take their medication like a anti hallucinogenic" Kathy tried to explain to the officer.

"So its clearly apparent that Raven doesn't take hers or maybe she has been on drugs" the officer said trying to understand.

"Yes it could be co morbidity also known as dual diagnosis" Kathy said.

"So what starts these manic attacks on people?" The officer asked.

"She may be responding to hallucinations or delusions, hearing voices and listening to them as voices of command instructing her to do something to someone. Her response is to kill especially if they think it's the voice of god, instructing them to destroy evil ones". Kathy said worried about Ruth.

All was quiet after the police officers left; Ruth appeared to be doing well interviewing Raven when suddenly the panic alarms went off on the ward. It was around the lounge area the staff came from all directions in response to the alarm, a fight between two patients was taking place. The staff were busy splitting up the fight and calming the situation, when Raven began to respond to the noise from the alarm. Raven's behaviour was changing and she was holding her ears and screaming, Ruth tried to calm her down but she pushed her away. Once the alarms had been silenced the more placid Raven became wild and began chanting at Ruth using words such as demon woman and fallen angel as she began to lurch forward and tear at Ruth with her nails. She then reached for Ruth's pen and stabbed her in the side, Ruth had seen the panic button but couldn't reach it, and Raven knew this as she kept her away from the button. Ruth felt herself becoming weaker as she began loosing blood, but although she was weak she continued to defend herself. Raven used all her strength to pull her down and screamed at Ruth "fallen angel!"

Ann was close by but just looked on she had reached the doorway but stopped and gazed at the incident. Raven got Ruth round the throat and blood was visible on Ruth's face and neck. Kathy noticed Ann in the doorway then saw Raven attacking Ruth through the window, she pushed Ann out of the was and hit the panic button. She pulled Raven off and knocked her to the ground, other staff soon came to the rescue and once

Raven was being restrained Kathy concentrated on helping Ruth. Ann was still standing around watching Kathy who was trying to keep Ruth conscious and at the same time mopping the blood away.

"Devil child" Raven kept shouting

Ruth tried to talk to Kathy her neck and arms dripping with blood "My god Ruth stay with me".

The doctor eventually sedated Raven then two of the staff removed her from the room. Once the paramedics arrived and began to help Ruth while Kathy

"Why didn't you help or press the panic button Ruth is badly injured and may not survive?" Kathy asked angrily. "What is wrong with you?"

Ann never answered just rushed out of the room and into the toilet. She ran into a cubical and began vomiting into the bowl, she was bent down for a while when another member of staff went in slamming the door behind her.

"Yes you bitch how could you, let your colleague get injured like that even if you didn't like her". The woman said.

"You don't understand Stacey, I froze I couldn't help her" Ann explained wiping her mouth.

Stacey pointed at her "You better hope she fucking survives that's all" Stacey said heading for the door.

Dr Geoff Gilbert was with the paramedics Kathy was holding her hand trying to control the tears but beneath her hard exterior was a soft interior with a heart of gold. Ruth was drifting in and out of consciousness the paramedics were fighting to stabilise her. Eventually they took her away to the casualty department. Kathy knew that she had to stay on the ward until the end of her shift and then visit Ruth wherever she may be by then.

Her Heavily pregnant daughter Emma at the desk at accident and emergency accompanied Ruth's mother Diane.

"Where is Ruth Ashley I am her mother Diane?" Diane shouted anxiously.

Emma was much calmer but eager to find her, she was trying to calm her mother down but struggled to stand up.

"Mother its ok they will find her for us" Emma said leaning on the counter.

The receptionist looked on the computer "Cubical five" She replied.

"Thank you" Emma said leading her mother to the cubicles

"Ruth is going to be the death of me" Diane said in a low voice.

The curtains were drawn around cubical five so they waited outside, the casualty department was busy people were rushing in and out of cubicles and you could hear the odd murmur or snippets of conversation, some patients were moaning others yelling out in pain. Patients of all ages lay on beds in cubicles or in the corridors doctors and nursing staff were hurrying from one place to another with equipment. Suddenly the curtain opened and a doctor in a white coat appeared in front of them, Ruth was lying in a bed in the background her head and neck was being dressed by a nurse.

"I presume you're her mother Diane Ashley?" The doctor asked.

"Yes and this is one of my other daughters Emma" Diane said pointing at Emma.

The Doctor shook hands with both of them.

"I am Dr Wilson, your daughter Ruth is a very lucky woman she was saved from a very nasty attack, the wound from the pen in her abdomen didn't do any real damage and the worst injury was to her neck, it seems her colleague Kathy saved her life".

"She's a good nurse and friend to Ruth" Emma said and her mother agreed.

"She called us and told us about the incident" Diane added

"So what next? Emma asked.

"She is going to be transferred onto a ward when she has been cleaned up and then remain in hospital for a few days on observation" Doctor Wilson explained.

"So why did the woman do it, my Ruth only wants to help patients" Diane asked.

"Who knows with psychiatric patients they just flip, I must confess I know very little about them" Dr Wilson shrugged his shoulders.

"So she's going to be fine?" Emma asked.

"She has suffered trauma and the physical scars will heal, but her mental health may suffer" The doctor said concerned.

"That I think is ongoing she has been through a lot in her lifetime and she's only thirty three" Diane said bowing her head

"Mother what has happened has happened

you can't alter the past" Emma said placing a reassuring hand on her shoulder.

"Well if you will excuse me I must tend to other patients" Dr Wilson said.

"Thank you Doctor" they both said as he walked away.

Diane and Emma entered the cubical and watched the young nurse place bandages on Ruth's arms, Ruth was awake and looked at her mother and sister.

"I made a mistake that caused me to get injured" Ruth said in a weak voice.

"Child you did your job who would realise that this woman was going to attack you" Diane said with anger in her voice.

"Yes Ruth you are not to blame" Emma agreed.

Tears were evident in Ruth's eyes, her brown eyes sparkled in the light and the tears rolled down her thin cheeks. Ruth was weak and very vulnerable at this stage, the nurse smiled at her and finished bandaging her left arm.

Diane reached her face with her hand and wiped away her tears "Come on Ruth we will get through this".

"Yes Ruth be strong and let us help you" Emma

added.

"Stay with me when you come out of hospital I will care for you" Diane said insistently.

The nurse left the cubicle taking all her equipment with her, she acknowledged them as she left.

"I will come back later ok" She said leaving.

Emma went to the other side struggling to kiss her on the cheek but her bump prevented her to get too close. "Damn your niece wont let me get too close".

"We are going to care for you Ruth" Diane insisted.

"What about Cheryl?" Emma asked.

"I am sure she won't mind Emma" Diane said.

The curtain was drawn back slightly and Cheryl stood nearby "Can I come in?" Cheryl asked.

"Of course" Emma said standing away from Ruth.

"Hi darling" Cheryl kissed her on the lips and began talking to Ruth "What a mess that woman made of you, my poor darling" Cheryl had heard what was said and she was over dramatising to make a point, as if to say why leave me out of caring for her.

Emma looked a little annoyed and seemed to recent Cheryl, she had got used to Pamela and remembered the experiences of her father's death claiming to see Pamela's ghost and also the experience on the ward when she saw Pamela in the toilets. She still insists that Pamela was present so many times and no matter what others say she was real and not part of her imagination. Pamela died tragically leaving a gap in a few peoples lives, her memory lingers and some of the fun times spent with Ruth and family.

Diane and Emma left Ruth with Cheryl although Ruth was getting sleepy not long afterwards Ruth was taken to a ward; she was in a side room just off the main ward. Kathy appeared later and managed to find Ruth awake and eating a biscuit.

"Good to see you eating Ruth" Kathy said smiling.

"It's fucking hard trying to eat with these dressings on" Ruth said smiling back.

"Geoff went mad when he realised what had happened" Kathy continued.

"The alarms went off in the ward so you were all busy, I couldn't reach the panic button to alert you" Ruth explained.

"That Raven is not to be trusted, I knew she was trouble" Kathy said.

"I was too trusting and look what happened, she seemed ok at first" Ruth picked up a drink and put a straw to her mouth. "Then when the alarm bells went off she flipped" She began sucking from the straw.

"Ruth you know how unpredictable they can be" Kathy said reaching over to help her with the glass beaker.

"Yes I know your right and I am wrong" Ruth said looking away from Kathy.

"God Ruth I am trying to help you, I was as trusting as you" Kathy admitted "I got injured and now I am cautious, learned my lesson I can tell you".

Kathy was the type of person who would tell it like it was and not hold back, she could tell that Ruth was listening by the expressions on her face. Ruth was looking up at the ceiling then she looked back on Kathy with a gentle expression on her face.

"Kathy I admire you as a friend and colleague and you saved my life, which is more than Ann did, but I see good in everyone you know me".

Ruth said holding Kathy's hand.

"Ruth I love you for your approach and trust with the patients just be more cautious and as for Ann what a waste of space she is I will never rely on her in a crises again".

"No she just hates me because of my ways and because of Pamela, she wont ever let that go".

"Well she is being moved next week so one more problem out of the way".

"And what about Raven?" Ruth asked.

"She was moved after another incident on the ward involving a patient" Kathy said.

"Another attack on staff?" Ruth asked

"No just another patient who she called a Devil worshipper, you know kitty who said she saw Pamela as an angel" Kathy explained.

"Oh yes Kitty is she ok?" Ruth asked.

"Yes Kitty can fight and gave her as much as she got and more" Kathy laughed.

"Good for Kitty, well done". Ruth laughed then let out a mighty "Ouch!!"

"Careful Ruth" Kathy touched her arm.

"I forgot about the fucking wounds" Ruth said smiling.

"My fault for making you laugh" Kathy admitted.

"I would love to shout" Ruth said.

"Shout, well you have plenty of time to shout honey" Kathy said loudly.

"Fuck off Kathy" Ruth said jokingly.

"Like wise Ruth you tart" Kathy said with a smile.

"Well I had better go and let you rest" Kathy said standing up

"Ok piss off leave me to shout" Ruth said smiling.

Kathy kissed her tenderly on the cheek and walked towards the door waving as she went. Kathy was reluctant to tell her about the fact that Ann had moved and was instrument in aiding Raven to escape knowing Raven would target Ruth in the hospital. She alerted the police who rushed to the hospital but Raven was more cunning and hid away for a while.

Kathy realised that Raven knew more than she realised, she mentioned Malcolm and Pamela as if she knew them personally. It was not the first time that a patient had pursued a member of staff, stalking them and attempting to harm or kill them. Mental health nurses had been in all kinds of situations in the past threatened on the ward and vulnerable at times which is why they have panic buttons on the ward and the staff watch out for each other.

Raven eventually did appear on the ward dressed in a white coat, the staff were rushing about the main ward past the side ward where Ruth stayed. Raven slipped into the room and saw a figure in the bed. She grabbed a pillow and placed it over her face, then watched as the person began struggling to breath. Suddenly the door opened and a nurse entered the room she noticed the person panicking with a pillow on her face, as she raced forward Raven swiftly left the room.

The nurse made sure the patient was safe and called for assistance. When the nursing assistance arrived the nurse was busy checking all the equipment and reassuring the patient.

"Alison it's alright everything is fine" The nurse said glancing at the other members of staff.

"But someone put a pillow on my face" Alison said anxiously.

"Okay we will investigate it" Another member

of staff said.

At that moment Kathy appeared on the ward and went straight to the nurse looking after Ruth.

"Hi Emily how's Ruth?" Kathy asked.

"Come into my office I did to tell you something" Emily said with a worried look on her face.

"It's bad isn't it? Kathy said preparing herself for a shock.

Emily led Kathy into a room and shut the door behind them, she then pointed to a seat.

"Please sit down and let me explain" Emily said with a look of gloom on her face.

"Jesus how bad is it" Kathy said sitting down.

Emily sat beside her and looked directly into Kathy's eyes.

"She was moved onto the ward for observation purposes and because she was self harming" Emily pointed to her own arms and legs.

"Not again" Kathy said turning her head away.

"You mean she's done this before?" Emily said surprised.

"Oh yes she does it in her sleep" Kathy said.

"Oh god she was doing it last night clawing at her legs and screaming its most distressing not just for her but the other patients" Emily explained.

"She has nightmares from childhood abuse from abuse from a previous relationship" Kathy gave a detailed outline of events.

"But you must understand we can't have a psycho patient on here this is a general ward" Emily insisted, "You're a mental health nurse you should know that".

"May I just say that Ruth is not a psycho, she is not mentally ill" Kathy said angrily.

"Well you could have fooled me the way she acted" Emily said shouting back at Kathy.

"I told you what she went through so don't give me that, she is a good nurse and in control of herself". Kathy said in Ruth's defence.

"Well I want her off the ward as soon as possible" Emily said heading towards the door.

"My god Ruth was right about general nurses your all callas bitches with no feelings" Kathy standing up.

Emily opened the door and stood aside while Kathy left the room.

Kathy walked towards Ruth's bed still upset by what the nurse had said, but tried to hide her feeling so that she didn't upset Ruth. Ruth had just returned from the shower room and was busy drying her hair with a towel, she noticed Kathy and seemed to know that she was upset.

"What's up Kathy is it that bitch of a nurse?" Ruth asked.

"Well yes" Kathy replied.

"I did warn you about general nurses, all bitches" Ruth said.

"They don't seem to understand anything" Kathy said sitting on a chair near Ruth's bed.

"Fucking ignorant more like" Ruth said making sure a nurse heard her.

"They want you off the ward" Kathy explained.

"So fuck them I will go I am ok now physically and mentally" Ruth shouted.

"So shall I help you pack and go back with you to your apartment?" Kathy offered.

"Yes please Kathy lets get ready to go" Ruth said.

Raven had left the hospital and headed for Ruth's apartment; once again she had avoided capture and lurked in the darkness by the park. When she thought it was safe she headed for the apartment, she glanced around the street before entering the building. Then when she entered the building she hid under the stairs and waited for Cheryl to appear, someone had obviously told her where Ruth lived. Raven had not waited long before two women appeared at the door; Cheryl was one of them and the other a neighbour.

"Hi Cheryl how's Ruth?" The lady asked.

"Hi Julie she's ok they moved her onto the main ward this morning" Cheryl replied.

"That was a nasty attack on her" Julie said concerned.

"Yes she really suffered" Cheryl said, "Some woman was said to be attacked in the side room where Ruth moved from but the woman was unclear about who actually did it" Cheryl said.

"Why unclear didn't she see them" Julie asked.

"No she woke up with a pillow over her face, if it had been Ruth lying there she could have been killed" Cheryl said concerned.

"Well she's safe now right?" Julie asked.

"Yes and the police are searching for Raven, she can't be far away" Cheryl said, "It's a matter of time before that maniac is locked away".

"Ok wish Ruth well from me" Julie said smiling.

"Yes I will take care" Cheryl said walking up the stairs.

Cheryl reached Ruth's apartment and attempted to put the key in the door, she dropped them and put down a bag of shopping a tin rolled out of the bag and stopped behind her. She opened the door then bent down to pick up the bag, as she turned to pick up the tin she saw the figure of a woman standing with the tin in her hand.

"Did you drop something?" Raven asked.

"Oh yes" Cheryl said then realised who she was, Raven pushed her into a wall inside the apartment and pinned her there with her elbow against Cheryl's neck. She then produced a knife from under her long black coat. Then kicked the door shut with her right foot without taking her eyes off Cheryl.

"Now don't fucking move or I will cut your throat" Raven said in a deep menacing voice.

Cheryl was quaking with fear knowing that Raven meant what she said and was capable of anything.

"Tried to kill Ruth and just had the pillow on her face, then I would have cut her up" Raven said.

"But now I discover it wasn't even Ruth but some other unfortunate bitch".

"What do you want from me" Cheryl asked in a

quivering voice.

"You are Ruth's girlfriend someone told me and that I would find you here" Raven said.

"Who would tell you this?" Cheryl continued "Have you killed them?".

"Tut tut Cheryl my dear I don't kill everyone only the wicked" Raven said with a sickly smile.

"Ruth is not wicked, neither am I" Cheryl said "Please let me go.

"Did you know Malcolm or Pamela?" Raven asked.

"No but I knew of them, Pamela was Ruth's ex girlfriend and Malcolm was a psycho" Cheryl said.

"Wrong Malcolm was a messenger from god and Pamela was a demon" Raven continued speaking in a rough voice

"Pamela was a fallen angel who killed Malcolm with Ruth, they are answerable to god and I am his slayer I have come to destroy all wickedness and kill the evil ones". Ravens eyes narrowed as she held the blade close to Cheryl's neck, so near blood appeared on the knife.

"Now the question is, are you a demon or are you going to help me?" Raven said.

"How can I help you?" Cheryl said feeling the

blade cut her and the blood trickle down her neck.

"I want addresses and phone numbers of her family" Raven demanded.

"Why, do you plan to kill them?" Cheryl asked.

"No my dear just make sure they stay out the way, so that I can just get those responsible" Raven said in a more relaxed manner.

Raven pulled away the knife and spun Cheryl around so that she was facing the lounge, then pushed her forward. "Go in there" she insisted.

Cheryl cooperated by walking forward towards a settee near the window; in front of her was a balcony.

"Malcolm was pushed off a balcony like this by Pamela and Ruth" Raven said.

"They were defending themselves" Cheryl said.

"Did Ruth say that?" Raven asked.

"Yes she did" Cheryl said.

"Then she is a liar, just like Satan the father of the lie" Raven became more hostile.

Raven thrust the knife forward narrowly missing Cheryl and ripping into the settee near Cheryl's shoulder. Cheryl realised that she had gone to far in defending Ruth and decided to remain silent for her own safety. Raven noticed the blood on Cheryl's neck, which had almost dried; she looked upon her frightened face.

"You can use the bathroom if you like and wash that blood away" Raven said pointing to her neck.

Cheryl went into the bathroom while Raven searched for an address book, she noticed a small book by the phone and put it in her coat pocket. At this time Cheryl was washing her neck and looking for an escape route out of the small window in the bathroom, but it was too small. At that moment a knock came at the door, Raven approached the door cautiously and peeped through a tiny hole in the door. She opened the door and Ann the nurse came in Raven was not surprised to see her. They entered the lounge and began a conversation, which Cheryl could just here from behind the bathroom door.

"Hello Ann you got here then" Raven said as if she were talking to a friend.

"Yes and I nearly got caught helping you to escape" Ann said complaining.

"Ann dear you did well not helping Ruth and helping me get away" Raven said.

"So what now have you seen Cheryl?" Ann asked.

"Yes and I will be finding Ruth again soon" Raven said confidently.

"So what happens next?" Ann asked.

During the course of the conversation Cheryl found her mobile phone and tried dialling a number, but she was unable to get a signal from the bathroom.

Suddenly she heard arguing coming from the lounge and put her phone away quickly, she ran out of the bathroom to see Ann on the floor and Raven holding a bloody knife in her hand.

"I had to kill her she knew too much" Raven said wiping the blood from the knife on a tea towel.

"Now I need to tie you up while I go and find Ruth's family" Raven explained.

She produced a washing line from her coat and tied her hands behind her back. She then used a rag and secured it around her mouth and bound her feet.

Then Raven left the apartment and raced down the stairs, she left the building heading for the park. She seemed to know where to go evidently familiar with her surroundings, following the footpath through the park. She eventually reached a clearing and looked around for a safe route to Ruth's mother's house. She waited for a police car to pass by and then headed for the house approaching from the rear entry over a low fence. As she limbed the fence she managed to scratch her wrist, the blood from her cut dripped onto the pavement.

Back on the ward Ruth was almost ready to leave when Emily approached her, Ruth braced herself expecting trouble.

"It ok I am leaving soon" Ruth said abruptly.

"Wait I am sorry" Emily said sincerely.

"What" Ruth said with disbelief.

"My sister Sharon tells me you helped her after she was attacked in the park" Emily explained.

"Yes I did, wait is she your sister?" Ruth asked.

"Yes and she spoke about you, I also heard from other nurses saying how good you are" Emily said almost with tears in her eyes.

"I do my best" Ruth replied.

"Well you don't have to leave" Emily continued, "I was a bit hasty" she admitted.

"It's ok I want to leave anyway" Ruth said

continuing to pack.

"Well I will see you before you go" Emily said walking away.

Kathy had been watching and seemed a little upset with Ruth .

"Honestly Ruth you could have been more polite she was apologising" Kathy said.

"Well pardon me but wasn't she going to kick me out before" Ruth said sharply.

"It took a lot guts for her to apologise, she could have just let you go" Kathy continued.

"I know I am sorry but I had a bad night and hate the fact that people saw my performance" Ruth admitted.

"Nightmares, were you scratching and screaming?" Kathy asked knowing the answer to this question.

"Yes I saw Malcolm the floating masks, Pamela and every other conceivable person in my past" Ruth looked at Kathy "When will these nightmares end?"

"I don't know the answer to that" Kathy replied.

"The nightmare are so vivid no wonder I react by screaming and gouging my flesh" Ruth suddenly sat on the bed and wept.

Sheena, Gloria and Angela came onto the ward and walked over to the bed. They looked at Ruth then Kathy Angela went over and hugged Ruth.

"Is this a bad time?" Gloria asked.

"No not at all" Kathy said smiling.

"Are you alright?" Sheena asked?

"Yes just being silly" Ruth replied.

"Are you leaving? Angela asked.

"Yes I need to be back home with Cheryl" Ruth said wiping her eyes.

"I must admit I am surprised that she's not here" Angela said looking round.

"She's probably tied up at present" Sheena said "Washing or cleaning maybe".

"Perhaps" Ruth said.

"You haven't had a row have you? Sheena asked.

"Sheena!" Gloria shouted kicking her in the ankle.

"What?" Sheena said rubbing her ankle.

"She might not want to tell you" Gloria replied.

"It's alright Gloria" Ruth said "We are fine Sheena, as you say she is probably washing or cleaning" Ruth was concerned about Cheryl but she didn't admit it.

They all spoke for a short while then walked to the end of the ward together stopping at the nurse's station. Ruth waited for Emily to appear looking around the area in particularly at the side room that she was originally nursed in. Emily appeared and looked at Ruth unsure exactly how she would be towards her.

"Emily thank you for looking after me, I do really appreciate it I am not the easiest patient to nurse" Ruth admitted.

"Hey I have had worse" Emily said putting out her hand.

Ruth shook her by the hand "I suppose not all general nurses are bad" Ruth said smiling.

"I am getting used to mental health nurses too" Emily said smiling back.

Raven was still outside the house looking into the window; she had been watching the activity inside. Emma had entered the kitchen making a drink for herself and her mother; she was unaware that she was being watched. Although she felt uneasy and kept looking over her shoulder, she opened the fridge and suddenly shuddered.

She left the kitchen with carrying two mugs

and then returned to switch the light off. Raven tried the door handle to see if the door was locked the handle went down easily and quietly so she opened the door. On entering the kitchen she crept in and hid behind the fridge, she could hear the television and a conversation between Diane and Emma coming from the lounge. Raven decided to listen for a while, intrigued by what was being said.

"Are we visiting Ruth later?" Emma asked.

"Maybe, but I need to tell you something first" Diane replied.

"So tell me" Emma said eagerly.

"Later I need to give it some thought" Diane said hesitantly.

"Mother you have me intrigued" Emma said teasing her.

"Anyway you need to rest" Diane insisted.

"I am fine" Emma said stubbornly "I do rest you know".

"Well you know what the midwife said" Diane said in a worried tone.

"I know you worry about me and Ruth" Emma said.

"Do you know I still feel hungry?" Diane said.

"I am craving for pickled onions again" Emma said.

"My first grandchild I can't believe it, I wish Ruth had wished that Ruth would have give me children, but that will never happen" Diane said sadly.

"Well don't put any pressure on her, you never know" Emma replied.

"Ruth is one on her own" Diane said smiling.

"Yes I was looking through some photographs she doesn't even feature you or dad, unlike us" Emma said.

Diane didn't reply and stood to her feet "I think its time we had something to eat" she said heading towards the kitchen. "I know what to get you" She said laughing.

"Do you need any help?" Emma asked.

"No like I said before rest" Diane said switching on the kitchen light.

As she walked towards the fridge Raven appeared brandishing a knife that she had hidden under her coat. Raven smiled wickedly and held the knife to her throat, making sure Emma heard her as she spoke to Diane.

"Nice to meet you Diane, do you know who I

am?" Raven asked.

"I can guess" Diane replied, "What do you want from us?"

"Why I am after Ruth, I plan to kill her" Raven said coldly.

"Well she's not here" Diane said trying not to show her fear.

"I know but you are" Raven said watching Emma enter the room.

"What are you going to do with us?" Emma asked.

"That rather depends on you" Raven replied.

"So why do you want us?" Diane asked.

Suddenly Emma began to walk backwards into the lounge, she wanted to get to her mobile phone, which was on a table beside the settee.

"Stop!" Raven shouted "Don't move any further or I will cut your mothers throat".

"Quick run" Diane shouted "Save yourself".

Emma froze on the spot and noticed the tension in the air, Ravens face suddenly changed as it did with Ruth on the ward. Diane ran forward to stop Raven attacking Emma and Raven responded by stabbing her by striking in the throat with the knife and then stabbing her in the stomach. Without thinking Emma raced to her mother's aid and was knocked to the ground by Raven using her left hand. At this point Raven raised her right hand holding a bloody knife to stab Emma, but to everyone's surprise she missed and stabbed herself in the arm. Raven then gazed in front of her and saw a image of Pamela standing in front of Emma. She screamed and raced out of the door, then out of the garden gate heading towards the park.

Emma also saw the image and smiled at her, Pamela smiled back and then vanished. Diane lay on the floor bleeding, Emma ran in to lounge grabbing the phone and contacted the emergency services for help. She rushed back into the kitchen to her mother kneeling down beside her and crying hysterically. Diane was trying to speak to her and managed to whisper in her ear, Emma was trembling and nodded.

"Mother stay with me, hold on the ambulance will soon be here soon" Emma said.

Ruth arrived at the apartment with Kathy; Ruth's other friends had gone home just after Ruth had discharged herself from the hospital. Ruth unlocked the door and walked into the hallway, she was swiftly followed by Kathy.

"Cheryl I am home!" Ruth shouted.

There was no reply so Ruth repeated herself, it wasn't until she entered the lounge that she realised something was wrong. She could see a body lying across the floor covered in blood and thought at first it was Cheryl.

"Cheryl!" She shouted.

They both rushed forward and knelt down towards the body, They soon realised it was Ann's body on the floor and both looked at each other in confusion.

"What on earth is Ann doing here?" Kathy asked.

"Yes especially as she hated me" Ruth replied.

"And where is Cheryl?" Kathy asked.

"Let's search around" Ruth said moving away from Ann's body.

They looked in the bathroom and Ruth's bedroom before looking in Cheryl's room and finding her tied to a chair near the bed. Ruth removed to gag from her mouth while Kathy untied the bonds around her wrist and feet. Cheryl hugged Ruth and began telling her about Ann and told her that Raven may have been heading towards her mothers house. Without hesitation Ruth and Kathy headed towards the house taking a short cut through the park, Cheryl phoned the police and remained in the apartment in order to explain everything.

They ran through the park using the main pathway, before long they noticed a dark figure coming towards them. The weather was getting worse as well as the wind and rain, a thunderstorm began, with claps of thunder and flashes of lightening. The figure came closer and it was soon apparent that it was Raven who noticed Ruth.

"What have you done to my family?" Ruth asked shouting at Raven angrily.

"I have attempted to destroy the evil that resides in your house" Raven shouted back at her.

"If you have harmed them I will kill you" Ruth exclaimed.

"Frank told me to destroy all evil and he is a messenger from god" Raven explained.

"Frank is dead your delusional" Ruth said.

"No he's very much alive and well" Raven continued "You are delusional to think Pamela is a good person when she is evil" Raven knelt to pick up a branch.

"Pamela was a good person" Ruth said also picking up a branch.

Both Ruth and Raven ran towards each other, Raven swung her branch and narrowly missed Ruth who swung her branch and hit Raven in the arm. Raven then made an attack on Kathy scratching her neck and part of her face, causing her to stumble and fall to the ground. Ruth went into a rage and hit her across the face, then punched her in the stomach. Raven fell to the ground and became very still for a while, at this point Ruth checked Kath's injuries. At that moment Raven recovered from her attack and headed towards Ruth her hands shaped like claws trying to scratch Ruth.

"I will claw you to death you evil bitch" Raven said knocking Ruth into the mud.

"Fuck you I will beat you this time" Ruth replied pushing her against a tree.

Raven came back at her and stumbled allowing Ruth to jump on top of her and grabbing her hair and pulling her down in the mud. They fought for a while until Ruth managed to break free from Raven's clutches and fall back onto the ground.

Raven picked up another branch and rushed towards Ruth noticed a figure above them in the trees, but found it hard to focus on her. A bolt of lightening hit a tree near them and a branch came crashing down on Raven, part of the branch entered her stomach and pierced her left eye. Raven lay lifeless with her other eye staring up at the sky, and then blood began to ooze from her mouth. Ruth looked up at the figure in the trees and noticed her blonde her and a radiant smile, this was clearly Pamela who was there to protect those she loved.

Ruth and Kathy headed towards Diane's home both tired after the battle in the park. They noticed the Ambulance and Police there and walked straight into the house where Emma sat crying. Ruth walked over to her and sat close to her, reaching out to embrace her not saying a word. Diane's body had been removed from the kitchen leaving Emma to tell Ruth about what happened, Claire and David as well as other members of the family and friends joined them.

Ruth went for a shower before joining Emma in the ambulance as she entered the ambulance Emma looked at Ruth and began to speak to her with a concerned look on her face.

"I need to tell you something" she began "Mother told me something before she died" She hesitated.

"Well tell me" Ruth said anxiously.

"Well" Emma said finding it hard to speak.

"Is it so hard to say Emma, is it that bad?" Ruth asked.

"It's about you Ruth, please it's hard for me to say this" Emma said weeping.

"Go on Emma for fuck sake tell me" Ruth said holding her hand.

"She said you were adopted, she was going to tell you" Emma explained.

"So after all this time she is not my mother" Ruth said disappointed.

"No it seems not" Emma said.

"So I wonder who is" Ruth said bewildered.

"Apparently Sarah is" Emma said.

"Sarah who?" Ruth asked.

"Pamela's mother Sarah" Emma said reluctantly.

"No I don't believe it, Sarah's my mother?" Ruth was shocked trying to work it all out.

"Ruth that's all I know but her cousin Laura knows the entire story" Emma told her sighing with relief as she had finally told her the truth.

"I am sorry that you had to find out like this Ruth" Emma said looking into her eyes.

"So that's why I look like Sarah" Ruth said looking back at Emma.

They arrived at the hospital Emma was taken out by stretcher and Ruth followed behind her. They were taken to the maternity department so that Emma could be examined after her attack. Ruth was also examined after her ordeal and found to be suffering from minor injuries otherwise she was well considering what she had gone through. After Emma was examined the results showed that her baby was well and unaffected by her trauma.

It was a sunny on the day of Diane's funeral, it was well-attended family and friends filled the crematorium. Amongst those who attended was Sarah's cousin Laura who was also a school friend of Diane's who wanted to see Ruth about her real mother Sarah. After the funeral she approached Ruth taking her to one side so that she could talk to her and explain everything.

"Ruth may I explain to you about your real mother Sarah" Laura said.

"Yes of course" Ruth replied eager to know the

truth.

"Emma explained what she knew, but I have kept this secret for over thirty years" Laura continued.

"I feel as if my life has been turned over, leaving me with a void that can't be filled" Ruth said.

"Well I know the full story and I want to tell you if you want to know" Laura said looking at Ruth's reaction.

"I think I need to know so please tell me" Ruth insisted.

"Well about thirty four years ago your mother Sarah was involved with a man that she grew up with called Kevin who was unfortunately involved with another woman. So she had an affair with Kevin for a while but between this time, she met a soldier and became pregnant. Kevin was still on the scene and she was worried that he might find out about her baby and finish the relationship".

"My god she must have been in such a state" Ruth said.

"Yes that's why when she disappeared she had you and had you adopted, Diane offered to take you in and you already know about Pamela who is Kevin's daughter" Laura paused for a response.

"Yes Pamela told me about her Father and Sarah my mother" Ruth said.

"So Pamela was your half sister and she was a year or so older than you, Sarah obviously kept her and brought her up, Pamela featured her father and she brought her up in modelling". Laura explained.

"Yes she loved modelling and got me involved in it, when we were in a relationship, you know in love." Ruth said awaiting a reaction.

"You were lovers?" Laura asked bewildered.

"Yes didn't Emma tell you?" Ruth asked.

"No but if you had found out that she was your sister what would have happened then?" Laura asked concerned.

"How can I answer that question, all this is difficult to accept at present" Ruth admitted.

"I understand it's a lot to take in at once, maybe we can visit Sarah's grave together one day I will give you my number and you can call me when you want to visit". Laura said finding her phone number in her mobile.

"Ok thank you Laura and I appreciate you telling me about my mother" Ruth said gratefully.

A few weeks later Laura decided to take Ruth to

Sarah's grave, for some unknown reason Pamela never took Ruth there although she visited there frequently. Laura placed a bunch of flowers on her grave and then Ruth did the same and spoke to Sarah.

"Mother I wish I knew you like Pamela did" Ruth shed a tear knowing how tragically she died.

"You are so much like your mother Ruth" Laura said.

"I know I have seen photographs of her, even Pamela commented on that she noticed it the first day we met on the ward". Ruth explained.

"You mean she was your patient?" Laura asked.

"Yes she was a patient and we got to know each other, I helped her and we became an item" Ruth said trying to explain everything.

"I bet that caused problems her being a patient and you being a nurse" Laura said trying to understand the situation.

"Well Kathy helped me to sort the situation out and I finished nursing for a while and entered modelling" Ruth said.

"I remember seeing something in the media, but didn't take in much, Diane never mentioned much about you either just that you were problematic". Laura said.

"Well I did have my reasons after all I was abused as a child and treated badly in a relationship with Malcolm an ex boyfriend". Ruth felt uneasy telling Laura about her past.

"I am sorry I believe Pamela was also abused" Laura said trying to empathise with Ruth.

"Sarah termed Pamela as cracked porcelain from perfection to imperfection due to the abused that she faced as the child model so beautiful on the outside but scared on the inside, I am cracked porcelain too". Ruth said hoping that her explanation was enough for Laura to understand.

The story continues in cracked porcelain

–acts of abuse part two

SRS BOOKS

CRACKED PORCELAIN FULL STORY

CRACKED PORCELAIN FULL STORY TWO -BROKEN WINGS AND LOST SOULS

CRACKED PORCELAIN FULL STORY THREE- REMEMBER ME

CONFLICT OF FAITH

STORIES BEYOND BELIEF

DOUBLE EXPOSURE

ULTIMATE PURPOSE

OPERATION BRAINSTORM

FOR THE LOVE OF CHARLOTTE

THE HARRINGTON CURSE

CURSE OF ZYANYA

THE CURSED

EIGHT SKULLS OF TEVERSHAM

THE ADVENTURES OF THE TIME WITCHES

FURTHER ADVENTURES OF THE TIME
WITCHES

USEFUL ADDRESSES

RACE FOR LIFE

http://raceforlife.cancerresearchuk.org/index.html

MANCHESTER PRIDE

http://www.manchesterpride.com

INTERNATIONAL GAY PRIDE

http://www.nighttours.com/gaypride

NEW YORK

https://www.nycpride.org

ABUSE

http://thisisabuse.direct.gov.uk

ABUSE U.S.A

https://www.childhelp.org/hotline

GENDER EQUALITY

http://www.equalityhumanrights.com/about-us/about-

commission/our-vision-and-mission/our-business-plan/
gender-equality

DOMESTIC VIOLENCE

http://www.helpguide.org/articles/abuse/domestic-
violence-and-abuse

BOOK CLUBS IN MANCHESTER

http://bookclub.meetup.com/cities/gb/18/manchester

INTERNATIONAL BOOK CLUBS

http://www.readerscircle.org

WHY BOOK CLUBS?

http://www.slate.com/articles/news_and_politics/
assessment/2011/07/book_clubs.html